Hammers, Strings,

And

Beautiful Things

By the Author

All the Worlds Between Us

Hammers, Strings, and Beautiful Things

Visit us at www.boldstrokesbooks.com

HAMMERS, STRINGS,
AND
BEAUTIFUL THINGS

by

Morgan Lee Miller

2019

HAMMERS, STRINGS, AND BEAUTIFUL THINGS

ISBN 13: 978-1-63555-538-7

THIS TRADE PAPERBACK ORIGINAL IS PUBLISHED BY
BOLD STROKES BOOKS, INC.
P.O. BOX 249
VALLEY FALLS, NY 12185

FIRST EDITION: OCTOBER 2019

CREDITS
EDITORS: BARBARA ANN WRIGHT AND CINDY CRESAP
PRODUCTION DESIGN: STACIA SEAMAN
COVER DESIGN BY TAMMY SEIDICK

For Julie

CHAPTER ONE

A lanna, I can't do this anymore," I said, and my telling her this had nothing to do with the cocaine I just bumped before she came into the green room.

"Blair, it's gonna be fine," she said, clasping her warm hands around mine. "This show is no different than all the other ones you've done. You're going to be great. This is what your grandpa would have wanted."

I closed my eyes and resisted the urge to take my hand back. The more I put up a fight, the worse this whole conversation would be, and I already had been putting it off for a month. Even if her hand squeezed mine in the most nurturing way, even if the dark silver in her eyes sparkled with support, this needed to happen. I couldn't have a girlfriend right now.

"No, it's not that," I said, a knot of emotions tightening in my throat. "I meant us. I can't do us anymore."

There. The words slipped right off my tongue and now hung in the open.

Her grip around my hands loosened. "What?"

"I'm sorry."

She took her hand back. "Are you seriously breaking up with me?"

"I'm sorry. I just...I can't be in a relationship right now."

"What? I mean, where is this even coming from?"

"I'm going through my quarter-life crisis, and it's not fair for you to go through it with me."

She raised a skeptical brow. "So...you're trying to save me from you?"

"Well, yeah."

"How heroic, Blair," she deadpanned.

She had every right to be pissed at me and tell me to fuck off. For the past five months since my grandpa was diagnosed with stage 4 liver cancer, she had stood by my side. She made her shoulder available for me to cry on and went to the hospital with me because I knew I couldn't handle watching the cancer eat him alive by myself. She was there for me and my mom while we planned his memorial service, cooking us food and doing everything she could to make it a little easier for us. She'd slept in my bed every night since he'd died, spooning me to sleep. She refused to leave me, knowing how much his death crippled me, and how did I repay her? By breaking up with her. It was awful. I knew it was awful, but my gut told me I had to do it. I knew what the right decision was. I needed to focus on me and take care of me, and look how well that was going.

"I'm not trying to be heroic, Alanna. I'm trying to do the right thing."

"By breaking up with me? After everything we went through?"

"How am I supposed to make you happy when I can't even be happy? I barely have a handle on my whole life right now. Clearly."

"I don't buy that. You're about to go on tour with the biggest pop singer in the country. You have a record deal. How many hit songs have you written for how many artists? I think you have a perfect handle on your life right now."

"That doesn't lessen the blow of my grandpa dying."

"I was there for you the last five months, getting, like, three hours of sleep some nights because I was at the hospital with you. I took an exam on two hours of sleep the night he died because you needed me, and I wanted to be there for you. I'm very well aware of how shitty things are right now, but they're going to get better. I told you that you wouldn't have to go through this alone, and you still don't have to."

My dad was never in my life, so my grandparents took my mom and me in. Gramps was the dad I never had. Just five days before, I serenaded two hundred people who came to Gramps's funeral to my own rendition of "Landslide" by Fleetwood Mac. He was still fresh in my mind. The clothes hanging in his closet still smelled like him. His last glass of water still sat on his bedroom nightstand. The last record he listened to was still on his record player. With him gone, I could hardly get myself out of bed. I could hardly go through a day without drinking or smoking weed, and most importantly, I couldn't even sit down at the piano and write a goddamn song. Writing was my therapy. Sitting at the baby grand piano or fingerpicking Gramps's '77 acoustic Hummingbird guitar cured me from whatever emotions were weighing me down. Instead of a diary, I wrote songs in my brown leather notebook. But I had felt so much over the past few months; it was like the words congealed into the knot constantly in my throat. I had nothing to contribute to my notebook. My therapy wasn't even working for me. If I couldn't even seek out the things I loved, how could I possibly be in a relationship? My life was still toppling into a disintegrated heap.

"Is this because you wanna hook up?" she was gutsy enough to ask.

"Oh my God, no," I said with a raised voice because her accusation was so ridiculous. Hooking up was the last thing on my mind. Cancer ruining your family doesn't really make you horny. Alanna and I used to have amazing sex. I guess that was what happened when you chased each other down for four years. All the tension we held in for so long exploded into months of blissful sex until my grandpa got sick, and nothing made me in the mood anymore. So, this definitely wasn't about hooking up.

"I can't believe you even think that," I continued.

"You're running because this is somewhat serious? Because we've been together for a year? After everything we've been through, you wanna end it?"

"How can you not see that I haven't been myself? I'm tired of feeling this way, and I need to focus on myself."

She got up from the couch as she dabbed her face. "You haven't been able to sleep by yourself for the past week because you didn't want to be alone, but now you actually want to be alone?"

All those sleepless nights provided me with clarity. Yes, I wanted to be alone.

"Alanna, you're not even trying to understand where I'm coming from. Have you really enjoyed our relationship for the past few months?"

"No, I haven't," she answered with another eye wipe. "But life happens, and it gets shitty. It doesn't mean I stopped loving you or stopped wanting to be with you. But clearly, that's what it means for you."

"Alanna—"

"If this is what you really want, Blair, then fine. I'll leave and set you free." I rolled my eyes. Nope, she wasn't going to try to understand where I was coming from at all. "You have a nice tour. I really do hope you find the happiness you're looking for." The anger in her voice didn't convince me that she was sincere. Right as she twisted the door handle, she turned back around with her eyebrows tighter together as if she was preparing for one last punch to the gut. "By the way, you're not fooling anyone. I know you're on coke right now. Real nice."

My stomach dropped. I just broke up with the girl who knew my darkest secret. Not even Miles, my best friend and bandmate, knew about the coke or the other times I did it in my life.

My heart thrummed faster in my chest. "What? How did you—"

"He would've been really disappointed in you, you know."

"*Don't* bring my dead grandpa into this."

"You've been self-destructing for months, and I still stayed by you."

"I never asked you to. I'm not some studying material for your thesis, okay? I don't need you to save me."

Things I just learned: breaking up with a girl currently getting her master's in social work would bite you in the ass.

"Fuck you, Blair." She wiped her eyes, but the tears wouldn't stop staining her face. "Seriously. Fuck you. You know, you never drank as much as you do now until your grandpa started getting sick, and now that's all you do. If you don't want your life to fall apart, how about you stay sober?"

And then she slammed the door shut. I rubbed out the tension in my face and then downed a shot of Southern Comfort and strapped my blue-green Fender electric guitar around my body as Miles came back from the bathroom. This happened every show. His nerves were like black coffee running right through his body, and even though we'd been performing together since high school, he still had the preshow bowel movement.

"Sorry," he said, sweeping his brown hair out of his face before he snatched his drumsticks off the couch. "I'm just thinking about how we're going from playing for two thousand people tonight to, like, ten thousand people in a few weeks, and it's really getting to me."

"You need to eat more cheese. We'll make sure to pack up the fridge with that. And Imodium."

His honey-colored eyes met mine, and clearly, a breakup showed on my face because his eyebrows creased when he studied me. "Did something happen? I saw Alanna crying in the hallway. She didn't even say hi to me. She ran past me."

I plucked a couple of strings on my guitar, making sure everything still sounded in tune, even though I tuned the guitar about a half hour ago. If Miles's preshow bowel movement was his nervous habit, then overtuning my guitar was mine. "Oh, yeah, I just broke up with her."

His mouth dropped. "What? Just now?"

"Yeah."

"In a green room?"

"Yup."

"Ten minutes before our show?"

"I know it wasn't ideal."

"Jesus, Blair, this is a big deal. Are you okay? You sound kind of cavalier about the whole thing."

I shrugged. "I'm fine. Just kinda numb. She hates me. She doesn't get why I did it, and she really didn't want to even try to get it."

"Did you tell her you've been feeling off for a while?"

"Yeah, I also think that's a given with the whole no sex and no writing thing." I hopped off the couch and made my way to the door. We would be called to take the stage any moment.

"Is there anything I can do?"

"Yeah, we're not playing 'Finally' tonight or, like, in the foreseeable future. So tonight, let's do a cover of 'My Friends Over You.' I think it fits my mood right now."

He placed his hand over his heart. "You know early 2000s songs are my weakness."

"I know, it's half of the reason why I chose it. Now, let's go rock this."

Miles and I formed our band senior year at our LA art high school. We'd been doing shows for six years, starting with college parties, to local restaurants and venues, to opening acts for smaller musicians, to now shows with a few thousand people packed into them, soon to be sold-out arena shows all over the country. Every show we'd done in the last six years, I was able to step on stage and leave whatever crap was inundating my mind backstage. So, this show was no different. Since Gramps took a turn for the worst, we canceled all of our shows leading up to the Reagan Moore World Tour. It was our first show in four months, and I was determined to give it my all. Nothing was going to hold us back. Not the death of my grandpa, who would have sworn at me if I sulked and sucked because of him. Not because of Alanna. Not because of anything.

The second we stepped on stage and the music we made poured through the speakers, the lights flickering on us and hearing two thousand fans singing along to our songs, it enhanced the high already running through my body. I forgot all my troubles, focused on the thumping music, the crowd, and making sure that the four months of not performing didn't take its toll on us. If we were going to open for the American leg of Reagan Moore's world tour, we couldn't settle for anything less than perfect for our comeback show in Silver Lake.

I worked the crowd more than usual and even crowd-surfed, which was always a thrilling time. It was even better when you were high. When I crowd-surfed during our cover of "My Friends Over You," I absorbed all the vitality from the crowd as their hands gracefully glided me over them. The warm rush of adrenaline pumped through my body as the music blasted through the speakers and enhanced their singing and cheering. When the show ended, sweat dripped down my face and stuck my shirt to my back. That was how you knew when you had a good show. You felt as if you got back from the gym on cardio day.

Afterward, I powered through the coke comedown while chatting with a few fans by the merch table, taking pictures with them, signing some autographs—and I even signed my first boob, so that was the highlight of my night. With the enhanced high feeling that got me through my performance came the enhanced low feeling. At least there was one thing I learned from my general education classes in high school and college that I could apply to real life. For every action, there was an equal and opposite reaction, and I'm pretty sure that when Newton came up with that, he meant being high on drugs. The high made me weightless and soar, and then when I came crashing down, it made me sink as much as I soared. The past few months squeezed on my chest; Alanna's cries stung my eyes. The emotions I kept suppressing to satisfy the fans balled up in my throat.

That was my cue to head back to my mom's. At least we had each other to lean on, and I really needed my mom just to scoop me up in her arms.

I'm not sure how I made it all the way back to Irvine from Silver Lake. I kind of drove mechanically on the 5 until I snapped out of my long daydream as I parked the car in front of the house I grew up in. I rested my head against the headrest; the radio faintly played through the speakers. I inhaled a deep breath to collect a few more moments for myself before I endured walking into a house barely recognizable without Gramps inside it. I let the radio continue to play because pure silence was something I didn't think my wandering mind could handle at the moment.

"This is WQRD, who is this?" the radio announcer said in the typical announcer cadence.

"This is Ashley. Oh my God, did I win?"

"You are caller twenty-one. Congratulations! You just won two front row seats to the Reagan Moore concert!"

Her screaming brought a little smile to my face. It was a nice reminder, given really shitty circumstances, that people were so thrilled to see the show Miles and I were going to open for. That was a positive I was going to cling on to like a security blanket. It reminded me that excitement was around the corner, that in two weeks, I'd be traveling all over the country with my best friend, performing in front of tens of thousands of zealous fans every night with the biggest name in music. That was something to look forward to. It was enough to twitch a smile out of me, knowing how excited Gramps had been when I told him the news.

"How do you feel, Ashley?" the announcer said.

"Amazing! I'm so excited! I couldn't get tickets because they sold out so fast."

"Lucky you and a friend will sit front row for the first show in Las Vegas for the Reagan Moore World Tour with opening act Midnight Konfusion. They're supposed to be great. You're going to have a great time, Ashley."

"Ah! I'm so excited!"

As Ashley screamed off air into a mattress sale commercial, I stared at the Spanish-style house, preparing myself for the vast emptiness that now made up the inside. Walking in and not seeing Gramps drinking a Johnnie Walker neat in front of his bookshelf, which housed hundreds of records, nodding to the music playing through his stereo headphones was still weird to me. It was a sight I'd seen every time I came home at night. It was his bedtime ritual. And for the past two weeks since his death, I hadn't gotten used to the empty chair and the silent record player.

Actually, it broke my heart every time.

I remembered back when I was a teenager and all those nights I snuck out of the house, creeping out of my window, butt sliding down the roof, and then leaping from the roof to perfect the two-story jump with my worst injury only being a sprained ankle. I was a little shit in high school. I had friends to meet up with and girls to make out with. But only once did I get caught sneaking out. This particular time, I ventured out to a party because this really hot junior wanted to make out with me. She was the kind of girl in high school you lusted so hard after that the lust would never go away, even long after you graduated. Sometimes, Dana Bohlen sprang into my head, and I ruminated about the furtive moments we shared and felt equally nostalgic and turned on at the same time. I was sixteen, and a hot "straight" girl wanted to fool around with me. Sign me right up, which I did. Pronto. But after Dana Bohlen and I used each other to satisfy our needs, I crept back into the house at one thirty in the morning, stopping dead in my tracks in the dark kitchen when I found Gramps in that computer chair, full-sized headphones around his neck as he searched the bookshelf for a new album. The lamp on the end table was the only light on the first floor, casting weak rays up the twenty-foot ceiling.

"Nice try," he said without giving me any eye contact.

I couldn't remember the last time Gramps was up past midnight. It was a crazy night if he was up past ten. But sure enough, there he sat, exchanging Marvin Gaye's "Let's Get It On" with Jim Croce's "I've Got a Name" with a full glass of Johnnie Walker neat sitting on the end table.

My heart pounded in my chest. Gramps was someone you didn't want to disappoint, and the sixteen-year-old me thought I was so smart and slick not to get caught by Mom, Grandma, or Gramps, but here I was with a light literally shining on my face.

"I, uh, I…"

"Yeah, you better be stuttering. Care to share where you snuck off to?" He finally gave me eye contact, his brownish-gray, furrowed eyebrows directed sharply at me.

Going down on Dana Bohlen, I answered in my head, and then the memory of my face in between her legs replayed, and God, I couldn't get turned on again in front of my grandpa.

"Just with friends," I replied way too quickly to be believable.

"And what kind of trouble were you and your friends up to?"

Alcohol, weed, and orgasms.

"Nothing. Just watching a movie."

He let out his loud, distinct cackle, and the memory of it pulled a smile from me. His laugh was contagious…except for when he laughed right before he lectured you. "You really think I'm dumb enough to believe my sixteen-year-old granddaughter when she sneaks back into the house on a beautiful summer night, that she just watched movies with her friends? Well, I'm not that dumb, but it's entertaining that you think I am."

The man was a genius. An actual genius as a musician, a songwriter, a music producer, and as a father to his daughter and granddaughter. Joseph Bennett didn't fuck around. I didn't know why I always challenged him growing up when deep down, I knew the truth.

"I had a wine cooler," I lied, but I knew what he was looking to get out of me. I had a few wine coolers and several shots of really bad-tasting vodka, but I would rather have admitted I had a Mike's Hard Lemonade instead of admitting that I gave Dana Bohlen an orgasm before she returned the favor. I was close with my grandpa, but not *that* close. Never that close.

"Scandalous," he said sarcastically. I was surprised by how much his strict Nashville upbringing was stripped from only two years of living in Southern California. "I always said if you're going to drink, A: tell me, and B: stay put and do not drive. So, you broke two of those rules. Oh yeah, and you're still grounded for getting brought home by that cop a month ago for pool hopping."

"I'm sorry."

"No, you're not. There's no reason to lie to me, Blair. I trusted you. That's why I always told you to be honest with me, and you won't get in trouble. I don't know why you disobeyed me when I thought we had a pretty fair agreement. You know, your grandma has gotten on my case for being this liberal with you, and now that you've proved me wrong multiple times in the last month, maybe I shouldn't have these lenient rules. If you're not going to respect them, then you don't deserve to have them. It's a privilege, not a right."

"I'm sorry," I said again, though looking back on it, his words resonated as much as any authority figure's words could resonate with a hormonal, broody teenager. I think it was because I knew that I was Gramps's weakness, and maybe because we had such an abnormally close bond for a grandfather and granddaughter that I sometimes took advantage of that. It wasn't until he was gone when I realized it.

"One day, when you're finally an adult, I'm going to be gone, and you're going to remember all these stupid antics you're up to now, and you're going to regret them. You're better than this. Don't disappoint me. I didn't raise my granddaughter to be disappointing. I raised her to be tough, independent, and most importantly, a loyal, honest, genuine person."

"I'll be honest next time. I'm sorry."

"Good. Until next time, no phone, no computer, and I'll finally get that security system installed, and guess what?"

I gulped. Okay, this was getting pretty shitty. "What?"

"I'll be the only one who knows the code to turn it off."

Out came the contagious cackle as he spun around to set the Jim Croce album on the turntable.

That memory repeated itself in my head as I stared at his huge house from the driveway. I started crying and then punched the steering wheel as I imagined going inside to see Gramps in that chair, telling me he warped through heaven or wherever the hell he was just to kick my ass for doing coke and breaking up with my girlfriend.

When I finally calmed down and wiped my eyes dry, I walked through the mudroom, and the security system dinged to let Mom know someone stepped into the house. Yes, Gramps was really serious about that security system. He got it the next week and kept his word about being the only one who knew the code. It wasn't until his final days when he whispered the code to me. It was my birthday. Zero five two three. The whole time, it was my birthday, and after he told me in the hospital, that infamous bellow of a laugh seeped out of him.

He got the last laugh, and I loved it and hated it at the same time.

Walking through the mudroom into the kitchen, I froze when I saw that end table light on, the computer chair facing the bookshelf, and music softly pouring from the record player. I blinked a couple of times, wondering and hoping that this was all a dream, and Gramps was really alive again. Maybe something happened, and I traveled back in time to when I was sixteen and had a chance to take back all the crap my petulant antics put him through.

The chair spun around, and I found Mom holding a whiskey neat in her hands as "The Way We Were" by Barbra Streisand played. My stomach twisted hearing the song and seeing my mother's tearstained face and puffy red eyes. It was the song Gramps sang on the piano during Grandma's funeral when I was eighteen. The vaulted, twenty-foot ceiling echoed the melody of the song in the house that doubled in size without him in it. Mom's dark brown eyes looked up at me through the gloss of tears.

"I broke up with Alanna," I said, my voice shaking from processing the scene in front of me.

"What? Honey? Why? Why did you do that?" she said through broken sniffles.

I gave a shrug, and I guess since the cocaine had left my system, all those emotions I buried came out in a cry.

"Oh, hon, let it out," Mom said. She downed the remains of her whiskey, set the glass on the end table, then opened her arms up for me. I curled on her lap despite being a few inches taller than her. But she took all my weight after letting out a small grunt and tightened her arms around me as if I was a little kid again, rubbing my back as I buried my face in her shoulders. "It's okay to cry. Just let it out."

"I really miss Gramps," I blubbered when I pulled myself away from her shoulder, noticing the tears staining her gray T-shirt. "At first, I thought he was in the chair."

Mom wiped away my tears. "I'm sorry to disappoint, hon," she said with a tiny smile. "Now, tell me why you broke up with Alanna."

"Because look at me. I'm a fucking mess. I'm leaving in two weeks. I need to be on my own." I ran my hand over my damp face. "God! I can't stop crying."

"How about we drink some whiskey and cry together? Let it all out."

"I don't need whiskey to cry when you're playing the world's most depressing song ever. Seriously, why are you doing this to yourself?"

"Because it's a great song and reminds me of my parents. Also, I need a good cry." She tucked a strand of hair behind my ear. "Gramps and Grandma might be gone, but we've still got each other. We'll always have each other."

"I'm sorry I'm leaving you in two weeks."

"Honey, don't apologize. You're going on tour with Reagan Moore. I might be in my mid-forties, but even I know that she's a big deal. I'll be fine. Now, come on. Let's have a glass together and maybe turn this off and listen to Jim Croce."

That garnered a grin from me. "I love Jim Croce."

"Me too. It reminds me of my dad."

She kissed my temple, and after fixing us both a drink, she continued to hug me as if I was a little kid as opposed to a soon-to-be twenty-four-year-old, but I let her. After months of taking care of her and Gramps, I needed someone to scoop me up and hold me, and since I snipped Alanna free from doing that, I turned to my mom, my best friend, my rock, my everything.

CHAPTER TWO

O h my God, my openers are here!" Reagan Moore exclaimed into her mic right as we took in the sight of the Las Vegas arena. In the midst of rows of folding chairs that made up the floor seats stood her enormous stage emerging from the concrete floor.

Her stage definitely proved we were all about to embark on a world tour with how massive it was. It took up the whole width of the arena, extending three-fourths of the way up to the ceiling and at least a quarter of the length of the floor. Plus, behind Reagan Moore and her band was a giant LCD screen for computerized digital effects and to show the close-up of her face while she performed.

This was the kind of stage every aspiring musician dreamed of performing on.

She looked so little in comparison to it, and when she found us soaking in the stage for the first time, she carefully hopped off, which had to have been more than a six-foot drop, but she did it without a grunt. Reagan Moore's head of wavy light blond hair bounced gracefully as she speed-walked over to us. Man, those magazine covers and billboards didn't do her beauty justice. That glowing smile of hers pinned me to the floor, and I wasn't sure if I was experiencing being starstruck or realizing that Reagan Moore had one of the most beautiful smiles I'd ever seen. Her face was free from makeup, her stud nose ring was in the same spot as my hooped one, and she wore a plain black V-neck and aqua track shorts, so the beauty was nothing but pure.

She first pulled our manager, Corbin, in for a hug, and then as she hugged Miles, her dark blue eyes met mine. That was when my armpits started sweating. Her facial features were so delicate, and her eyes were so soft that I don't think she had the ability to ever hurt anyone. I'd met her once about a year ago at a label party Gramps's business partner hosted at his house, and I didn't remember sweating. Even though back then we only exchanged pleasantries, somehow, I made it through that first conversation without armpit sweat.

After greeting Miles and Corbin, she opened her arms for me and took me in as if I was a longtime friend. "It's nice to see you again, Blair. How are you doing?"

When she broke the hug, her stare held sympathy, and I almost missed it because I was too busy smelling her designer perfume. She smelled as beautiful as she looked.

"Pretty good," I responded, which was half true. At this particular moment, knowing that in four hours, the place would be packed with roughly thirteen thousand people and Miles and I would perform our first ever show in a sold-out arena, life was pretty good. Gramps would have wanted me to focus on this, not the crap outside, so I would push away my grief for him.

Her hand landed on my shoulder. "I'm glad. And I just want to say that I'm so sorry to hear about your grandpa's passing. I was fortunate enough to have met him a couple of times, and he was always so kind and funny."

"Thank you. Yeah, he was a pretty amazing guy."

"I'm glad you're doing okay, though. I'm so excited to have you guys come on tour with me. I think you both are absolutely brilliant."

"And we feel the same way about you," Miles said. "We can't wait until we get on that stage."

"Well, I'm done sound checking, so she's all yours now. Oh, and after your sound check, we're having a feast. Come hungry. There will be champagne."

"You don't need to ask us twice," I said.

"I'm gonna go shower up, but I'll see you two in an hour!"

❖

Reagan Moore wasn't lying when she said they were having a feast. It made sense because she had to feed her opener, her band, her dancers, and all of her crew. And that meant about fifty people. Yes, fifty people, which made sense when I saw the fleet of buses that came with her. Reagan Moore came with a stage that took up practically half an arena floor, eight sleeper buses, four tractor trailers, and a whole army.

Four long tables of every single kind of food I could imagine stretched across the entire wall. Sandwiches, fruit, vegetables, salads, and cases upon cases of water. Her manager, Finn, informed everyone to grab a flute of champagne for a toast. Her army separated into cliques, her dancers in full concert makeup and coifed hair circled around each other with small plates of food since they were about to endure an hour and a half of dancing. The stage crew in their black T-shirts loaded up on sandwiches after all the hauling and setting up they already did for the day.

As Miles, Corbin, and I fixed our plates, my eyes fixed on Reagan Moore as she entered the room and eyed all the food in front of her. I couldn't control myself from scanning her head to toe. Her blond hair with loose, natural waves cascaded down to breasts that were slightly revealed by the dip in her long-sleeved, sparkly black bodysuit that ended right at her bikini line. And if that revealing black bodysuit wasn't enough to kick-start impure thoughts, she wore black knee-high boots to highlight the toned legs her bodysuit accentuated. The blue in her eyes popped even more from the dark dusting of her eye makeup. My lips parted as her beauty swept me up in a hazy cloud, and once I realized my mouth was open, I closed it and swallowed.

And then without warning, she turned around and met my gaze, and that was when I realized Miles and Corbin weren't beside me anymore.

"You skipped out on the salad?" she asked and looked up at me with a teasing grin. I stood there, heat attacking my cheeks, forgetting what I even put on my plate despite the fact I was just at the food table thirty seconds before. "What?"

She pointed to my plate, free from any sort of vegetable but loaded up with tiny sandwiches, fruit salad, and a nice handful of potato chips. "No salad. I caught you."

"Oh, yeah, I kinda hate vegetables."

"Seriously?" She acted as if I told her I hated ice cream, which was way more shocking than someone hating vegetables.

"I mean, carrots are cool."

"Carrots are cool? I didn't know a vegetable could be cool."

Who said vegetables were cool? God, how she repeated my lame comment made it seem as if she really thought I was lame. And I didn't blame her. But the grin still firmly intact made me wonder if she found my dumb carrot comment endearing.

"Yeah...I didn't know that either until I said it," I said shamefully.

She laughed. "Wanna go join Miles and Corbin at the crew table?"

We ate with a handful of guys from the crew, all built as if they could do some heavy lifting. I caught Miles eyeing one of the guys who had to be around our age: styled brown hair, a scruffy five o'clock shadow, with long, thick eyelashes and gray eyes. I knew exactly where his mind was.

"Down, boy," I whispered to Miles.

He snapped his attention to me. "What?"

"I see you drooling."

He wiped his mouth as his cheeks turned pink. "I'm not drooling."

But he was. He went back to eating his salad, but I still caught him ogling. When I moved to LA, Miles Estes was the first friend I made. We had first period history together, and I'd smelled the remnants of stale weed emanating from him, which I didn't expect coming from this skinny kid with a kind, fresh face, rocking black skinny jeans and a gray sweater over a white collared shirt. He looked too straight edge. I asked him if he had some, and he told me to meet him under the football bleachers during lunch. That was how our friendship started. But then once we were comfortable enough to ask about each other's dating life, I found out Miles was bi at the same time he found out I was a lesbian, and both of our eyes lit up as if we had just found our person. At fourteen, we didn't know a lot of people who were out, so knowing that we were queer really solidified our friendship.

His eyes lit up with the bearded crew guy the same way they lit up when he found a gay friend.

"Okay, maybe a little," Miles admitted when he took a sip of water. "He has really nice eyelashes."

After we all ate, Reagan grabbed her champagne flute and stood on her chair. "Hey, guys! I'd like to make a toast," she said over the chatter.

But my gaze went straight to those sexy legs and black knee-high boots. She circled her attention around the room. "So, tonight is the big night," she said, and everyone in the room "wooed" and clapped. "Ten months of planning this tour and working tirelessly to perfect every note, every dance move, every light, the stage, and it's finally here, and I couldn't be more grateful to have all of you by my side. This tour wouldn't be possible without you. This show is sold out, over thirteen thousand people are going to be in that arena tonight. Take in all the sights and sounds. Live in the moment because we're so lucky that this is what we do for a living. We'll look back on these days when we're older and wish we could relive all of this. We'll remember the friendships we made on this tour, the smiles on the fans, the energy running through us. Don't take this for granted. Enjoy every second of it. And to my wonderful opener."

She turned to us with a full smile, and her stare caused my stomach to do backflips again, something I'd never felt until Reagan Moore stood in front of me with that glowing smile; piercing, dark-blue eyes; and those damn boots practically waving hello. It was so hard to look at her eyes instead of her long, built legs that begged for my attention. "I've been a fan of you guys for quite some time, and I knew once I heard your EPs that I wanted you guys to open for me someday. So badly. The fans are going to love you just as much as I do, I know it. You never forget your first arena show, so enjoy it. It's one for the record books." She raised her glass. "And, everyone, today is Blair Bennett's birthday, so that means we have to sing and embarrass her."

Her manager, Finn, came to the table with a giant chocolate cake, the number two and four candles already lit, and in white icing, it said "Happy birthday, Blair." She was definitely right. I was embarrassed that all those people looked at me and sang "Happy Birthday," but it was a good embarrassment. I only expected some beers with Miles and Corbin on the bus ride to Vegas, which had happened, and then my birthday would go completely unnoticed in the shadow of the excitement of the first show of the tour and the fact that this was my first birthday with Gramps gone and no family around me.

But the gesture was really sweet, given the fact Reagan Moore and I hadn't exchanged more than ten sentences up until that point.

An hour and a half later, Miles and I consumed our preshow shots of Patrón and Southern Comfort. We stood in the darkness of the side stage, calming our pounding hearts with deep breaths. Miles drummed on his black skinny jeans as I plucked each string of my Fender to make sure they were perfectly in tune, then wiped my clammy hands on my faux leather pants. Miles and I practiced at least four hours a day, and being confined to a bus while traveling all over the country, I was eager to go out and take the stage, strum my first chord, use my looping station, and play all the other seven instruments I brought to wow the fans. As much as I was excited and bursting at the seams to get out there to play, I also felt so hollow knowing that Gramps wasn't alive to witness this. When I told him that Reagan Moore wanted us to open for her, his smile took up his whole face, and his dark brown eyes sparkled in the fluorescent hospital lights. The first round of chemotherapy drugs ran through the tubes into his body, and it was only a matter of time before he started to feel the awful side effects of it, but that didn't seem to matter to him. He reached for my hand, clasped it tightly, and said, "I haven't been prouder of you than I am right now. My little Piglet is going to be a rock star." And his voice repeated that same comment from wherever he was in the universe, bringing tears to my eyes that I forced back down in my throat because I couldn't afford to have mascara run down my face.

This performance was for Gramps, the man who raised me, the man who always encouraged my love of music, the man who taught me everything about life, and the strong, intelligent, caring person I hoped to one day be.

This is for you, Gramps.

The lights of the arena hid us in darkness until my Fender ignited the lights for our opening song. It was our job to warm up the crowd for Reagan Moore. In three years, our band made three EPs and we were currently working on our first full-length album. Our song "Tomorrow"—a song about procrastinating and drinking on the beach instead of dealing with the real world—never failed as the opener. And it didn't fail that night in Las Vegas either. Just a few measures in with the wailing of my Fender, the lights burst on and revealed the thirteen thousand people exploding into a cheer I knew I'd never forget. I remembered Reagan's pep talk and took in the sight of the faces in front of me and the bodies extending to the far back of the arena, phones in the air, glow sticks bouncing around in the low and high levels; all of it only encouraged me to run up and down the stage to hype up the crowd, encouraged the adrenaline to pump faster, and my fingers to push harder on the strings for extra oomph.

By the end of the seven-song list, I found myself hammering away at the Fender on top of one of those five-foot speakers on the end of the stage, teasing the crowd on the floor and the lower level as I improvised some riff, feeding off their energy and loudness that pierced my in-ear monitors. The crowd on the floor shifted over to me, their hands in the air, sweat sticking to their foreheads a tad less than mine, and their cheers begging for more. As the last chord rang out, I thought, damn, this is fucking amazing. Now this is a high.

That night in Las Vegas, I realized that my love for music and performing might be the cure I needed to sew my life back together. The energy the crowd gave off was addictive. It was even more addictive when they sang the words to our songs right back at us. As an opener, I kind of assumed many people out there in the audience used my stage time as a buffer between bathroom and beer breaks and the main show. And sure, plenty of people did that. Seats were still empty around the arena that slowly filled up the further into our set list we got. But with about three-fourths of the seats already filled with fervent fans, the sounds of them singing to us was a magical cocktail of all the right emotions for me to feel hopeful about the next year on tour. As much as it hurt to know that Gramps was gone, and he wasn't here to witness the biggest show we had to date, I knew that he would kick my ass if I didn't take every detail in or fully bask in the glory that was performing in front of people.

And that was what made me smile when I fell asleep in my bunk that first night. This tour? I knew it would save me and put me back on track for this little thing called life.

CHAPTER THREE

B oys. I hated them.

Corbin and Miles were velociraptors when they slept. Miles would say it was because of his deviated septum, but honestly, I was sick and tired of people in Southern California blaming everything on a deviated septum. It was liberally self-diagnosed as with doctors diagnosing kids with ADD in the nineties. Deviated septum or not, the dude kept me up at night and really needed to go to a Walgreens to find some breathing strips. Or a sleep clinic. He needed to go to the sleep clinic.

The cadence of their snoring refused to be in sync, and it was the hellish version of the *Jurassic Park* theme song in the bus. How our bus driver, Tony, was able to even drive through those snores was beyond me. I guess if you lived life as a hippie in the sixties, going on tour with all the rock 'n' roll greats, you learned to live through any kind of madness.

The sun was my enemy in Salt Lake City. For someone who only had four hours of sleep, that bright, strong Utah sun felt as if I was being smote in a Catholic church.

I opened the storage door on the side of the bus to grab as many instruments as I could. My Hummingbird, mandolin, ukulele. I almost had the electric violin when I felt a hand on my shoulder. I jumped straight up to find Miles's crew crush with the nice eyelashes laughing at my flinching.

"You're doing my job," he said with a smile, pointing to the gear.

He held out his palm to save me from carrying any of my instruments. I guess we really weren't in Kansas anymore. Gone were the days of me and Miles shoved in a hand-me-down white passenger van with all of our equipment to load and unload, and hello to the days Reagan Moore hired two full sleeper coaches of roadies to do it for us.

I handed him the instruments. "Right, sorry about that. I'm still getting used to this."

"I've been with Reagan since the beginning, and I'm still getting used to it."

"Just be careful with this one. Most prized possession." I pointed to the Hummingbird case.

"I'll handle it with all the love and care. Promise."

Then Miles's beau walked away, and I almost felt bad that Miles was still on the bus, missing his chance to gawk at his dreamboat. But then speaking of dreamboats, out of nowhere, Reagan's blond hair grabbed my attention more than the bright summer sun. She smirked at me with her eyes hidden under her black Gucci glasses, and she clutched a steel coffee container in her hands. My scowl must have given something away because when she looked at me, she laughed.

"Late night?" she said, and I could hear the caffeine humming through her perky voice.

She was decked out in yoga attire that could definitely serve as a shot of espresso for me. The mandala, ocean-printed yoga pants hugged every muscle of her quads and calves while her black racerback tank top showed off those arms. Now I understood how she seamlessly jumped off that enormous stage without a grunt.

Any remaining moisture in my mouth was sucked up by Reagan Moore in her yoga outfit. How did I sign up for that yoga class?

"Yeah, uh, I guess you could say that," I answered through my arid throat.

"Too much Southern Comfort?"

"Oh, no. More like Corbin and Miles make it sound like we're living in *Jurassic Park* in there."

She laughed. "Yeah…sometimes I have FOMO with no bus mates. And other times—like this one—I'm totally glad that I don't. Especially boys. They're loud."

"And they smell," I added.

"And they sweat constantly."

"And they never put the seat down."

Reagan laughed and tucked a stray hair that didn't make it in the ponytail behind her ear. "If you ever need to escape the snoring, I have a noise machine that I don't use because well, not to brag or anything, but I have a whole bus to myself. Don't really need it."

"Ouch," I said and threw a hand over my heart. "Rub it in a little more, will you?"

"Hey, I'm just saying. Oh, and coffee. I have more coffee." She jiggled her travel mug, and I could hear the coffee sloshing around in it.

"Oh my God, coffee. I need some."

She offered me her mug. "Take the rest. I don't need any more. It's my second mug."

"Really?"

"Really. It's yours."

I gladly accepted. "You're a lifesaver."

"Swing by after the show, and the sound machine is all yours."

She winked and headed back into her bus.

With that wink and the blazing sun, I melted right in my spot.

❖

I went and got that noise machine the next night after we finished our Denver show, where we took full advantage of the legalization of weed. Miles set aside his "deviated septum" card for the "I smoked too much" card when it came to providing an excuse as to why he sounded like a T. rex in heat. The ceramic llama cookie jar that we carefully wrapped in a blanket for extra padding and stored on one of the three empty bunks was now filled with edible gummies, suckers, and plenty of buds, like a stocking on Christmas morning. The only downside to all of the weed was that Corbin's and Miles's bodies really reacted well to it when it came to sleeping. And that meant a cacophony of snores.

So, when the meet and greets were over and while the crew packed up the stage, I decided to take advantage of Reagan's offer. I knocked on her bus door, and Martin, her driver, called to her somewhere in the back of the bus that she had a guest, and I watched her messy bun make its way over to me. She'd already changed out of her concert attire into her more comfortable pj's, a loose Bonnaroo Music Festival T-shirt from last year and neon green track shorts that showed off those damn legs.

It was a struggle to look her in the eyes.

"So, I'll make you a deal," I said and held up an unopened bottle of rosé and a pan of homemade lemon bars I baked for my bus before the tour. "These delicious treats for that noise machine?"

"Wow, wine and lemon bars? Did you make those?"

"I did. I like baking and thought I'd give the headliner a stash, so they're all yours. We ate some of them, but I also made a lot, so these ones are yours."

She accepted the pan with a grin. "Thank you, Blair. That's really sweet of you. I might have one right now."

"Go for it."

"And the wine? I'll be honest, I'm kind of shocked that you have rosé."

"What's wrong with rosé?"

"Nothing at all. I just expected you to offer, like, tequila or weed or something else."

"Oh, I totally have all those things if you want me to get some—"

She raised her hand. "I'm kidding, Blair. I would have never taken you as a rosé chick. Or a Southern Comfort gal, more importantly."

"Janis Joplin always drank SoCo before her shows," I explained.

"So SoCo is rock 'n' roll?"

I paused for a moment to think about it. "Well, I don't know. Janis Joplin liked it, so maybe."

"Your sleeve tattoo?" She gestured to my right arm, which was designed with textured black flowers and geometric mandalas coiling from about an inch from my wrist up to my shoulder. "Pretty rock 'n' roll. Your nose piercing? Pretty rock 'n' roll. Your Fender? Definitely rock 'n' roll. SoCo? Not in the slightest."

"The fact that Janis Joplin didn't fall into any rock 'n' roll cliché or stereotypes makes SoCo rock 'n' roll," I said.

"Whatever you say, SoCo girl. Come on in."

When I stepped in her tour bus for the first time, I inhaled cleanliness. I almost forgot what that smelled and looked like because living with boys meant that man musk would quickly take over. And man, did man musk quickly suffuse. I found myself spritzing perfume at Miles's and Corbin's bunks every morning as if splashing holy water on a possessed body. But Reagan's bus smelled like the inside of a candle store and looked like a Beverly Hills mansion on wheels. Mahogany cabinets in the kitchen, tiled floors, LED lights lining the path to the master suite. A sectional couch in the front. Two matching recliners next to it. A kitchen table with loveseats serving as the booths. A freaking electric fireplace.

I was afraid to walk on the tile because my flip-flops probably had specks of dirt caked on them, and her bus was so clean and beautiful. I noticed ocean breeze-scented air freshener beans on the granite countertop as I twisted the cork out of the bottle. Though she appeared to act like a normal twenty-three-year-old, it was the little things that reminded me she was anything but. Little things meaning her designer glasses, roadies to carry all of her tour equipment, and twelve-bus tour parade on the highway. And now her sumptuous set of wheels. Yup, her tour bus was exactly what I would expect an A-list celebrity tour bus to look like inside, and I definitely wasn't worthy enough to be in it.

"Is that a Winnie-the-Pooh tattoo?" she said and gestured to the back of my left tricep.

I poured us some wine into the plastic wine glasses. "Winnie and Piglet to be exact."

She laughed and took a generous sip of her wine as if she needed it for fuel. "That's pretty adorable."

"My grandpa used to sing 'Return to Pooh Corner' by Kenny Loggins to me every night when I was little. He always called me his Piglet. It was my first tattoo. He wasn't a fan. So, it's not a surprise he wasn't a fan of the sleeve or the nose ring."

"Okay, that's actually pretty adorable. But not rock 'n' roll."

"Man, you're giving me a beating tonight. And here I thought you were nice."

"I am nice. You just have to go through initiation. I like to blame it on my brothers. All they did growing up was tease me, so it's a sign of endearment."

She gestured for me to sit down. So, I opted for one of those recliners as she took a lemon bar and then stretched out on the sectional. She bit into the dessert, closed her eyes, tilted her head back, and let out the soft moan that activated my brain.

"God, Blair, this is amazing," she said in mid-chew behind her palm. "The crust on this…perfection."

Could she take another bite and moan again? Talk about perfection.

"I'm glad you like it," I said and pulled a large gulp of wine to wash away all those carnal thoughts.

"You bake a lot?"

I nodded. "Yeah, my grandma got me into it. She owned a bakery for the longest time when we used to live in Nashville."

"Nashville baby?"

"Yup, up until I was thirteen, and then I became a California teen."

She put her hand on her heart. "Aw, we're both going to have the same hometown shows." She took another bite of the lemon bar. "Hmm, God, between this and your birthday cake, I'm really gonna have to do some serious yoga tomorrow."

"Thank you for the cake, by the way. It was really sweet."

She waved a hand. "Oh, please. It's your birthday! Everyone deserves a cake on their birthday." She swallowed. "And a crowd of thirteen thousand people."

"It was quite the birthday to remember."

"We're three shows in, and everyone loves you guys. Like, I'm completely amazed by you guys. You know how long I've been a fan?"

I blushed and hid my cheeks behind my wine glass. It was pretty great being complimented by the most popular musician in the music business. "How long?"

"For at least two years. Isaac Ball got me into you guys."

"Oh yeah, Isaac. I cowrote with him on his last album."

"I know. When it came out, we grabbed some dinner, and he raved about you. The very first song, 'Tomorrow,' had me instantly hooked. And I had no idea that you played, what, eight instruments?"

"Right on the dot."

"List them."

I looked up. "Piano and guitar. Learned from my grandpa. Played violin all throughout school. First chair violin in the symphony orchestra right here."

She laughed and took another sip of wine. "So rock 'n' roll."

"Hey, let me bust out the electric violin I have, play a couple loops, and then change your mind."

She grinned. "Please do. That actually sounds intriguing. What about the other ones?"

"Well, my grandpa started giving me instruments to learn so I would stay out of trouble, and I became obsessed with them and taught myself. So, I learned ukulele, mandolin, harmonica, drums, and the bass guitar. Hoping to learn the banjo next."

"Wow, you're practically a musical prodigy. It's no wonder that you're Joseph Bennett's granddaughter. You inherited all his talent."

Who needed wine as a pick-me-up when I heard Reagan Moore relishing my music?

"Oh, well, thank you. That means a lot."

"And where did you learn to loop?"

"Honestly, I saw a street performer doing it in West Hollywood when I was a teenager. I stopped and asked him what he was doing, and he told me everything. I asked for a station for Christmas, and the rest is history."

We both took another liberal gulp, our eye contact never breaking, and because it never broke, my stomach did another backflip. Seriously. What was up with my stomach lately? Her stare drew me in to catch a closer look at the depths of her eyes. At one glance, I'd just catch a beautiful pair of blue eyes. But at a closer look, I almost caught a glimpse of a million stories she tucked way back in those depths. Stories of joy, sadness, hope, and heartbreak. I wanted to know them all.

"You look like you're in deep thought," Reagan said with what looked to be curiosity forming a half smile.

She caught me in deep thought about how beautiful her eyes were. I wasted a moment to think about what to say next.

"Just thinking about how I need another glass of wine."

From Denver to Santa Fe to Tampa to Miami, it was a lot of driving. A lot of music playing. A lot of fans singing back to us. A lot of fans we met and signed autographs for. The excitement of touring didn't get old. We hosted a party in a different city and venue every night. Drank and socialized with Reagan's dancers and crew after. I wondered if people ever got sick of touring because I didn't think I would. No part was boring. Not even all the driving. The driving days, Miles and I drank beers while writing songs, recording demos, and purposely annoying Corbin because it was easy and fun to do. We hadn't written in months due to my intense writer's block from Gramps's cancer and death, and though I still didn't feel one hundred percent back in it, I felt as if I was on the right path.

I was thankful when we reached Miami, a bustling city with a backdrop of tropical waters, beautiful people, and lots of booze and dancing. The bright blue waters were a wonderful sight after driving through the cornfields of Middle America for the past week.

Miles and I were so ready for the beach…and to be anywhere besides a bus. I got the hint that everyone else on the tour felt the same way because every time we landed in our next destination, we spilled from our buses, formed our cliques, and went off to sightsee if we had even two hours to kill before we had to start getting ready for the show. Everyone except for Reagan, who went straight to her hotel room to do God only knew what until she emerged again at the arena.

I hated that she never went out while all of us bonded, formed inside jokes, and took in the different sights of each city while she locked herself a hotel room, which I'm not sure was drastically different from her bus. She spent a lot of time being alone and cooped up. I don't know how she did it.

Miles made progress with the cute bearded guy during our adventures with the dancers and crew. Turned out, the bearded guy had a name. Ethan. A political science major who didn't want to do anything political science related, so he joined Reagan Moore's tour as a guitar tech. And when Miles, Corbin, and I decided to storm South Beach for some fun in the sun, he invited Ethan. Since Miles would be too busy flirting with a guy who might or might not be into him, I decided to take a risk by texting Reagan about our plans. I knew she would reject them given her history of all the other stops we made in the first week and a half. But even one of the most famous people in the world deserved to enjoy the fresh air, the fun, and to feel included on her own tour. It was worth a shot.

So, I texted her. *Miles, Corbin, and I are going to the beach at 11. Come join and have fun with us.*

She responded about a minute later. *That does sound really fun. I wish I could join but I can't.*

Me: *Oh, come on. It's beautiful out.*

Reagan: *Last time I went to the beach I got chased off it. True story.*

Me: *Wear a disguise. We can go find one of those fake mustaches to put on you.*

She texted me a smiley emoji, followed by, *I would love to, but I really shouldn't. I don't want to ruin your fun. Plus, I have a book I should finish.*

Me: *No! You never come out with us. I refuse to let you be a grandma at 23.*

Reagan: *Hey! There's a reason for my madness. It's called a stampede.*

Me: *We want you to come out! You deserve to have fun. Try it for a little, and if it's too much, then we head back. Promise. Enjoy the sunshine and the water. You know you want to.*

Reagan: *I really do. It sounds wonderful.*

Me: *Then join. Pretty, pretty please.*

I didn't get a response until two hours later when I heard a knock on my hotel door. When I opened it, I found Reagan in the worst possible disguise. Celebrities and their disguises. Did they really lose all perception of concealing identity once they got their million-dollar check and Twitter verification? The top half of her face was swallowed by a white floppy hat and those oversized black sunglasses, and the rest of her body hid underneath an aqua cover-up dress.

"Ready to hit the beach?" she said with a smile popping through her costume.

"Wait, is that your disguise?"

Her smile dropped. "What?"

"I mean, you look wonderful. No one will ever know it's you. You're just a regular gal in Gucci glasses underneath a cloud, I mean, floppy hat," I said and smacked the brim.

"Are you making fun of me?"

I laughed because she was actually dead serious, as if she legitimately thought it was a good attempt to disguise herself.

"No, why would I do that? It's not like you made fun of me on your bus, so that would be so cruel and unfair. Now, let's go. We're missing prime sun time."

We made it to one of the last open spots on South Beach without anyone recognizing her. Walking from our hotel to that spot, it felt as if we were helping a prisoner sneak out of jail. But as we laid our towels down, we were still safe. Miraculously.

"See, my disguise worked," Reagan said and dropped her designer bag down in the sand.

"Yeah, but how are you gonna get in the water with the hat?"

"Why do you keep going after the hat?"

"Um, because you went after my tattoo and alcohol choices."

I pulled out my sunscreen and attempted to apply it. Miles already was on it with Ethan. By the time I got my sleeve lathered up, he was rubbing sunscreen on Ethan's back, the two in their own little world and poor Corbin the lone man out, just waiting for a bottle.

"You need help with your back?" Reagan asked.

Miles and Corbin exchanged amused looks and then roared with laughter. Both of them knew better than to offer to help me with sunscreen. It freaked me out when people massaged the lotion into my skin. I didn't want their grimy hands touching every inch of my body the same way I'd use sensual oils to arouse my partner right before sex. Nope, it felt too intimate. I always did my own back. Also, if someone did your back, it was an unwritten rule that you did their back, and I really didn't want to lather someone up with sunscreen. Nope, I didn't want to touch their zits, hairy moles, or back hair. I kept my hands to myself, thank you.

But all that changed when I turned around at the sound of Reagan's question. There she stood in a white string bikini. My stare went right to her flat stomach and the lines that curved around her abs, probably from yoga and the dancing that was part of her set. And then my gaze fell to her very small bottoms and her muscular legs and then wandered up to her chest. The curves of her breasts were even more perfect than when they appeared in the dip of her black, sparkly bodysuit.

And there I stood, forgetting how to talk, frozen on South Beach on an early June day.

"Huh?" I meant to say, but the sound ended up coming out as an inaudible noise.

"Do. You. Need. Help. With. Your. Back?" Her question was filled with sass, but she eased it with her smirk.

"Oh, yeah, sure."

I held out the sunscreen mechanically, as if my arm was controlled by an unknown force. That force being her white string bikini. She grabbed the bottle, eyeing me suspiciously, and I hoped that it wasn't because she noticed my scanning every inch of her body. She squirted the lotion in her hand and motioned me to turn around. Right before she put her hands on me, she stopped before saying, "This is beautiful."

I sucked in my breath when her fingers touched the black dream catcher tattoo on the side of my ribs. As she traced along the feathers hanging down to the top of my obliques, this electricity hummed from my ribs straight down.

I suddenly needed to guzzle the water bottle I brought in my bag.

"Thank you. Second tattoo."

"Out of how many?"

I shrugged. "I don't know. I lost count when I got this done." I wiggled my right arm.

That was when her hands landed on my shoulders, shocking me with the cold lotion and the wonderful, gentle touch of her hands massaging that stuff into my skin. Slowly, gently, and methodically. It was almost as if she was purposely trying to make skin care sensual. And it worked because I inhaled from each touch, closing my eyes and basking in her hands wandering all over my back.

"Oh, so Reagan's allowed to put lotion on you, but you get creeped out when anyone else offers?" Miles whined.

I opened my eyes and found Miles standing there with crossed arms. Sunscreen painted his shoulders that hadn't been rubbed in by Ethan yet. He was also staring with a crooked grin.

"Okay, Miles." I tried to shut his trap, knowing the next words to follow.

Reagan laughed behind me as she squirted another round on my arm. Yup, there was no saliva left in my mouth when her boobs leaned into my back as her arms wrapped around me. "You don't let people help you with sunscreen?" she asked, and her question tickled the back of my neck.

"No, she doesn't," Corbin added and was too dumb to notice me shooting daggers right at his flapping mouth. "She thinks it's too sexual."

"No, I don't—"

"Last summer, when we went to Huntington Beach," Miles continued, "you refused to let us help you with sunscreen. You even turned down Alanna when she offered—her girlfriend, for the record," he informed Ethan and Reagan, "and then you got that giant-ass burn on your back that had you bedridden for four days. Remember that?"

"Wow, you really don't like sunscreen, do you?" Ethan said as he returned the sunscreen application to Miles, whose smug smirk grew even wider when Ethan resumed.

"She doesn't," Miles said. "And then she begged her ex-girlfriend to put aloe all over her back after that."

"Remind me to kick sand in your face when she's done, okay?" I said.

Reagan playfully slapped my shoulders. "All done, SoCo girl. I'm honored to have been allowed to help you prevent skin cancer. Now, do you mind returning the favor? Or is that too weird?"

"She won't do it," Corbin said. "It's another part of the reason why she hates people putting lotion on her back. She doesn't want to rub anyone's skin—"

I snatched the bottle out of Reagan's hands before Corbin could finish. "I got this. Nice try, though."

Reagan welcomed my lotion-covered hands by lifting her beach-curled hair. I applied the sunscreen on her back the same way she did mine. Slowly kneaded it in her skin, making sure the neck that collected all her stress really got protected from the UV rays. Her skin was so soft, and feeling each curve of her upper back created a low burn in my stomach that radiated down to underneath my bikini bottoms.

"I think Blair has a crush on Reagan," Corbin chanted not so quietly to Miles and Ethan, who rewarded him with teasing laughter.

"I think we're past the 'like' level," Miles said. "I've known her since we were fourteen, and not once have I ever seen her allow people to rub sunscreen on her. It has to be *love*."

I lowered the bottle and glared at all three of them. "Stop making this weird. Seriously."

And I could see the tug of Reagan's lips from her ears, only encouraging their banter. "Yeah, guys," Reagan said. "I'm getting a great massage out of it. Plus, I really believe in exposure therapy, so shut up."

I ignored their banter because the woman who basically owned the radio and the music charts needed to be protected from the strong

Florida rays, or she would be too sunburned to perform, leaving thousands of people devastated and their whole summers ruined. So, basically, I was doing the world justice by touching her skin.

Slowly, my oily hands slid down her back, making a pit stop halfway down where her bikini top tied together. I glided my hands underneath the knot and then to the side, sweeping down the curve of her stomach, then to the small of her back. She leaned her head to the side, and I could have sworn she let out a heavy sigh. A similar sigh to the one that escaped her when she tried my lemon bars.

When I was all finished with the best task ever given to me, she let her hair down and faced me, revealing a satisfied smile. "Well, that was probably the best sunscreen application I've ever received."

"Had to make sure your skin was thoroughly protected."

"Oh, it's thoroughly protected. Thanks for the massage," she said and placed a hand on my shoulder for a brief second.

After that low-key, arousing moment, I made it my mission to be by her and her string bikini for the rest of the time on the beach.

I couldn't believe her floppy hat and Gucci glasses worked like DEET to mosquitoes, but it did. The five of us spent an hour making a crappy excuse for a sandcastle without having any buckets. Miles and Ethan worked on the moat while Corbin, Reagan, and I sculpted the castle. During the whole sandcastle building, no one spotted her. Granted, she still wore her floppy hat and sunglasses, so it was pretty difficult to make out her face, but Reagan even made a comment how wonderful it felt to go unnoticed and do something as simple as building a sandcastle on the beach.

"You know the last time I did something normal like this in public?" she asked. "Two years ago, I stuck my hair up in a beanie and wore a baggy shirt and sweatpants and no makeup and saw a movie. Those two hours were wonderful. I got a large buttered popcorn. A fountain soda. Sat in the darkest corner like a creep. No one bothered me."

I started to feel bad for her. Part of me didn't because everything she had going for her in her career was something I'd dreamed of having ever since I successfully played the treble clef part of "Heart and Soul" on the piano with Gramps when I was five. But the other part of me couldn't fully understand what it was like worrying about going to the beach or the movies or the convenience store down the street. I still had that luxury.

"So, you're glad you risked it and came out?" I asked.

"Yeah. Thanks for dragging me out. It's nice being invisible for once all while getting tan." She winked.

But by the end of our art sculpting, the five of us took a step back to admire our mediocre work with sweat dripping down our faces. It was a hot day in Miami, with only a few clouds shielding us from the sun. When we finished our sandcastle, we were ready to take a refreshing dip in the bright blue water. The only one who was hesitant was Reagan, knowing she would have to leave her invisibility behind when she removed her floppy hat and sunglasses.

"Remember what I told you," I said. "We can leave anytime. I'll kick sand at anyone who tries to bother you."

That pulled a smile from her. She tossed the hat on the towels and joined Miles, Ethan, and me in frolicking to the water like little kids, while Corbin volunteered to stay behind to watch our stuff. Miles and I fully committed by diving into the crashing waves, allowing the water to wash away the sweat from our faces and bodies. Reagan stayed behind with Ethan waist deep, while Miles and I spent the next few minutes challenging the waves each time they curled forward.

Something about getting tossed around by the ocean waves was thrilling to me.

After I popped my head back up after a few dives and blew the salt water out of my nose, I searched for Ethan and Reagan only to find them back where our towels were with Corbin. A group of teenage girls huddled around Reagan with phones extended in their arms. Despite warning me how she couldn't go out because of this very reason and despite her subtle complaints about always being noticed, she still bent down to appease her fans, wrapping her arms around them. Ethan and Corbin did nothing but take pictures.

Being invisible only lasted so long for her.

"Oh shit," I said and trudged through the water.

The snickering high school girls spread the word, and by the time we got back to our towels, the sandcastle had been trampled over by at least a dozen fans asking Reagan for her picture. She entertained most of them by taking selfies, but I caught her eyeing other people nearby on the beach, doing a crappy job at hiding their phones sneaking a picture.

"Hey, let's head out," I said to her, tugging her arm before the next round of fans stumbled over.

This time, we didn't make it to the hotel unnoticed. Even with the floppy hat, bathing suit cover-up, and sunglasses, the fans from South Beach had chased us all the way onto the path toward our hotel.

"Reagan! Reagan! Just one picture, please!" the crowd said.

Without permission, people lurched forward to snap a selfie, immediately looked at how it turned out, and if they didn't like it, they tried it again. They acted as if she was a zoo animal who they could constantly take pictures of until they got it perfect enough for an Instagram filter.

"Okay, I think you got enough," I told one fan. I didn't care if she was only sixteen, she attempted a selfie with Reagan about five times, and every time, Reagan tilted her head forward to avoid the camera lens. The girl gave me this heartbroken sulk, but I wasn't buying it. "I'm sure one of the twenty-seven pictures you took will be good enough for your Instagram."

"What a bitch," she muttered to her friends, but I couldn't have cared less because she backed away from my bite.

"Stalking and shoving your phone in her face. Classy," I said back to her, and she flipped me off.

When I opened the hotel doors, a few fans attempted to walk in with us. Luckily, the hotel was already on it, and security came running out and pushed them back outside in the heat. As we sprinted to the elevators, I knew the damage had been done. They knew where she was staying and would probably spread the word to internet message boards. I felt responsible for all of it. I was so angry that our good time building sandcastles and the genuine happiness emanating from Reagan about being normal for once was ruined by stalking fans.

In the elevator, she was silent. She held her glasses in her hand, but her eyes were hidden by her floppy hat.

"I'm really sorry," I said. "I guess I had no idea how bad it could get."

Finally, she looked up at me. Neutral expression firm and steady on her face. She seemed just as disappointed as I felt. "It's not your fault, Blair."

"But I dragged you out of your room—"

"You didn't, though. I chose to come, and I'm glad I did. This wasn't anything for the record books. I'm fine." She attempted a smile, but I knew it was forced.

The elevator dinged for my eleventh-floor room. As I stepped out, I felt her fingers grab hold of mine, instantly shooting something magnetic into my body. "Can we do wine after the show?" she asked, and when I met her stare, it was like something passed through us. The connection sizzled. "I don't feel like being cooped up by myself."

"I think you deserve it," I said.

With that, she let go of my hand, a satisfied grin etched back on her face, and the doors closed.

CHAPTER FOUR

The Miami crowd was insane. They were loud. Rowdy. Knew more of our songs than I thought they would. I guess Reagan expected it because she brought out giant beach balls that she kicked into the crowd and shot all the energized fans on the floor with a foam gun. I didn't even know she brought a foam gun on tour with her, so I immediately started planning on how I could steal it from one of the tractor trailers and use it for our next show in Orlando.

Between the energy from the Miami crowd and watching Reagan perform, I was in no mood for a calm night with wine. Miles and I continued our party on our bus, taking more shots, blasting music, eating weed gummies, pissing off Corbin because he thought we were too loud, rowdy, and intoxicated, and I told him to stop being a thirty-two-year-old grandpa.

When I got back to my hotel room, still buzzing from alcohol, weed, and the awesome crowd that was Miami, my phone chirped with a text message from Reagan.

Her text read, *Soooo is this wine still on the table?*

I furiously texted back, *Wine is never off the table for me. Want me to come up now?*

Yes, please.

I wanted more than just to sit around and drink wine. My hotel room overlooked a completely empty pool. If my past was any indication, pools on summer nights were my weakness, and taking a nice swim was the best way to unwind, in my opinion.

I ventured up to the penthouse suite in my robe and flip-flops. A few moments after I knocked on her door, Reagan opened it with a glass of white wine in her hands. She was already in a loose T-shirt and track shorts, so I knew I needed to do some convincing to get this girl back into that white bikini and into the pool.

She thoroughly scanned my robe, and my stomach jolted when those eyes traced the dip down to my cleavage. She actually did that. Her eyes went straight to the bare skin of my chest the way mine kept going to her legs and butt anytime she wore her bodysuit.

My heart raced with excitement. Was Reagan Moore checking me out?

"Oh, wow," Reagan said breathlessly, still taking me in everywhere but my eyes. "I literally don't even have to raise a finger and a pretty girl in a robe comes to my door?"

She leaned against the doorway and sipped her wine, the corners of her lips tugging upward. My eyebrows folded. She was checking me out. She was hitting on me.

"I'm not really sure how to take that," I said.

"Take what? You're literally in a robe."

"I have a bathing suit on underneath." I pulled my bikini straps up to show her. "Let's go swimming."

Her smile unraveled. "Swimming? It's one o'clock in the morning."

"So?"

"So? I'm pretty sure the pool is closed."

"That's why you whisper."

"I'm not gonna break into the pool after hours."

"You know you can't get arrested for sneaking into a pool?"

"You can. It's called trespassing."

"I got caught sneaking into a neighbor's pool in high school. Wanna know what happened? The cop brought me home to my grandpa, and I got in a lot more trouble with him than the cop. So, you're fine."

"Oh, that's reassuring."

"You're famous and loveable. Nothing will happen to you. Enjoy that famous privilege. Come swimming with me." I grabbed her hand and tugged her toward me.

"Blair," she said through her laugh.

"I already scoped out the pool. It's empty. Coast is clear. Throw on your suit. Chug the wine. Let's go!"

After debating it for a few more moments, she rolled her eyes and then tossed back the rest of her wine. "You're a bad influence, I hope you know that."

"You know you like it."

"A little. Must be the sleeve."

Drop it. There's no way she's hitting on you.

Ten minutes later, I led Reagan to the outdoor pool on the seventh-floor deck. Below us, the humming of cars driving by filled the air, and the sweet summer breeze gently blew the fake palm trees on the pool deck. The lights from the pool crawled up the side of the building. I'd almost forgotten how thrilling it was to sneak into a pool. Reagan Moore, on the other hand, had almost forgotten how to live like a normal human being. And I was determined to bring back the simple things in her life without anyone noticing.

But that would be easier said than done with her current pace. She tiptoed behind me, curled up in her white hotel towel as if that was her invisibility cloak, and surveyed the scene over her shoulders every other step she took.

Breaking into the outdoor pool was easy. You literally just lifted the gate and tossed your towel to the side, which I did with my robe. Not getting caught was the harder part. Miles and I always snuck into my Irvine neighbors' pools in the dead of night when we were teenagers. We had almost become professional pool hoppers at sixteen before getting caught. Eight years had passed, so I was a little rusty.

As I slowly eased into the shallow end, Reagan peeled off her towel so slowly that it was as if she was hoping we'd get caught before she exposed the red-handed evidence of her bathing suit.

"Oh my God, girl, live a little," I said as I trudged through the shallow end.

"I do live a little. I live a lot. Usually on the other side of the law."

"You do realize you're just going into a pool for an innocent swim. I'm not asking you to strip naked or have sex with me in it."

I continued trudging farther into the pool like an eager child until I glanced back to check on her. When our gazes met, her stare fell to the concrete deck. And then I hesitated. Because she hesitated. And a warm feeling dove low into my chest. Was it something I said?

"Get in," I said to break the silence.

"Maybe we should whisper?"

"Maybe we should stop being wimps and just get in the water," I said a little louder to irk her. "If it makes you feel better, I really don't think *TMZ* is interested in you sneaking into a hotel pool. I am, though."

She let out a long, frustrated sigh and tossed her towel aside. She took one cautious step at a time until she reached the shallow end, and a shiver ran through her when the water hit her waist. The pool lights illuminated her face, and the reflections danced on her skin. I loved how tiny beads of moisture stuck to her as she doggy-paddled over to me, and something about the way she swam stripped the "Big A-list Celebrity" title from her. Maybe because she wasn't standing on an enormous stage the size of her celebrity status. Maybe because she wasn't wearing her Gucci sunglasses or sitting in her luxurious tour bus or hotel penthouse. In that Miami pool, she didn't have anything luxurious surrounding her. She was a normal twenty-three-year-old girl swimming in the pool after hours.

There was just something so pure about her as she found her spot in the four-foot-deep pool, and then she looked at me quizzically as if waiting for me to make the next move.

"How you doing, James Dean? Rebel without a cause?" I asked.

"This is actually kind of…nice."

"Uh, right?"

"It's so peaceful. Just listen."

A wind blew through the air and ruffled the faux palm trees surrounding the deck. The city and cars below us continued to sing to each other, and the whole scene was nothing short of the sounds I'd fallen asleep to on Reagan's noise canceling machine.

The sounds pulled the corners of her mouth to the night sky as she leaned her head back, allowing the pool to take in her messy bun. She closed her eyes, and the chlorinated water lifted her body to the surface. After a hectic day of running around from the stampede of fans, kicking oversized beach balls, and blasting foam guns at the twenty thousand people, she finally found the peace she'd been looking and hoping for. Something normal she could enjoy without a single person to ruin the moment.

But after a few shots of tequila right before, I didn't want my pool-hopping buddy to relax into the ripples and enjoy the peace and quiet. So, to capitalize on the energizing liquid running through me, and also for my own entertainment, I ducked underwater, and pushing through the chlorine burning my eyes when I opened them, I flipped her around.

I heard her shriek. When I emerged, her hair was soaked, and she wiped away the pool water dripping down her face. Her messy bun was ready to dismantle at any time, and I couldn't control the laughter I'd bottled up in my lungs in order not to breathe in water.

"Blair! What the fuck!" She sent a wave of water my way.

I laughed, and she threw a glare at me, pressing her finger against her lips, but I couldn't stop laughing. The look she gave me when she pulled her face from the water, so disappointed I ruined her quiet moment, was hilarious to me. It gave me a good laugh, something I hadn't had in a while.

"That was priceless," I said to her, holding my stomach from the laughter tightening my muscles.

"Want me to splash you again?"

"No, I'm sorry. Truce." I put my hands up to surrender. She relaxed into a tread as a victorious smile took over her face. "Honestly, I wanted you to come out here to enjoy this. A pool. No one around. I just wanted you to feel a little normal since you can't build sandcastles or go to the movies, so I'm just trying to give you that."

Her lips pursed in amusement. "God, you're so soft, you know that? I thought a whole sleeve tattoo was supposed to make you a badass."

"Are you calling me soft because I care about how you feel?"

"It's a compliment, Blair. You surprise me, that's all."

"I surprise you?"

"Yeah."

I straightened my back, intrigued by where this could possibly go. "Oh yeah? How so?"

She looked up at the starless, city maroon sky, biting her lip playfully, before looking back at me. "I, uh, I don't know…"

God, was she blushing? Or did the light highlight the pink she got from the sun? Just the thought of her blushing about me made me blush.

"What? Tell me!" I begged, dying to know if it was the blush or sun that reddened her face. Did Reagan Moore get a sunburn in Miami, or was she blushing over me in Miami? This was a detail I wouldn't be able to fall asleep without knowing. "Tell me! Tell me! Tell me!" I chanted and splashed her.

She winced as she fought the splash, but her quiet giggles added to the rustling palm trees and talkative streets. "Blair! Stop it!"

"Tell me!" One last splash.

She looked at me. "You just look...you...you're fun to hang out with, even if it sometimes means that you drag me into doing things against my will."

I grinned. I looked something, and I was determined to dig out that secretive adjective until dawn broke out in the sky. "I look what?"

"I said you're fun to hang out with—"

"After you said I look 'something' and then you stuttered."

"Are we really making this a big deal right now?"

"Yes, because you're not answering my question."

Yup, that was definitely blush, not sunburn. I could tell because it crawled up her face the more I begged. I loved it.

"Ugh!" She slapped a hand on the water. "You look nice in a bathing suit, that's all. See. Nothing."

But it was something. I only had a few straight friends, and they didn't go around telling each other how nice they looked half naked. Her compliment held some weight. Good weight. And it made me relax into the pool because Reagan Moore said I looked good in a bathing suit.

"I look nice in a bathing suit?" I repeated for clarification. "Is this a second part to your robe comment earlier? Are you hitting on me?"

She let out a mirthless laugh. "Because I said you looked nice?"

"You said I look good half naked, so yes, I take this as you hitting on me."

She could deny it all she wanted, but I knew she was hitting on me. I would frame those words in my mind forever. Reagan Moore, world tour headliner, *Billboard*'s number one singer, the girl who won three Grammys for Best Album, Best Pop Record, and Best Pop Song a few months before just told *moi* that I looked good in my bathing suit after two weeks of insulting my taste in alcohol and tattoos.

Frame that shit like her platinum albums.

I raised a skeptical brow. I had to get to the bottom of why she was hitting on me. "I'm going to ask you a personal question."

She rolled her eyes. "Ugh, okay."

"Have you dated a woman?"

"Oh my God, Blair. You went in for the kill right there."

"You literally just said I look good in a bathing suit, so the question is nothing but fair."

She started to swim away from me. "I'm never complimenting you again. Seriously."

"Answer the question."

"I really hate you."

"Oh yeah, it shows," I deadpanned. "Now, answer the question."

She stopped swimming for a moment to toss me major side-eye from over her shoulder. She sighed and then looked skyward again as if debating whether or not she should answer my question. "I've dated a woman, yes."

My mouth dropped. How the hell didn't I know this? How the hell did Alanna not even know this? I was almost positive—with the two of us combined and dreaming about hot celebrity women coming out as a lesbian or bisexual or anything in between—that we would have known something about Reagan Moore. But nope, I could only tell that she dated a famous heartthrob actor, Zeke Fowler, for a highly prolific few months, and that was it. The rest of her love life was a mystery, and I think that was the whole point she was trying to get at by how she cautiously tiptoed around her highly publicized life.

"Holy shit." The shocked words slipped right out of me. "Who? When?"

"She was the last person I dated."

"The last person you—holy shit."

She coughed up a laugh. "Okay, Blair. It's really not that groundbreaking."

"I didn't even know you were into women."

"That was the point. The media was all over Zeke and me. Everywhere we went, we had cameras in our faces and were constantly in the tabloids. You know I once saw on a tabloid that I was pregnant?"

"I didn't know that."

"I was nineteen. Stalked by grown men and my sex life written as entertainment for everyone before I even had sex. It was mortifying. Once we broke up, I swore to myself I would be smarter about what I put on my social media, and any relationships weren't going to be on my accounts. Especially dating a woman. All those men would be fantasizing about it." She shuddered.

"That sounds pretty awful."

"It kind of is. The past seven years have been great in terms of my career. I love it so much, and I'm truly thankful for it. But with great success in this industry comes a great sacrifice, and that means your dating life tanks."

"How so?"

"Well, besides the stalking? I don't trust anyone. No one. All my past relationships have given me a reason not to trust a single person who seems interested in me. Even platonically. Are they using me for attention? Are they going to be intimidated by my success? Are they using me for fame? Hollywood ins? When I was recording my first album, I had a boyfriend, this kid from my high school. Right when my album came out and it was getting all this praise, he treated me so differently. Like, he always wanted to be around me. He wanted me to bring him to every little thing I was invited to and then he would be pissed when I wouldn't."

"He sounds like a tool."

"He was my first boyfriend, so I gave him about ten chances to change his act before I was completely drained from the relationship. And then I broke up with him, and he was pissed, to say the least, because he had no in to the Nashville music scene. Don't worry, though, my older brothers, Colton and Hunter, ran into him and gave him crap. I was satisfied. But after that relationship, I told myself I would only date people in the industry because they wouldn't use me. So, a couple of years later, I met Zeke, and we dated for a few months. I thought it would be different since his career was already established and booming."

"You guys were, like, the It couple for that whole summer. The internet wouldn't stop talking about you two."

She rolled her eyes. "I know. It was probably the most stressful six months of my life. That's when all the stalking and the rumors happened. I guess that's what happens when you date an It boy, right?"

"You know, it was Zeke Fowler's show that put us on the map. They played one of our songs during their season two finale."

"Seriously?"

"Yup. It was our first claim to fame. Got people buying our music."

Zeke Fowler was an actor in this TV show about superheroes. He played a character inspired by Lex Luthor, and his evil ways on the show just enhanced his tall, dark, handsome looks...if I was into that. I sure as hell wasn't. And I wasn't into superheroes, but I was all into them using our music. Once the show used our EP song on their finale, it was a hit, and we found ourselves on the top one hundred most downloaded songs for a few weeks.

"So, what happened with you and Zeke then?" I said.

"Well, he's an actor and a model, and you combine both of those, and you get one melodramatic narcissist. My second album came out, it won a few Grammys, I had my first headlining tour, and he didn't feel that high and mighty anymore. He felt intimidated. I think he wanted to be more famous and successful than me. Like, he got off on the thought of taking this Hollywood noob under his huge biceps and parading her around to parties like fresh meat but instantly hated when I started winning Grammys and sold out big venues, and he wasn't winning any awards. So, he broke up with me."

"He dumped *you*?"

She laughed. "Yeah, can you believe that? Men and their fragile egos."

"And then you swore off men and found yourself a woman? Nice."

"Well, I didn't *swear* off men, but a really hot woman bought me a drink at the Grammys, and it went from there."

"I still can't believe you dated a woman, and I didn't even know!"

"Seriously? 'By the Way' is about my ex-girlfriend."

She caught me. I didn't know the songs on her second album. "By the Way" was this upbeat, poppy breakup anthem everyone listened to with a really catchy bass line. Except for me, apparently. It was also her opening song to her show. This whole time, I had a lesbian song dancing in front of my face, and I had no idea.

I was the worst lesbian in the world.

"Who's your ex-girlfriend?" I asked eagerly. I needed to know the type of women Reagan Moore fell for…since she was complimenting my looks in robes and bathing suits. "Is she famous?"

"A little. Jessie Byrd?"

My mouth met gravity once again. Jessie Byrd was a solo act, singing pop folk that found its way onto the Top 40 radio stations. I loved her music, then secretly hated her because she was so good at songwriting and playing the guitar. She was our competition and completely destroying us at it. She wasn't selling out arenas, but I don't think she cried about that at night. She was one of the most popular, relatively unknown singer-songwriters that all the TV shows wanted to use for their dramatic moments. She was very pretty, with memorable hazel eyes, but had some mysterious swagger that I didn't know how else to describe. Just something about her was edgy and cool. I followed her on Instagram because I had a crush on her face and her career. They only shared a few Instagram pictures of each other, but those pictures gave no indication that they were dating.

I so envied Jessie Byrd. On top of her writing and musicianship, she was actually rewarded with Reagan's smiles, more than what I had—the smiles I liked to pretend were because she thought I was pretty.

"I thought you guys were just friends," I admitted. "Honestly. Maybe even writing a song? I kind of was hoping for that."

"Yeah, we definitely weren't friends. She was my girlfriend for seven months, and those seven months were really fucking electric."

Describing her relationship with a woman as "fucking electric" should have sparked something in me, like a rush of excitement that my tiny little crush used such words about a woman. Instead, it was a painful shock of pure jealousy to my core. I didn't even know she had the ability to make me feel that until she said Jessie Byrd was "fucking electric."

"Then what happened?" I asked, fishing for more details to settle the envy in my stomach.

Reagan huffed. "Guess she got bored. I don't know. She kinda has a track record of going through girls, so I don't know why I thought I'd be any different. I was pretty devastated. Not heartbroken but devastated in the sense that I was so emotionally invested in it and felt all these intense feelings whenever we were together or texted or FaceTimed, just for her to drop me like a dime. Knife to the heart."

All that information made me look at her in a different light now. I always thought she was intimidatingly beautiful but so far out of my league that I didn't let more than a thought or two of making out with her consume much of my brain.

Until she told me her ex-girlfriend was Jessie Byrd and that I looked good in a bikini. Then the woman who I thought I was used to seeing was someone totally different. Someone who liked girls. Someone who was interested in dark-haired singer/songwriters who liked to brood in their music while drinking beers on stage—except that Miles and I didn't drink on stage at the Reagan Moore concerts. The average age she attracted was much younger than our own shows.

Damn it, one snap of a finger and I had a full-blown schoolgirl crush on the headliner of the tour I was on.

"So, now I know how to shut you up," she said to break the silence, gently flicking drops of water at my face to snap me out of my trance.

"So, you definitely *were* hitting on me earlier?"

"When you allowed me to put sunscreen on you, were *you* hitting on *me*?"

"I, uh, well…"

"Who's stuttering now?" she said with an aggressive point at me.

I blushed and sunk farther into the pool to hide. "You look good in your bikini too, if it makes you feel any better."

"It does. You can enjoy it while I head on out now."

She winked. As if my face couldn't feel any warmer. She whisked herself around and walked up the steps of the shallow end onto the deck. I felt anchored to my spot as I watched water drip, down her back, and off her bikini bottoms. She dried herself with her towel before wrapping it around her waist.

"You coming, or are you gonna stay there and drool in the pool?" she asked.

Man, was she a thorn in my side, but also the excitement I needed to revive the life back in me.

Two could play this game. She was the one who first said I looked good in my bikini, so as I got out of the pool, I grabbed my robe, quickly dried myself off, slung the robe over my shoulder, and refused to wrap myself up. She thought I looked good in a bathing suit? She could watch me until the elevator carried her up to her penthouse suite. I strutted to the door and held it open for her. Those eyes trailed from my lips, down to my breasts, down to my waist, to my legs, then all the way back up to my eyes.

"You're not cold?" she said after that really long and obvious glance over.

"It's hard to feel cold when your compliment makes me feel so hot," I said with a facetious wink.

She blinked a few times, accepted my invitation inside the hotel, and we didn't say a word until the elevator closed us inside tight quarters. I could feel her looking at me from her peripheral, and I sensed that she saw me looking at her from the corner of my eye by the way her lips curled upward as if she felt victorious.

By the time we got to my floor, I regretted my decision to not bury myself in the robe. Goose bumps broke all over my body, and the thought of cocooning in the duvet on my comfy, king-sized hotel bed felt amazing and wonderful. But what also felt wonderful was, when the elevator doors opened, Reagan's eyes fell back down to my breasts before flitting back up to me as if she accidentally dropped her gaze like a wet bar of soap.

"See, swimming after hours wasn't that bad," I said.

This crush developed at rapid speed. Her eyes churned my insides in the best possible way, a way that made me automatically smile as a reflex.

"No, not at all." She scratched her nose. "Um, yeah, thanks for the good day, Blair."

"I'm here anytime you need a spontaneous adventure."

I stepped out of the elevator, and as the doors started to close, I stopped one with my hands. "Oh, and, Reagan?"

"Hmm?"

"Just so we're even on the compliments, you have a really nice smile. Just thought you should know."

CHAPTER FIVE

"Mom, you sold the house?" I whined, sitting up straight while FaceTiming her as the Reagan Moore fleet traveled from Charleston to Raleigh.

A mountain of cardboard boxes containing our Irvine life towered behind her as she showed off the empty house where I grew up. Grandma and Gramps's house. The last remaining thing we had left of them.

And she smiled at me as if this was an accomplishment. As if she was actually glad to rid herself of the home we spent ten years in.

"Why are you telling me this now that the whole house is packed?"

"Because I knew what your reaction would be," she said and sat in Gramps's computer chair with the vacant bookshelf behind her cleared of all his records and record player. Now, it really was only a memory.

"But it's their house," I said.

"It doesn't feel like home to me anymore, and I don't need a four-thousand-square-foot house just for me. It's too much. You'll love the condo I bought though. It has a loft."

"You already bought a condo?"

"Yes, in Los Feliz. Oh, Blair, it's so beautiful. You'll have your own room when you come visit me."

I couldn't believe it. We spoke on the phone at least twice a week, and now I was finding out she was moving out of the Irvine house when the house was already packed up? I was furious at her. But as much as I wanted to yell and express my frustrations, seeing her smile beat all the angry emotions in me. As much as my gut twisted from moving on from the place that would serve as a time capsule for all my wonderful memories I had of my grandparents, Mom looked hopeful.

"Honey, I know you feel attached to this house because it's your grandparents'," she said with much more sympathy than before, "but if I'm going to live by myself, I'm not gonna do it in something too big for me. This is the first time in my life I'm able to buy something for myself, and it's scary and exciting at the same time. I'm forty-four years old and haven't had anything except for a Chevy Cruze in my name."

She guilt-tripped me without really trying. Mom was right. She'd spent eighteen years trying to raise me as she matured throughout her twenties and thirties. Then right when she finally got her bachelor's degree in business, after taking classes for years while juggling administration jobs, her mother was diagnosed with breast cancer, and she stayed in their Irvine house to take care of her rather than follow through with the plan of buying her own place. She didn't want to leave Grandma, even though both of her parents insisted that she still move out. But she never did. After Grandma died, Mom wanted to keep her grieving father company since he was just as miserable without Grandma as I was miserable without both of them.

Mom spent the past twenty-four years taking care of everyone but herself. She'd never been married. Never had a serious boyfriend since my shitty father. In six years, she lost both of her parents to cancer. I guess I didn't blame her for wanting to sell the house to start a new life in her control. I just really hated to let go of the one last thing that still smelled like my grandparents.

"Yeah, you're right," I said through a heavy sigh.

"Just because I'm moving out of the house doesn't mean I'm forgetting about them, hon. It means I'm trying to move on and continue upward."

"I know, I know. It's just—I really loved that house."

"I know you did. But selling the house is what I need to do. My therapist says I should consolidate because having all this space is a reminder of what I've lost. Oh, and guess what else?"

I pressed my lips together for a moment, hoping that she wasn't going to deliver more bad news. "What?"

"I have a date later this week."

My eyes widened. My mom had only dated two men that I knew

of. My dad and then some guy named Mark for about a year when I was fifteen. The rest of her time she spent working her ass off, taking care of her family, finishing her education, and taking extra hours as a receptionist at the hospital.

"You have a date?"

"Yes!" She squealed like a little girl. Was this really my mother I was talking to? I could only remember the rage burning in her eyes when she found out I was suspended for three days because during a drug lockdown, one of those drug dogs sniffed the eighth of weed I had in my car. I didn't think they were so cute after that. That memory of her jaw set firmly, eyes drilling in how disappointed and angry she was totally belied the shriek and school-age grin that consumed her face over a man. Gone were the days of tossing glares at her rowdy daughter, and hello to the days Mom acted like a little schoolgirl because she had a date. She informed me she actually had three dates with three different men the past three weeks. A lot of threes for me to remember. I'd never been prouder of my mother until hearing about all her dates. And here I thought my life was thrilling because Reagan Moore said I looked good in a bathing suit. But seeing my mom's smile and her voice climbing up an octave was a great moment for me to witness.

I guess there was more to Mom than just being a mom.

Apparently, his name was Greg, a business executive who lived in Beverly Hills, which meant he was probably some obnoxious rich dude who voted for Donald Trump because of his "fabulous tax plan." Mom lectured me about how I needed to stop assuming things about people who I'd never met.

While Mom's love life was booming like a Fourth of July fireworks display, mine was utterly confusing. While the Reagan Moore fleet traveled up Georgia and the Carolinas, I couldn't tell if it was my dreams causing me to act weird around her or if something started swelling between us. Since our time in Miami, our post-show wine chats brought us together on the same sectional couch in her bus, or she'd invite me to her hotel room. Each show, I'd noticed the space between us close the more comfortable we became around each other. Her insults became harsher, but still, that beautiful smile eased her words a little bit. In return, I'd playfully hit her arm or leg or whatever body part was closest to me because I just wanted to have an excuse to touch her.

As I tried forcing myself to go to sleep, still hearing murmurs from Miles and Corbin snorting in their sleep, my mind would go back to Reagan's bus and she'd finally kiss me, like, push me up against the kitchenette, kiss me. Imagining those lips on me stirred the warmth underneath my clothes and jolted a flutter in my chest. Damn it, it really sucked living with two boys plus our bus driver because all those nights kissing Reagan over and over in my head really collected tension in my body that needed to be released.

❖

To continue the nostalgia train that kept chugging in circles in my brain thinking about Mom moving, our next stop was the first city I ever called home: Nashville, Tennessee.

When I was thirteen, Gramps moved us from Nashville to LA when he started his label with his longtime friend and former bandmate. Although when asked where I was from, I always answered Irvine, a part of my heart still belonged to this city, and I was so glad to be back for the first time in eleven years.

It was also Reagan's hometown, and my body craved being next to her so it could soak up all her attention, but her parents and two older brothers lived right outside the city in Franklin, so she was spending the day with them.

So, third wheeling it with Miles and Ethan, I showed those Southern California boys the very little culture that America had, and the best culture—in my opinion—was Southern culture. Forget about the animal-style burgers at In-N-Out Burger, fish tacos, and avocado toast, Miles's stomach had never been introduced to proper barbecue or hot chicken before. And I didn't know about Ethan, but the lack of twang in his voice and lack of knowledge about hot chicken proved to me that his stomach hadn't fully lived. So, I took them to my favorite barbecue spot that Gramps always treated me to on the best days, indulging in slathered ribs, hot chicken, warm, buttery biscuits, and banana pudding with vanilla wafers.

We eventually waddled our full bellies down Broadway Street to a scotch saloon that served as our nightcap while we listened to live country music. I pounded back scotch after scotch, wondering what Reagan was up to, and how empty the Irvine house was, and reliving the first memory of Gramps introducing me to Nashville hot chicken and always laughing when I managed to get barbecue sauce all over my face.

I really missed his laugh. And all the scotch I drank filled my nose with the smell of Gramps. Nashville, scotch, and live music. If that wasn't Gramps's heaven, then I don't know what was.

Everything leading up to that moment in the cramped, dingy scotch bar was great, so why the grief stacked on top of me like bricks when I was with my best friend in a city I absolutely loved and missed was beyond me. I sat there in my own corner of the table, watching Miles and Ethan carry on effortlessly. Actually, it felt as if everyone carried on effortlessly. Mom too, even though I knew that wasn't the case, but her tossing that house to the side for a new one still clung to my brain. Even though I knew it was the right decision for her, and I was genuinely happy that she was excited about having a place to herself and finally entering the dating scene, it still made me wonder how she did it. I carried the weight of Gramps's death with me every night, and anytime it became too much, I poured myself another large glass of wine while I was talking to Reagan after shows, or I pounded back another shot in the green rooms, or I lit a joint and relaxed into my seat, but none of those were working.

I wanted a breath from it all.

I told Miles I was going to go back to the hotel. He gave me that concerned look, reading my face perfectly like he always did. That kid was so intuitive and knew me like the back of his hand; sometimes it annoyed me when I wanted to suppress my feelings. But I gave him a small smile that I was fine, just tired and needed to go to sleep, encouraging him to stay out as long as he wanted.

Every time the days morphed into night, my mind spun around like a carousel. What was it about the night that made people overthink everything? Their whole lives? The meaning of their existence? Why the hell they did that one weird thing in third grade, and why were they dwelling about it now? It was only the bad memories that seemed nocturnal, insecurities and self-doubt that sprang to life at night, louder than they were during the day. Sometimes, I felt as if I couldn't hide from my own voice.

When I got back to my hotel, I searched through my orange prescription bottle filled with Xanax, Ritalin, and the remaining eight ball of cocaine I scored a few days before I broke up with Alanna. Since I knew I wasn't going to fall asleep, and I was going to continue to ride on that carousel in my mind, I took a Xanax and then passed out.

A breath from it all.

❖

I spent the next day alone in my hotel room, relying on the cocaine to numb me in every way I needed it to. By the time we made it to our green room, I felt as if I was sunbathing on a cloud. I was so eager to get on stage and run around, jump on a five-foot-tall speaker, wail on my guitar, and soak up all the cheering from the fans.

After I tuned my Fender with fidgeting hands, Mom texted me a picture of a red-heeled pump on one foot and a black flat on the other, asking me which one was the best option for her date with Greg from Beverly Hills and the world of online dating. I stared at the picture, feeling the chemical energy controlling my body and mind. I had no idea what the hell kind of shoe my mom should wear. So, I used that as an excuse to see Reagan. I was in a pretty talkative mood anyways.

I marched down the hallway to her green room, letting the confidence from the two preshow shots and lines soak in my blood. Her green room door was always cracked open before shows. Usually, the only time I walked past her door was right after we got off the stage. The number one rule of live shows was that you didn't disrupt a musician's preshow ritual. So, I never bothered her.

But those rules didn't really exist when I rejuvenated the depleted elation running through me. Plus, considering that she was the woman who built her career on three double platinum albums filled with love songs, I think my interruption was justified. She knew exactly the shoe my mom needed to find love.

When I poked my head through her room, I found her stretched out on the couch in her concert hair, makeup, and attire. An aromatherapy diffuser scented the room, and whatever the weird smell was, Reagan seemed to enjoy it, eyes closed, and hands folded over her sparkly bodysuit.

"Knock knock," I said as I tapped the door.

"Oh, hey," she said with a smile, pushing herself up on the couch.

"What's the smell in here?"

"Clary sage. Helps calm your nerves, your stomach, and anxiety. You're more than welcome to breathe some of it in since it's our hometown show."

Not like I really need to breathe in any more, but if it gives me an excuse to be next to her…

"Well, if you really insist. Mind if I come in?"

"Not at all."

She moved her legs to give me room to join her on the loveseat. For whatever reason, she looked extra good today. I loved the natural shade of pink lipstick on her lips and the soft smoky shadow brushed on her eyelids.

"So, uh, my mom is going on her first date, in like, six years," I explained, scratching the back of my head as Reagan's beauty and the tension that kept following us around warmed my cheeks. "She doesn't trust me with fashion, and I don't trust myself in picking out the right shoe for her, so I'd thought I'd ask your advice on what she should wear on her date. Care to give it?" I wiggled my phone.

"Uh, always!"

As I opened my mom's text message, I noticed the lack of space that separated us. She scooted over until there was only an inch separating our legs. While she studied my mom's mirror selfie, I studied the tension reverberating between us. Instead of resisting, I let my leg follow the tension. It relaxed into hers ever so slightly, and the humming recentered to my knees. I couldn't focus on anything else except the friction. I wasn't the only one who felt it. Reagan completely lost interest in my phone. As I caught her stare, her gaze slipped down to my lips, and then her stare jumped right back up to my eyes.

"You smell really good," she said while leaning forward and sniffing the air close to my neck.

God, the things I would have done for her lips to touch me. If only we could close the inch of space. Could we forget about my mom's shoe dilemma just so she could continue to smell me? Maybe rest a hand on my thigh? Kiss the spot on my neck where I spritzed my perfume?

I swallowed hard. "Oh, thank you. New perfume."

"You smell immaculate."

"Don't make me cocky."

"Oh, yeah, that's right. Your ego. It's a thing." The corner of her mouth tugged upward as her eyes went back to my phone screen at my mom's mirror selfie. My mom, living her true, twentysomething self by taking an awful selfie with two different shoes on in a sexy black cocktail dress.

"Damn, your mom is hot," she said with much surprise.

"Tone the libido. She's all about the D."

"Sorry. Sage is an aphrodisiac. I can't help it." She nudged me in the arm. Yup, that had to explain the tension sucking our legs together like a magnet. Or my wanting her lips on my neck and her hand crawling up my leg. The aphrodisiac. Nothing else.

"You guys look alike, you know that? You've got the same dark brown eyes and perfect dark eyebrows."

"Are you saying I'm hot?"

It took a second for her face to turn bright red. "What?"

"You said my mom was hot, and then said we look alike, which means you think I'm hot."

"I…you…I said you looked good in a bathing suit, didn't I?"

"Oh, you did. I'll never forget you said that either."

"Just…shut up. Take a compliment and shut up."

My face started to heat up too just seeing how bright her cheeks turned because of me.

Then she typed back to Mom at lightning speed. *Red pumps! Black always needs a pop of color. Plus, the shoes are cute!—Reagan.*

"Really? She's going on a walking tour," I said skeptically.

"Blair, they're like three-inch heels. She will be fine."

"You can go on a walking tour in three-inch heels?"

Mom replied back. *Red heels it is! Thank you, Reagan! Hope you and my daughter have a great show.*

Reagan handed me back my phone with a crinkle by her eyes when my mom sent her a winky face emoji. "See. Your mom loves me."

"Mom loves everyone."

"I should send some sage her way."

"Please do. She hasn't had sex in, like, eight years, and before that, the last person she slept with got her pregnant, and he's a piece of shit."

Her eyes grew. "I'm not sure what I'm more shocked about. The fact you know your mom's sex life that well or the fact she hasn't had sex in that long."

"She's my best girlfriend. We tell each other everything. If anything, she's more disturbed by *my* sex life."

Her eyebrow rose as she gave me an intrigued smile. "What's so disturbing about your sex life?"

"Wouldn't you like to know. The sage has gone to your head."

She playfully grabbed hold of my knee, sending a jolt through my black leather pants and underneath my underwear. She started singing "You're So Vain" by Carly Simon until a knock interrupted her.

My chest swelled with jealousy when I saw the person knocking, and from the corner of my eyes, I saw Reagan's grin loosen.

"Jess?"

It was none other than Jessie Byrd herself, looking like a true hipster rock star: skintight maroon jeans that ended right above her ankles, a black leather coat, white V-neck T-shirt, and a black Panama hat resting on the top of her dark brown hair tousled in loose curls down to her breasts. Her lips stood out in bright red lipstick as a reminder that those lips once belonged to Reagan.

If I was amused in Miami about Reagan dating Jessie Byrd, I felt anything but amused sitting in that Nashville green room. It was one thing to imagine it—the sudden information about their relationship opened the door to all these scenarios in my head. But Jessie Byrd in the flesh? At Reagan's show? I'd just spent a few minutes tweaking out a smile from Reagan that was all for me. Only me. And one sight of her debonair ex-girlfriend washed that smile away and really diluted my high.

No, I wasn't a fan of it.

"Hey, stranger," Jessie Byrd said in her sexy Australian accent.

I'd only listened to Jessie Byrd sing her indie folk-rock songs on Spotify. I had every song off her two albums downloaded to my phone. But I never heard her speak or went out of my way to watch videos of interviews so I had no idea she wooed girls with her accent.

Talk about a disadvantage for me.

"What...what are you doing here?" Reagan said, still completely baffled by the appearance. From the sound of it, she wasn't a fan of the surprise leaning confidently against the side of the entryway.

"Seeing a concert. Is that all right?"

"You should have given me a heads-up or something."

"I wanted to surprise you. I couldn't miss out on this. You sold out your hometown show. It's a pretty big deal. You got a wicked crowd out there."

It seemed like the sage easily affected Jessie Byrd by how both of them looked longingly at each other. She either still had feelings for Jessie Byrd or was ODing on clary sage. I could almost see them practically undressing each other with their eyes from the apparent desire they still had. And here I was feeling excited that this beautiful, charming woman was giving me attention by grabbing my knee, nudging me in the arm, and telling me how great I smelled, only for her to completely melt at the sight of a girl who made her feel "fucking electric."

All that magnetic force I felt when I sat next to her really wasn't anything compared to whatever she had with Jessie Byrd. Their stares flushed me right out of there like the piece of shit I felt like.

"I'll leave you two alone," I said and got off the couch to breathe in something less sagey.

Reagan's soft hand clasped on to mine as I stood, and just that one touch from her froze me in my spot and sent some kind of shocking force into my stomach.

"Wait, Blair, no, you don't have to go," she said, begging with her eyes for me to stay.

That feeling that she caused moved from my stomach straight to my heart. The hypnotic stare she gave Jessie Byrd for that split second had completely worn off, but it was still sketched in my mind for me to analyze for the rest of the night. As wonderful as it was to hold on to her hand for just that moment, I knew I had to let it go and get myself and my mind ready for our show. That needed my focus. Not something unrealistic as me kissing Reagan. I'd save the scenarios I played in my head right before bed, hoping they could turn into a wonderful dream.

"Blair Bennett, right?" Jessie Byrd smiled at me.

I swallowed the starstruck lump in my throat and retrieved my hand from Reagan. "Hey. Yeah. I really love your music."

"Right back at you. I was listening to you guys on the ride over here. Studying for the concert."

My cheeks warmed and I really hope they didn't turn a traitorous red. I couldn't let myself cave at the sight of her too. "Oh, thanks. I've had your music on my playlists for years. You're phenomenal."

"Oh, please. I only play guitar. You play every instrument in the book *and* loop. You've got heaps of talent, mate."

You're caving...that accent...that face...the talent...

I offered her a friendly smile. "We could probably go back and forth with compliments all night, but I gotta get going and get ready for this crowd. It was nice meeting you."

"You too. Good luck."

I needed to delete all those Jessie Byrd songs from my Spotify. ASAP.

Miles was in the bathroom when I got back to our green room. Already feeling my mind start to cave, and still uneasy from my depressive moment the night before, I fished out a Ritalin from my bag. I really wanted to savor the remaining coke, so I decided to switch it up for something very close. The doctors prescribed it when I was in high school. I couldn't keep my mind occupied for too long. They said I had a lot of energy, and it would help me focus, which it did, but it also gave me some extra cash selling it to my classmates, and then occasionally, it was a nice high and break from reality.

I could feel the littlest things life handed me poke at my anxiety, so I thought to nip it in the bud and pop two Ritalin before we took the stage.

I usually watched some of Reagan's show from the side stage, but I had no interest in doing that in Nashville, knowing that Jessie Byrd was on the opposite end of the stage doing the same thing, fixating her ravenous eyes on her. So, after our set, I headed back to the bus where I forced Miles to drink with me. But when he stepped onto the bus, he said, "I made some friends with some hotties. Wanna smoke with them?"

He had me at hotties.

We dug through the llama cookie jar for pre-rolled joints we stocked up on in Denver and met a guy and girl around our age wearing VIP lanyards and yellow shirts that said "Staff." Both of them were pretty attractive, especially the girl, whose eyes skimmed me from head to toe.

I loved it when cute girls gave me that look. I knew how I was going to get over Jessie Byrd's sudden appearance.

Naturally, with enough weed, clary sage, and plenty of time to spare, the next thing I knew, I tossed my Reagan Moore World Tour lanyard right outside the back lounge door, the universal signal that Miles, Corbin, and I used as a sign of hookups happening in the back room. We started making out on the couch, and since it had been at least three months since I had a girl's mouth on me, tingles broke out all over every spot Weed Girl touched with her hands. I was currently going through my longest dry spell since the first time I'd ever had sex—Dana Bohlen—so it didn't take much to prime me. It was even better because this girl was more dominant than I thought she would be. A girl who knew what she was doing and what she wanted in the bedroom was so sexy to me, so I welcomed any dominant girl in my bed...or tour bus, in this instance.

She clasped her legs around my waist to flip me over on top of her for better access to take off my shirt. Once she tossed it aside, she sucked on my neck, pulling soft moans from me as I relaxed on top of her body. She flung me on my back again, and I loved how physical she was, throwing me around so easily as if my body was a toy. She kissed down the middle of my body and then dragged her tongue across my skin above the waist of my leather pants. She flipped open the button of my pants like a pro, and it was quite the workout getting those skintight pants off me. But Weed Girl was determined to free my legs. Once they'd escaped, her lips attached to the side of my knee, and she slid her tongue up to my inner thigh. I slapped a pillow over my face, biting into the fabric as I muffled the noises I wanted to let out without Tony hearing us because, God, I had a lot of pent-up energy that needed to be released.

"Get rid of that pillow," she said, gliding her hand on top of my underwear to assess if I was ready or not, and when she made the determination, she slipped my underwear off and then slid her fingers inside me.

I let out a sharp gasp at the sudden insertion, and her fingers undulated faster. The more I clenched the pillow, the harder and faster she moved. She was so assertive and rough with exuberant confidence that it all pushed me closer to the edge. I rocked my body against her as her thumb pressed against me. But with my eyes closed, the scenarios I thought of before I went to sleep played in my head. It wasn't Weed Girl fingering me, helping me christen the back room of the bus. It was Reagan. Reagan's fingers danced inside me; her tongue traced delicate circles on my inner thigh; it was her face I sandwiched in between my legs to hold her in place. It was her name I wanted to bellow as I climbed over the edge. Reagan was the one who made me combust after three months of celibacy as my fingers white-knuckled the pillowcase as I came.

But as I let my heart slow back down to a resting rate, I opened my eyes and saw some stranger between my legs, tasting my center as the aftershocks of my orgasm rang through me. None of that was the girl I kept thinking about.

To be honest, I wanted Becky gone. Was that even her name? Who really knew? Call me an awful person, I really didn't care. As necessary as the orgasm was, it didn't kick Jessie Byrd back to Australia where she belonged. It didn't get Reagan out of my head.

I pulled my underwear back up my legs, flipped her over, and just as I was about to kiss her stomach, the girl tugged on my bra strap for me to come up to her mouth. She held the back of my neck to control me, so I followed her demands only for her mouth to feed me a sample of her tongue so I could taste myself on her.

I wasn't a fan of it. No sir, I was not. I never was.

"I want your mouth," she whispered into my ear before nibbling on it gently with her teeth. I tried not to seem too freaked out that my own taste was in me. If I couldn't rub sunscreen on people without getting grossed out, then no, I didn't want any part of what just sprung into my mouth. Now I wanted nothing more than for Becky to leave. I really had a good reason now.

But then, the bus started moving, rocking back and forth as someone stomped down the hallway, approaching my door. Thank God for that lanyard—

"Oh my God! Wow!" Reagan said. The door opened, and light shone down on me in my bra and underwear on top of a half-naked stranger.

I sprang off Becky, who remained casually on the couch, making no attempt to cover her red lace bra. Both of their eyes widened.

"Oh, shit! Oh my God, I'm sorry," she said so quickly I barely made out the words until she was already running off the bus.

Becky's face lit up in the shadows as if this was the greatest surprise that ever happened to her. "Oh my God, that was Reagan Moore? Holy shit!"

I rolled my eyes and recovered my shirt and leather pants. Becky finally got off the couch, and her foot stomped on my pants to prevent them from covering my legs like the modest woman I really wanted to be at that moment.

"Nuh-uh. It's my turn," she said in a flirtatious tone.

"No, we're calling it a night," I said. While she kept my pants trapped, I put my shirt back on. "Sorry."

"But we just got started…"

I yanked on my pants to no avail. "And the show is over, and we have to head out. Sorry, Becky."

Her foot released after I gave one last tug and stumbled backward until the wall caught me.

"Seriously?" she said with a glare that cut through the darkness. "My name is *Brittany*."

Oops.

"Cool. Time to go, Brittany."

She snatched her stuff off the ground and made sure I heard her huffs of displeasure. "Fucking musicians," she muttered as she stomped down the bus steps and onto the asphalt.

Since those pants were too difficult to put back on, I found my pj shorts, threw them over my legs, and went to Reagan's bus. Luckily, Beck—I mean Brittany—and her friend were long gone, so I had a clear path to find out what the hell Reagan was doing on my bus. Her bus was our home base. She'd never even been in mine. Not once. So, I needed to find out why the hell she stormed onto my bus without warning.

Her bus driver, Martin, let me in after I knocked. When I slid open the door to her room, I found her on her bed in her pj's, knees tucked into her chest, and her forehead resting against her knees.

"Hey, you all right?"

She lifted her head. Her eyes hung in tiredness, and her face was cleared from that usual jovial smirk she always had on. It was the first time on tour she stared at me with the most maudlin expression. It killed me. Whatever reason forced her to come on my bus was bad enough to erode her beautiful smile.

"I'm *so* sorry," she said. "I didn't mean to interrupt—"

"Eh, it's fine. She needed to go anyways. Are you okay? You look upset."

She studied me for a second as I took a seat by her feet. "I'm fine."

"Really? Because you've never been on my bus before."

She shook her head slowly, and I sensed her hesitation in telling me whatever was bugging her. Maybe Jessie? I wiggled her knee in an attempt to shake a little smile out of her, but I got nothing. Not even eye contact.

Something was seriously wrong with her. The most serious I'd ever seen her was that one moment while we were building our sandcastle on South Beach when she told me how she wished she was normal just for one day.

"Hey, talk to me," I said. "Is it about Jessie?"

She drew out a long sigh that sounded as if it came from the pit of her stomach. "She showed up to my show unannounced," she said, her tone annoyed, angry, and hurt. "Like, she doesn't get to do that when she broke up with me for no reason. What in her right mind made her think she could just stroll into my green room so she could ask me out for drinks after the show to 'clear the air.' It's a game. She's playing a game. Clearly, she had nothing else to do tonight and wanted to watch me squirm."

"Well…did you squirm?"

She shot me a glare. "I'm not in the mood for jokes."

Damn, her tone was sharp. She really wasn't in the mood for the usual sass we gave each other. I could tell she needed something to loosen up her mood. So, the speakeasy light bulb went off in my head.

"Wanna drink? I could grab some wine from my bus."

"I don't know what I want. She hurt me so much, and she's acting so casual about it. Still. Just like when she broke up with me."

"Well, she's an idiot for breaking up with you," I said. My sincere comment got her to look at me with wondering eyes. "Really."

As much as it pissed me off that Jessie Byrd stole all her thoughts and I didn't, I knew she needed someone to be there for her. So, I would be that person. Us girls had to stick by each other, no matter how much our stomachs twisted from hearing the juicy details of the lives we weren't a part of.

"I have a bottle of Chardonnay in my fridge," I said. "How about I go get it, and we can have a glass before we roll out of here, all right?"

As I got off her bed and headed out of the room, I heard a soft, "Blair," coming from her.

I turned around, and Reagan's eyes rounded at me like a

whimpering puppy. It was the same eye look she gave me in her green room with Jessie Byrd behind me, begging me to stay. A sad Reagan Moore was really contagious, and if she wasn't her bubbly, annoying, yet extremely adorable self, then life was a real bummer.

"What?"

"Can you, um, would it be weird if I asked you, uh, to spend the night? Here? I really don't want to be alone tonight."

Was I dreaming, or did she really ask me to spend the night? Even after having a long moment of deep eye staring with Jessie that I hoped to God was not deep eye fucking. I'd take it. She didn't have to ask me twice.

"Will that make you feel better?" I asked, and she replied with a nod. My stomach did a celebratory backflip at the knowledge that my presence was the very thing to make her feel better. "Then let me grab that bottle of wine and my toothbrush. I can do an amazing job of taking your mind off her." I stopped when I noticed her raising a suspicious eyebrow. "I mean—wow—that really didn't sound right at all. I just meant that I've got wine and ears, and that makes a great combination of forgetting ex-girlfriends."

Then her mouth curled upward, and my rambling that wasn't supposed to be cute or funny instantly died at the sight of the smallest trace of a smirk. "I know what you meant, Blair. Do what you need to do. I'll be here, processing the night."

Out of the bus I ran. A pretty girl wanted me to sleep in her bed and keep her company. I would most certainly do that at record speed.

"I'm spending the night with Reagan," I said as I took a quick hit from a joint.

"What?" Miles shouted as he threw his body forward on his bed, banging his head against the top of the bunk. He whelped and rubbed the pain out.

"Don't get a concussion," I said and inhaled another puff.

"You're spending the night with Reagan? What does that mean? Are you guys gonna hook up?"

"I wish." I snatched the toothbrush out of my bathroom bag to find him lying back down on his pillow, still rubbing out the pain on his forehead.

"Wait a minute…so you do want to hook up with her?"

"Dude, have you seen her? She's hot."

"Yeah, but…" He made a face, the kind of face that said I should know exactly what he was implying without saying the words.

"But what?"

"But should you? What happens if it gets weird on tour?"

"Blair," Corbin said and poked his head out of his bunk, pulling out an earbud from his ear. "Are you seriously going to hook up with Reagan?"

"There's not gonna be any hooking up tonight. Calm down, dudes. She's upset that her ex-girlfriend came to her show tonight, and she's distraught."

"Because I don't know if hooking up with her is wise—"

Miles's eyebrows scrunched. "Her ex-girlfriend? She has an ex-girlfr—" Then it finally hit him, and his eyes lit up the same way they did when I told him I was gay all the way back in high school. It was exciting to know when someone was a part of our cool kids club. "Oh my God! Did she date Jessie Byrd?" He sprang back up and bashed his head yet again. "Jesus! Fu—"

"Gotta go. Snore as loud as you want tonight."

By the time I got back to Reagan, she was curled up in the fetal position on the left side of her bed, staring out the tinted window. I had a feeling she'd decided no on the wine, which was fine with me. The Ritalin I popped a few hours before was still working, which benefited her because I was really all ears, ready to focus on whatever she had to tell me. I poured myself a large glass of Chardonnay, took a few gulps, topped off the glass, and then sat on the empty space that dominated her king bed, not going under the comforter because I wasn't sure where the lines were drawn. We both liked women, we both found each other attractive, but allowing myself to fully sink into her bed could be a little too presumptuous. Maybe she'd think that I was trying to hit on her or something.

I didn't need covers anyway.

"You can have some covers," she said with a laugh. "I don't bite."

And then I felt stupid.

I crawled underneath, and as I positioned myself, my right leg brushed up against Reagan's smooth, warm leg in her pj shorts; the touch of her ignited those butterflies inside me that didn't come out once when kissing Becky—fuck, I mean Briana? It was a mere accident, and as much as I loved that my leg brushed against hers, I was the opener on her tour. It could be complicated. She was confused about her ex-girlfriend. My sole purpose for being here was to be a friend to her and listen to whatever she needed to say to feel just a little bit better. So, I retrieved my leg. Now wasn't the time to acknowledge that buzzing between us—that always seemed to be between us. Now was the time to listen.

"You smell like weed," she said and flung her body in a one eighty turn so she could face me instead of the window.

"Shit, I'm sorry. Do you want me to go grab some gum?"

She gave me a thin smile and shook her head. "No, you're fine. I'm just going to use it against you."

"Oh, great." I let out a sigh. "It helps me relax. Especially now. My mind seems to wander a lot. So, it's weed that helps me forget."

"Your mind wandering because of your grandpa?"

I nodded. "Yeah. Being in Nashville is bringing up all these old memories of us around the city. That and the fact that my mom sold the house in Irvine and downsized, so I feel like I lost even more of him, you know?"

She placed her hand on my arm. I sucked in my lips to hold in that relieved sigh that was desperate to leak out of me. And then when her thumb started rubbing my arm, I almost disappeared into her bed.

Just listening was going to be pure torture.

"I'm sorry, Blair."

"My dad abandoned my mom when she was pregnant with me, so my grandpa was much more than a grandpa. He was my dad and my best friend. It's just…well…the past two days have been kind of hard, hence the smell of weed."

"This is the first time you've said anything about him."

I shrugged. "I don't know what to say. He's dead and never coming back."

"I don't know. I've never lost someone close to me, but I'm here if you want to talk about it. Don't feel like you only need weed and alcohol to make you feel better."

"I know, and thank you, but the weed helps me sleep and calm the fuck down in general. My mind gets crazy sometimes with thoughts and anxiety."

She retrieved her hand and her rubbing thumb, but as that sigh seeped out of me, I could already feel an immense absence where her hand used to be.

"I mean, I get it," Reagan continued. "Maybe not on a generalized anxiety level, but my job and trying to keep my life as normal and private as I can constantly takes up a lot of head space."

"That must be really hard. Having such a successful job and loving it but hating that you can't just enjoy going to the beach."

"It is. Or if I wanna date someone, I freak out that it's all going to go down like it did with Zeke. It was awful, Blair. Being stalked by adults, having to run away from them on the street; they have no respect for personal space, and they would literally get up in my face with a camera. Sometimes, I was afraid of getting hurt. God, I was so miserable. In a way, I was glad that relationship ended."

"And that's why you hid Jessie Byrd from everyone?"

"One hundred percent. The media would flip their shit if they knew I was dating a girl because that's what they do, so the amount of stalking would skyrocket, you know? I don't care if people know I'm dating a woman. It's not the nineties anymore, but I do care that I'd lose even more privacy."

Martin started up the bus, and the floodlights in the hallway flicked off. The only light illuminating the back of the bus was the small table lamp on the nightstand right next to Reagan. As the bus pulled out of the venue, beginning its journey to Atlanta, her eyebrows furrowed as if she was trying to solve the puzzle that was me.

"So…you hook up with fans a lot?" she asked with bold confidence.

Well, I knew that question was coming.

I rolled my eyes thinking about Bethany. Her assertiveness wasn't sexy anymore. It was borderline creepy. "Not usually," I said. "But every girl has needs."

She laughed. "With fans?"

"Don't slut shame me."

"I'm not! I'm genuinely curious. We just talked about my dating life, and I never got the chance to put you in the hot seat. We have all the time now since I'm holding you hostage tonight. So, spill."

"What do you want to know? I'm an open book."

"Oh, well, this is gonna get good." She lifted up to get comfortable for all the questions I could tell she crafted on the spot, tapping her fingers against her chin. It was pretty adorable, actually. I shouldn't have smiled right before a hot seat questionnaire, but I did. "How many fans have you slept with?"

I sucked in my lips so my smile didn't show. I loved how much she wanted to know about my sex life because the more she wanted to know, the more I knew she was interested in me, and the more my body floated up to the clouds with swelling happiness.

My goal was to be as vague as possible to make her squirm.

"Wow. A super personal question off the get-go. A few."

Her face scrunched in a judgmental frown. "A few? Really?"

"The more you judge, the less I say."

"Okay, okay. How many is a few?"

"Under ten. Next question."

"Under ten! God—"

"Hey! No judging. This is a judge-free zone."

She threw her hands up to surrender. "You're right. I'm sorry. Not judging, just impressed...and slightly jealous?"

I laughed. "I'm well aware of the jealousy. Next question?"

A blush hit her cheeks, and she paused for a moment. "How long were you with your ex-girlfriend?"

"A year."

"Why did you guys break up?"

"Because I wasn't really into it. My life is kind of a mess right now, and I was going on this tour. It wouldn't have worked out."

"Okay, Jessie," she said with an eye roll.

I opened my mouth to defend myself and then closed it. She was completely right. Jessie Byrd needed to focus on herself, and so did I. There was nothing wrong with that, and I think Reagan would have agreed if it wasn't for the freshness of the wound Jessie gave her.

"And how was the girl tonight?"

I shrugged. "Okay. I got what I wanted. But you barged in just in time so I didn't have to reciprocate."

"You didn't reciprocate? God, you're an awful lay!"

I playfully hit her arm. "Whoa, I'm not an awful lay. If you're gonna hook up with a touring musician, you gotta know there's an itinerary they follow, so there might not be enough time."

She let out a bellowing laugh. "You're so full of shit. You just didn't want to reciprocate."

I thought about it for a hot second. "Yeah, you're right."

"Wow, never thought Blair Bennett was a pillow princess."

"Whoa, not usually, okay? Tonight was different. I'm definitely not a pillow princess if I'm actually into the girl. This girl was someone to pass the time with."

"You're an asshole," she said but still had a smile on her. She then lay back against the pillows. "Well, at least someone's getting laid on this tour. I've already accepted the fact that I'm gonna die alone."

"Have you looked in the mirror lately? I find it really hard to believe that you'll die alone. You're gorgeous as hell."

Her eyes drifted to the liberal space between us. Through the dim lighting, I noticed her cheeks reaching peak pink levels, and my stomach did another twist. I guess even after running into her ex-girlfriend, I could still make her smile and blush, and I hoped that meant something.

"Oh, thanks," she said and bashfully tucked a strand of hair behind her ear. "Still doesn't shake the feeling off me though. Like, running into Jessie tonight—or I should say, Jessie hunting me down in my dressing room. That's doing a really good number on me, making me think I'm incapable of finding someone good for me."

"You looked at her like she was everything."

"She's *not* everything," she said defensively. "I wasn't even in love with her. I guess I was really infatuated. I think it was mostly physical."

"She *is* pretty hot."

"Yeah, I'm well aware. So, if I looked at her like she was everything, then it must be because I'm probably sexually frustrated, and I need to get laid." That warmth on my cheeks radiated down my whole body. For a split second, that cliffhanger thickened in the room. And then when the moment fizzled, she looked at me with curious eyes. "So, you really think I'm gorgeous as hell?"

Her tone subtly begged for a compliment that was so easy to give, and she seemed genuinely shocked that I'd said that to her. I was genuinely shocked that she was really oblivious to it all. How did she have no idea how beautiful she was? Anytime that girl walked into the room, my body was overcome with so much warmth, I was shocked no one noticed.

"I told you in Miami that you have a really nice smile," I said. "Was that not a hint?"

"Sorry, I'm having a moment right now. Seeing Jessie is making me all sorts of insecure and reminding me how long it's been since I've been with someone, and it's driving me crazy."

"You haven't been with anyone since her?"

"Hey!" She hit me in the arm again. "I thought this was a judge-free zone?"

"I'm not judging! I just find that incredibly surprising."

"Do you understand why I'm frustrated now? I don't even want to hear you complain about having needs. I completely know and understand more than you right now."

Her eyes drifted off mine and found a random spot on the wall to look at. That was when a light bulb clicked on in my head, and as much as the rational part of me desperately reached to flip it right back off, the other part of me currently controlled by the weed, Chardonnay, and residual Ritalin wanted to leave it on. Let it grow brighter. It was risky, but with great risks came great rewards.

Don't say it. Don't say it. Don't say it. Don't say it...

"Well, you know, since we both have needs, maybe we should just use each other."

Oh my God, no! You said it. How do we escape this moving bus?

Her eyebrows climbed up her forehead at the same time her mouth parted to the smallest degree. "Are you serious?"

"Uh..." Yup, tongue-tied now. "I mean—it was a joke?"

"Was it, though?" Her tone was skeptical. Even she didn't buy it. I didn't either.

"I didn't mean for it to come off as creepy as it did..."

The more I babbled, the more her smile grew through her blush. The more she smiled and blushed, the more my face and body felt as if it'd been hit with menopause.

"Blair Bennett, are you coming on to me?" she asked, giggling.

"I, uh, were you coming on to me in the pool? When you said I looked good in a bikini?"

"Oh God, here we go," she said and twisted herself to her other side to give me her back. With a turn of the knob, the nightstand light flickered off, and the two of us were draped in darkness with the occasional highway light sweeping by us in a blink of an eye. "Narcissism is contagious in Hollywood. I would stop going there."

"It's a legit question," I said.

She flipped back over to face me, now mere inches away. "So was mine!"

"You answer first. You hit on me first."

"How did I hit on you first? You allowed me to put sunscreen on your back."

"I didn't want second degree sunburn again." I held back a grin, knowing that her diversion to my question gave me all the answers. The girl knew how to work the media and their questions. If she didn't want to answer the question, she diverted. And boy did she divert. "Just answer the question," I continued. "Were you coming on to me in the pool?"

"You literally just offered to give me an orgasm right now," Reagan said. "You know what, you don't need to answer my question. I already know the answer. You *were* coming on to me, and you're only acting like this because you're not sure how I took it. So, to torture you, I'm going to leave you with this: good night, Blair." She tossed back over on her other side.

"What? No! You can't do that!"

"Oh, I think I can."

Silence. Nothing but silence and the faint humming of the bus engine. I let out a frustrated moan, knowing I wasn't going to get my answer. Her PR team did a great job sealing up all her secrets and making sure that frontal lobe of hers never cracked under pressure. Sexual pressure included.

"Ugh, I shouldn't have agreed to this," I said. "I'm not gonna be able to fall asleep now."

"You shouldn't be going to sleep frustrated...or Random Girl isn't doing you right."

Everything below my underwear flared up with so much desire just thinking of Reagan doing me right.

I inhaled way too much clary sage that night in Nashville, Tennessee.

CHAPTER SIX

Ever since I made that horrible proposition that we sleep together, whatever weird tension that glued us together became even stronger. But weird in an exciting way, as if we had this secret we kept from my band, the crew, the fans, the press, and the whole world. And I loved that added thrill.

Since Nashville, Reagan asked me if I wanted to spend the night with her again under the guise of avoiding Miles's snores, but I had a feeling it was more than that. If she felt anything like I did from our first sleepover, she was searching for the rush of exciting uncertainty of where the night would lead with the vulnerable backdrop of a darkened room and warm bed. Nashville to Atlanta to Birmingham, I found myself lying next to Reagan, discussing everything and anything. She told me about her life growing up in Nashville, the youngest with two older brothers, and how her oldest brother, Colton, who was five years older than her and was expecting his first child with his wife in November, and she went on about how she was going to spoil her niece and couldn't wait to spend Thanksgiving with her family. She asked about my family, and I went on about my grandparents. How Grandma was the disciplinarian and the woman who got me into baking, who would always bake her amazing cookies for my friends who came over or for school bake sales. I told her how Gramps gave me different instruments to learn to distract me from getting so bored that I found trouble—like sneaking off with Dana Bohlen or pool hopping in all the ritzy neighborhoods with Miles and my other high school friends.

The morning we arrived in Richmond, I woke up to my arm slung over Reagan's body, her back snuggled into my front, and my face buried in her shoulder blades. It took me by surprise, and as much as I wanted to push myself to the farthest corner of her bed, the more I adjusted to the knowledge that we were in a perfect spooning position, the more comfortable it felt. It pulled a smile from me as I caught the smell of her shampoo emanating off her. The sounds of her deep breaths I'd grown used to over the course of a week told me she was still asleep, but that was okay because it bought me more time to enjoy her in my arms. I held her for a few more moments, holding in my pee so it could last a little longer. By the time I returned from the bathroom, she was already stretching and smiling at me.

But that spooning session I'd keep to myself.

Since the start of the tour, Reagan and I had a collection of shared moments of secret flirting and the undeclared war we were playing with each other to see who would break in making the first move. Every night I crawled into her bed, I hoped that it would be the night we would have our first kiss. There were plenty of silent opportunities. When our eyes securely locked in between conversations, moments of playful arm slapping, subtle comments about attractiveness, and accidental cuddles. I wasn't sure how long it would go on, but it was pushing me over the edge. My lips were screaming for the touch of hers. My body was screaming for the touch of hers.

Actually, every fiber of my being was screaming for her.

During our sound check in Richmond, Reagan was back at the soundboard with the sound technician, curiously watching him adjust the microphone and instrument levels as she sipped on her green tea through a straw. Miles and I already tested our opening song and planned on playing around with two more before our sound check was completed.

"Let's warm up with a cover," I told Miles.

Everything was already sounding good. The mics were at the perfect level. The instruments. The bass. Why not have fun?

"What are you thinking?" Miles asked behind his drum kit.

"'Jessie's Girl.'"

He frowned. "Really? Rick Springfield?"

Without letting him voice his opinion, I went ahead without him, strumming the opening chords on the Fender and making a face at him. He flipped me off, our usual banter. When I turned around to face the soundboard, I found Reagan's stare on me as the muted chords spilled out of the speakers and filled the empty arena. When I sang the first lyric, I could feel her zero in on me quizzically. And when the bridge came around, she lowered her straw, crossed her arms, and squared her body to us with a wide smirk partially hidden by the bite in her lip.

It was a perfect song to warm up to. It was the perfect song to get Reagan's damn attention.

But of course, we didn't talk about it after the show when we ended the night drinking wine in her bed. I think she did that on purpose for more torture.

The next night in DC, a local restaurant catered food for us before the show, and all fifty-something of us loaded up our plates. Reagan waited her turn for the tongs as I plucked the right sized lemon-pepper marinated chicken from the tin catering pan.

"That's a nice breast you have," she said with a slight hesitation before she gestured to the chicken clasped in the tongs in front of my chest. Her tone sounded anything but innocent. Her single cocked eyebrow and the pull of one side of her lips insinuated that she knew exactly what she was trying to imply. The worst part was that she caught me so off guard with that comment I didn't have anything to dish back to her. My throat went dry, my tongue was tied, and my cheeks felt so red; I handed her the tongs and scampered away to Miles so I didn't have to look like an idiot that much longer.

During our performance, I told Miles I wanted to switch up our set list and do a cover. It was nice to change things up a bit, right? Since I spent a lot of time inhaling the faint clary sage permanently stuck to Reagan's skin and hair, I told Miles I was going to play "Crash Into Me" by Dave Matthews while he stayed quiet on the drums. The song was about Dave Matthews's wet dreams over a girl, which sounded a lot creepier than the romantic, sexy sound of the song. So, while the lights dimmed on Miles, I started the song off by adding a few layers to my looping machine to add some flair. The first loop was a lick on the Fender, and the second loop was a few slides of quarter notes. Then I quickly threw on the acoustic baby Martin and played the guitar part we all knew and loved against the loops. I could see Reagan in her concert attire, standing in the shadows of the side stage with her eyes glued on me as I sang to the twenty thousand people of DC. But really, I sang to her…even though I pretended not to notice her watching me.

In response to my impulsive cover, Reagan stopped halfway

through her set list and checked in with the crowd, asking them how they were doing, and they responded in a roaring cheer.

"You guys don't mind if I sing a cover, do you?" Their cheering told her they didn't mind one bit.

A cover wasn't part of her set list at all. She'd never played any cover since the beginning of the tour, and she didn't even spice up her sound check to play a cover with her band. It was one thing for a two-person band to switch up their set list. It was an ordeal for Reagan to switch it up and tell her band, her dancers, and her crew that she would add a song they never prepared for.

She broke out into "Cool for the Summer" by Demi Lovato, a song that was sexual and all about girls hooking up with girls. But she sang and performed it with her usual innocent disposition. I never thought a pop song would turn me on so much. She made it a point to walk over to the side of the stage where I stood unnoticed as she sang. Hearing her sing those words made me so dizzy. The crowd on the floor pushed closer to her, tossing their hands up, begging for just a finger graze, and after she satisfied a few begging hands, she turned to the side stage, looked straight at me, and winked.

That pretty much did it for me.

After begging me to play the song all freakin' day, I caved and granted Miles's wish for the second cover song for our next show in Philly. As much I wanted to play "Electric Feel" by MGMT to passive-aggressively sing to Reagan, Miles vetoed because he said only seven people in the crowd would know that song, and we had to cover a song everyone could sing along to. So, on stage in front of our Philly audience, I first looped the jingle of a tambourine, followed by a few bluesy chords layered with some subtle synthesizers on the keyboard, and then the third loop was the famous bass line at the beginning of the song. On the acoustic Martin guitar, I played live a sultry fingerpicking melody with some Latin spice reverberating in each note. And that was how we created "You Drive Me Crazy" by Britney Spears with a Midnight Konfusion flair. From the sound of the crowd cheering and singing every word back to us, I could tell they enjoyed it too. Reagan followed our cover with "Dress" by Taylor

Swift, wearing the sparkly purple dress she always wore during that portion of her set. I never heard the song before, but apparently it matched us to a T. Our secrets, how no one suspected anything going on between us or that I shared her bed. Since Miles was one of the biggest Swifties out there, he told me that not only was it a Taylor Swift song, but it was her most risqué song. According to him, when Taylor Swift first shared the song with her most fervent fans at her Rhode Island house, with her parents also present, her dad walked out because it was too much for his ears. I had no idea that Taylor Swift had the ability to do that to her poor father.

Of course, this new juicy knowledge drew my attention back to Reagan as she sang the chorus. She didn't want us to be best friends; she dreamed about me ripping that dress off her. My mouth dropped to the floor. I totally got why Taylor Swift's dad had to walk out now.

That purple sequin dress took on a whole new meaning that I would never be able to shake off.

I'd been buzzing from the past two days of intense flirting with Reagan. We had a day off in Manhattan before Reagan's sold-out Madison Square Garden show. Since a bunch of lyrics clogged my head, I dedicated some of that time freeing those lyrics into my journal. I cracked open beer after beer to fuel my thoughts, filled the fresh pages of my journal with all the lyrics until I hit a good stopping point and my right wrist cramped up. That was when you knew you had an amazing writing session. Wrist cramps were good cramps.

The night before the big show, after a whole day of writing and resting, as I brushed my teeth before I surrendered to bed and sleep, my phone buzzed with a text from Reagan. The time flashed 12:18 on my screen with Reagan's name right below it.

Her text read: *Room 2213. I have 180-degree view of Central Park and the whole city. Plus, a Jacuzzi tub. Just saying.*

I beamed as foamy blue toothpaste dripped down the sides of my mouth. As I clenched my toothbrush between my teeth, I typed back, *Is this a formal invite?*

My invite from Nashville never expires unless verbally addressed, which it hasn't.

I responded to her eagerly. *Coming.*

And she quickly responded. *I wish.*

My toothbrush fell from my mouth and into the sink. Toothpaste splattered on the counter and my chin as I reread that message. Yup, she really said that. This was happening.

I sprinted to room 2213 without even cleaning up the mess.

On my walk to her suite, I prepped myself for what this could turn into because I knew exactly what this was. I was always so terrified of making the first move that I went through my whole twenty-four years of existence having never made it. Hence, why Reagan and I were in this game. All my past girlfriends? They kissed me first. It was great because I didn't have to put too much thought into it. But Reagan was the first girl who stole all my thoughts and injected them with so much analyzation. I had a feeling that if I didn't initiate a kiss, we'd be playing this game of cuddles, talking about orgasms, and singing songs about sex on repeat for the whole tour. I had to do something because I wasn't sure how much longer I could let my brain keep wondering how her lips tasted.

When I stood outside her door, my pulse thumped against my skin, and I hoped that maybe we wouldn't kiss tonight so she couldn't feel the movements if she sucked on my neck. I was so nervous. The only time I remembered being this nervous with sweaty palms and my pulse twitching this rapidly was when I was about to lose my virginity to Dana Bohlen, and I hoped that my inexperience wouldn't scare her away from me or sleeping with girls.

With a deep breath, I knocked on the door, and a few moments ticked by as I waited. I was hoping she would answer faster, then part of me wondered if she purposely kept me waiting to keep me on my toes. She always did a good job of that. And it worked because the longer it took her to answer the door, the more my pulse panicked under my skin.

She opened the door wrapped up in a white robe, her damp hair up in a messy bun, and her collarbone teasing me from underneath the cotton fabric. She let me inside her lavish suite which seemed even bigger than my apartment in West Hollywood. And sure enough, two floor-to-ceiling windows overlooked all of New York with Central Park right below us, the dark blob encompassed by glimmering building lights.

"Wow," I said, taking in her suite, then taking in her in that robe. "And wow. You're very forward." I gestured to her robe.

"I was just about to change into pj's."

"You don't have to do that."

"No?"

I shook my head. "You can sleep in your robe."

"I could. It's really soft. Feel it."

She tugged on the front of the robe just a bit for my grip to catch. Her tug teased me, showing more of her collarbone and the swell of her breasts. She wasn't doing this to show off her robe. She was doing this to tease me. This was the lasso to pull me into her lips.

"It's really soft," I said through my arid throat, and I couldn't keep my eyes from trailing the soft skin down to her breasts. "Feels comfortable enough to sleep in."

"Well, if you really want me to sleep in this, as my guest, I'll do what you want."

"Then as your guest, I get dibs on little spoon."

Her eyelids relaxed into a side eye, and she blew out a long sigh as if granting my wish took up all the energy inside her. "Okay, but it's only because you have a nice face and nice sleeve."

I flashed her a smile before I jumped on the left side of the bed, burying myself underneath the white duvet and curling my body into a perfect little spoon position. When Reagan joined me, the leftover heat from her warm shower wrapped me up with her embrace, and the smell of the hotel shampoo and body wash permeated the air around us. Her body fit snug around mine, and my stomach fluttered when her arm hung in front of me, then wandered around until she found my hand to hold.

When our fingers interlocked for the first time, I could feel my insides ready to burst. I should have just kissed her. I mean, she laid out all the clues face-up as if showing off her royal flush, knowing she was going to win the whole pot. She was in her robe with nothing underneath, and I was one knot away from seeing what I could only imagine was the most beautiful naked body—toned from yoga and dancing, with pores cleared from clary sage. All I had to do was roll over and kiss her, but knowing that all the pressure and control was on me, I froze. Was it because I'd never made a move before? Was that the real reason why girls kissed me first? Because this whole time, I'd thought it was because I didn't have to try, and instead, I really was just too much of a coward to do it myself, and those girls knew it, so they had no other choice but to kiss me?

She clasped my fingers tighter as her forehead pressed between my shoulder blades. I knew if I didn't take advantage of this moment, I'd be walking into Madison Square Garden the next day—the most famous arena in the world—beating myself up because I didn't kiss her when the perfect opportunity presented itself. My mind would be more wrapped up in blaming myself for missing an opportunity to kiss her than taking in every moment I should while performing in front of a sold-out Garden. I'd rather have my mind clouded with the wonderful feeling of her lips dancing on mine than the ghost of them.

I flipped over to face Reagan. Through the darkness, I watched as her eyes narrowed on me as if I was the only thing in the room. I looked down at her full, kissable lips, then at her collarbone and where the robe met in front of her chest.

Don't overthink. Just do what you want to do.

I grabbed the robe, feeling the soft Egyptian cotton in between my fingers as they slowly trailed down the hem toward her breasts, barely grazing her skin. "I liked your song choice last night," I said softly.

"Oh, you did?"

Instead of full confidence embodying her tone, it sounded like it wilted down to half. Darkness blanketed us, a romantic view of the city adding speckles of light outside. Our faces were mere inches from each other, and the more I felt the robe in between my fingers, the more the silence pushed itself into bed with us.

"Yeah. I liked both song choices, actually," I admitted. "They were pretty direct."

"I feel like I have to be direct with you."

"You do? Why?"

"Because I'm lying here in my bed, completely naked underneath this robe, and you still haven't kissed me yet."

My heart actually skipped a beat. It stuttered multiple times in a row, and in that moment of stuttering, my brain and stomach did a synchronized flip like Olympian divers off the ten-meter platform.

I finally reached the knot in front of her stomach and began untying it. Slowly. Because she had no problem going slow with me. "Because you never answered my question."

"What question?"

"The one I asked you after the Nashville show."

The knot fell open, and I glided my hands onto her warm, naked skin. At the touch, I heard her suck in a gasp. I felt the little abs as I slid my hand down her flat stomach to her upper thigh. Just doing that, the air around me heated considerably.

"And I responded with two weeks' worth of cuddling," she said, and I could feel her tense up as if holding in any other gasps that needed to come out. "Thinking that maybe one of those nights, you would actually do something and make a move."

I stopped exploring her skin. "Seriously? It was all on me?"

"Hey, you were the one who proposed it." The tension evaporated from her tone, and full confidence took over. "Like, I know for a fact now that I'm going to die alone because I've, like, aged twenty years just waiting for you to make a—"

I jumped on top of her pelvis, pinning her to the bed. She finally stopped yapping and looked up at me with shock. Thank God. Reagan Moore stopped running her mouth. To reward her, I let the robe fall to her sides, finally revealing her beautiful body, and I reminded myself that I needed to keep breathing if I wanted to enjoy more of her. But it was so hard to when so many things were happening in my stomach, and I couldn't focus on what to take in first. Her perfect breasts that I knew would fit right into my palms. Her perfect stomach. Her perfect collarbone. God, how was someone this beautiful? I had no idea.

I moved my hands up her stomach to her chest so I could skim my thumbs over her nipples, and her breasts did fit perfectly in my palms. Gently. Slowly. Her nipples hardened against my fingers as I traced the tops of them. I swear, all Reagan had to do was lie there naked, her stare tracking mine wandering over every inch of her body. She elicited a rush that made me shiver, and she hadn't even undressed me yet.

She reached for my T-shirt and slid her hand underneath so her fingertips ran along the waist of my shorts. Closing my eyes, I pulled in my lips and released a pleasured sigh, trying to revel in the wonderful and thrilling anticipation of the first kiss. She pulled my shirt toward her, and I lowered myself on top of her, studying the way her eyes begged me to stop teasing and to finally kiss her. But I wasn't done taking her in yet. Someone as beautiful as her needed to be appreciated.

Patience.

I could feel her nipples pressing into my shirt, and God, did I want my shirt off so I could fully enjoy the touch of them against my own.

My cheek moved hers to the side so I could finally kiss the soft skin of her neck. Inhaling the clean smell of the body wash, I worked my way up her neck, nibbling, running my tongue in circles, and then moved to the other side of her neck to do the same thing. Her hands clasped on to my back, and with one suck at the right spot, a muted moan stopped at her tightly closed lips as her fingers dug into my back.

My heart raced as I kissed underneath her ear and then her cheek and then finally her lips. Those lips I spent weeks fantasizing about every night finally kissed me back. My whole body ignited like I'd taken a drug I'd never tried before, a drug forever superior to all the ones I had. The kiss quickly turned passionate, picking up aggression and speed, proof of how ravenous we were for each other. Feeling her tongue against mine sent a sharp warmth to my center. She breathed a faint moan into me, and hearing the sound of pleasure coming from her forced me to position my leg in between hers to elicit more. That was when she aggressively pulled my shirt over my head as if it was the most insulting thing she'd ever touched. Finally, I was topless, and wasting no time to close the gap so my nipples could meet hers, and God, her warm skin touching mine was even better than I imagined. I found her lips again and sucked in her bottom lip before caressing my tongue with hers, feeling how much we needed each other with every movement. Her fingers slipped into my hair and firmly held a bunch of it, demanding me to continue kissing her and welcoming the subtle, undulating rocking my waist made against hers. Her tongue trailed across my bottom lip before sucking it into the grip of her teeth, and the feeling her kiss injected into me was something so wonderful and warm and rousing, I had no idea what to do with all the feelings raging inside me other than to pull my mouth away from hers so I could kiss all the other parts of her body. Because it needed to be done.

My chest burned with all these different desires: all the ways my hands wanted to touch her, all the ways my lips wanted to kiss her, and all the ways I wanted to move my body against hers. As I thought about the infinite possibilities, I went straight for the source that spiraled a jolt of electricity through my whole body, her breasts. I took them into my mouth and lightly sucked on each until my suction pulled a moan out of her, and then I moved to the next one to do the same thing. With each movement my mouth made, her head tilted back a little more into her pillow, and she let out sighs while her nails raked along my back.

"Blair," she muttered through a moan. I glanced up at her, and she clasped desperately on to my face. "I really need you. Right now."

"Patience. I'm busy."

"I've been patient. For seven months. And then some."

"You need to be properly warmed up." I lifted upward to kiss her collarbone while I played with her hard, protruding nipple. "I gotta fuck you right."

She let out an erotic whine and then tossed her arm over her eyes in defeat. I kissed her body from her neck to the valley of her breasts down to her flat stomach, and then slid my tongue across her waistline. At that, the fist she had in my hair became tighter, and her whole body relaxed.

I drew circles around the fabric of her underwear, teasing down to her center where I realized she wasn't lying when she said she didn't need to be warmed up anymore. Feeling the wetness I was shocked I could give her, I pressed my thumb into her, and her lips parted to expel a groan. Her fingers tightened in my hair as I bit the top of her underwear and used my hands to assist my teeth in taking them off. After I tossed her pink panties aside, I spread her legs open, positioned my body comfortably on the bed, and started kissing the inside of her thighs as each kiss led the way closer to her.

And when I put my mouth on her, she let out a loud gasp, pulling my hair in the sexiest way, and her back arched off the mattress.

I swirled my tongue in circles on her, alternating between motions and pressures, but each stroke generating a different sound and movement from her body. When I knew she was ready, I glided my fingers into her and felt myself become wetter the more I felt her. She secured my head right where she wanted me, and I relished each aroused cry and undulating movement against my mouth. The whole time I went down on her, I could hear my heartbeat drumming in my ears. My throat was so dry, the exact opposite of what was happening underneath my underwear. I felt insecure, even though the way her hips moved against my mouth, how her hand applied more pressure on the back of my head, how she breathed and vocalized her pleasure should have been an indication that there wasn't a reason for me to be nervous or insecure.

"Oh God," Reagan belted out, and that plucked me away from worrying and back to the present.

Her breaths got shorter. The movements of her hips became faster, circling around my mouth, searching for what she'd been needing for seven months. She clung to the headboard, and the sounds I was able to pull from her went straight to my center; it was almost as if she was pleasuring me through her noises. And just as I moved my fingers faster and sucked on her, she let out the release she'd been waiting for, the release I'd been waiting for. The sounds she made caused me to melt into her bed, and a part of me was disappointed that it was over because I wanted to listen to her longer. She shivered as she rode out the rest of her orgasm, until her body collapsed. I waited for her to gather her thoughts, kissing the inside of her thighs while I enjoyed the lingering, pulsating movements around my fingers still inside her.

"Oh my God," she said breathlessly while resting her hands on her forehead. "God. Seven months I've bottled that up."

"Hopefully, it was worth the wait?"

"It was…it…yes…worth the wait."

"Let me do you again."

Her head tilted downward, and I had to admit that her gaze looking past her breasts and in between her legs was the best viewpoint a lesbian could ask for. I lightly kissed the top of her, wanting so badly to replay the last five minutes all over again.

"But I want to do you—" she said.

"No, I need to get you off about two more times. And prove to you I'm not a pillow princess."

She tossed her head back, acquiescing. "God, I'm gonna die tonight."

Her hand slipped through my hair and gently directed my head back down to her to shut me up. I loved how she still took the reins and told me what to do in the gentlest and not so gentle way. I could have melted and died at that point. She could direct my head wherever, and I would have equally been aroused.

I gave her two more, and by the end of it, I couldn't wait anymore. I swear one more moan from her or one more rock against my fingers and mouth, and I would have lost it.

After I kissed from her center up her stomach and to her lips, she wrapped her sexy legs around my waist, flung me on my back, and stripped my underwear off. Then she paused. As her bare bottom sat on my pelvis and pinned me to the bed, her eyes took in my naked body, as if she really needed this moment before she could continue. The way she scanned my body sent a powerful hum to every nerve ending that comprised me. She reached for my dream catcher tattoo, and those delicate fingers sent chills all throughout me as she traced the feathers up to the dream catcher, where she drew invisible circles over the ink. Just as I closed my eyes to fully enjoy her touch, her fingertips went to my sleeve and skimmed along the designs of flowers and geometric patterns until they cut off at my shoulder. Her hand kept going, flattening so she could feel my collarbone and my neck that wouldn't stop twitching from my pulse. Her palms ran across my breasts, slowly, going back to the nipples to feel them once more.

"You're really pretty," she said so softly, and something inside me burst open, hearing the vulnerability in her voice. If I wasn't already ready for her, that would have done it completely.

"No, that's all you," I said, and once the words left my mouth, I hoped to God she couldn't hear the subtle tremble in them.

She shook her head and continued to wander all over my body. "Nope. You know I've always had a crush on you, right?"

"What?"

She nodded. "I mean, I always thought you were hot, and the fact that you're so crazy talented made it better, but when I saw you again in Vegas, I felt like I couldn't stop looking at you."

I was so glad it was dark in the room because my cheeks warmed up. I couldn't wrap my head around the fact Reagan Moore thought I was attractive.

"Kiss me," I said and caved in to the overwhelming desire to kiss her.

She lowered herself on top of me, and our naked tops met once again as she kissed my lips. As the kiss deepened, her bare center grinded against me. I could still feel her arousal as she rocked back and forth on my thigh, lighting me up in erotic shivers from the surface of my skin to my bones. Just a few moments of grinding against me, she knew I was ready. Her damp hair and sturdy lips trailed my skin until she finally made it past my stomach, my waist, and spread my legs apart.

"Who would have ever thought that Ms. Insults was going to sleep with the very person she was insulting?" I said as Reagan kissed my inner knee.

She pressed her thumb into my clit and triggered a surprised gasp to fly right out of me.

"Fuck," I yelled and tossed my head back into the pillow to surrender myself.

"Do you ever shut up?" She rubbed circles on me as if it was my punishment for speaking out of turn. My fingers curled over the pillow. God, she was touching me. I didn't have to fantasize about it anymore. She was touching me; she was sending warm shivers up me from the firm circles she pressed into me. "The noises I want to hear coming from you don't involve words."

"I can give you that if you just go—"

I sucked in my breath when her warm mouth took me in, and her tongue replaced her thumb, deepening the circles. After going down on her three times, my body had never been more ready. Moments later, another gasp left me when she slid her fingers inside me. Honestly, it didn't take long for me to come. She knew exactly what she was doing, when to speed up, when to go harder, when to change up motions. It was as if my body and her mouth and fingers spoke the same language.

Our bodies just fit together perfectly.

And then I lay there, completely defeated, out of breath, and depleted from the release of all the frustration that had accumulated inside me. She kissed my inner thighs again before slowly inching up to me as her nipples grazed my skin.

"There," she said softly, and I could hear the smile in her voice. "Now you can talk."

I shook my head. "Can't."

"Good. I did you right, then."

I was up at the crack of dawn. Processing. There was a lot of processing. I guess we were a little too distracted to pull down the blinds to hide the morning sunlight that shone right on us. The rays pouring into the room streamed on Reagan's face nestled on my right boob, arm across my stomach, and breathing the adorable heavy puffs she did in her sleep. As much as I wanted to enjoy her, my mind went straight to what today was. A sold-out Madison Square Garden show. The pinnacle of every musician's dream. The most famous arena in the world. And I was playing on that stage tonight. Without my grandparents or my mom in attendance.

The thought quickly made the bed uncomfortable, despite it being a king with a fresh duvet and the most beautiful girl I'd ever seen. After an hour of twitching in my spot, I noticed that my lungs suddenly became smaller; the breaths became shorter. I darted into the bathroom, locked the door, and sat on the toilet, wrapping my hands around my head. A powerful heat overcame my body as the blood pounded in my ears and the anxiety snaked around my chest. It terrified me. I lost the ability to breathe regularly. I automatically started crying as I tried to keep my heart pumping, but it was as if my lungs wanted none of that.

I flipped the faucet on and splashed my face a few times with cold water. When I saw myself in the mirror, it was like looking through a fish-eye lens. I blinked several times to push away this distorted reality feeling. Closing my eyes tightly, I leaned against the bathroom counter as I took deep breaths to familiarize myself to where I was—in the hotel bathroom, water dripping down my face, fingers wrapped around the sink counter—trying everything to slow my pulse to the right rhythm.

It took a few moments to go back to a regular breathing pattern. I tiptoed out of the bathroom to find Reagan still passed out in the same position I'd left her in, which lifted one of the weights off me, knowing I didn't have to explain myself.

It was hard explaining a panic attack to someone when you didn't even understand it yourself.

I found my phone and decided to tell Miles what happened. Even though we met because of weed and started a friendship because we were both queer, our friendship deepened because of our anxiety. He got attacks more frequently than I did, so he was my rock when I had one. We made a promise to each other junior year that we would say anytime we had one because that meant we had pent-up anxiety we probably needed to talk about. I was still confused as to why I'd had one, but panic attacks came up over the smallest things. It was performing at the most famous arena in the world without my family that was the kerosene to the fire I kept suppressing for the last few months.

I texted Miles. *Just had a panic attack. I'm fine now but still freaked out.*

He responded right away. *Seriously?! What's wrong? How are you doing? Need to talk?*

Me: *I think performing at MSG tonight is making me miss my grandpa and my family even more. He always talked about MSG and how huge it is for any musician. Just wish he was here to see it.*

Miles: *I'm sorry, Blair. Where are you now?*

Me: *...Reagan's bed.*

Miles: *As in finally naked in Reagan's bed?!?*

Me: *Yes...which makes this so much worse. Like, how can I have a panic attack after the wonderful sex I just had? Wtf is wrong with me?*

Miles: *OMG I'm dying! I need all this info! Go drink water. Eat something. Take a few more deep breaths. Maybe lie down and close your eyes. And then give me ALL the details!*

Since Miles knew all too well about panic attacks, I listened to his advice, needing some kind of food in my system to regulate my blood sugar. After I popped a Xanax, I went downstairs to fix up two plates of breakfast. When I got back to Reagan's room, I found her in the exact same position as I left. Still passed out, curled in the fetal position, facing the indent of my body on the bed. I started the coffee and mindlessly ate a banana while staring out at Central Park waking up along with the rest of the city and feeling so empty that I couldn't share this huge night with my family.

The sounds of stirring came from the bed. When I turned around, I watched Reagan sprawl out in a full body stretch with her eyes squinting from the morning sun and tiredness. Even the little grunt she made as she stretched tugged at the corners of my mouth.

"Oh, hey," she said in her dream-drenched voice, so casual it made me laugh. "Do I smell coffee?"

"Oh, hey. Yes, you do. Want some?"

"Yes. Two creams and two sugars, please."

I fixed her coffee exactly as the princess ordered, bringing her plate that consisted of a spoonful of a fruit salad, a banana, a hard-boiled egg, a scoop of scrambled eggs, and three sausage links.

"Coffee and breakfast," I said.

Her eyes widened as she propped herself up. "Oh God. You treat all your girls to this the morning after?"

"Actually, no. You're my first."

"I feel so special. What a wonderful way to wake up. Hot coffee, hot breakfast, and a hot girl." She accepted the cup and plate, and I grabbed my coffee and food to join her in bed. "Thanks for getting this for me. That was really sweet of you."

"We have a big day, so I thought it should start off right."

And, you know, make up for the panic attack.

"You sound stressed," she said, swallowing her first bite of scrambled eggs as she reached for my knee. "You all right?"

"I'm fine," I lied. She didn't need to know about my panic attack. She had a big day too, and the last thing she needed to worry about was me. "Just a little nervous. It's Madison Square Garden."

"I'm right with you. I've never headlined a show there, and my stomach is already starting to hurt. I was going to do some yoga and meditate after breakfast. You can join me if you want."

"You'll be wearing yoga pants, right?"

She winked. "Right."

"Count me in."

In the silence, the sounds of the city from twenty-two floors below vibrated between the steel giants outside. Angry cab drivers. Sirens from police cars and ambulances. The two of us nibbled on our breakfast and nursed our steaming coffee, and she gave me crap for drinking my coffee black. She said serial killers drank their coffee black, and I shouldn't be trusted now. But once I finished everything on my plate, the Xanax started to kick in, bringing the nerves from a boil to a simmer. The things I would have done to bake something at that point. Something more difficult than chocolate chip cookies. I needed to make French macarons in five different flavors. I probably would have given up the opportunity to see Reagan in downward dog in tight yoga pants just so I could bake to ease my mind. It helped distract me. Sometimes, if I couldn't sleep, no matter the time, I'd bake. I baked those lemon bars before the start of the tour because I couldn't keep my thoughts still enough to go to sleep, and hey, they came in handy when I gifted them to Reagan.

"You know what we haven't done yet on this tour that we need to do?" she said as she peeled the banana.

"If you asked me this question twenty-four hours ago, I would have thought of a few things, but since we accomplished that multiple times last night, I honestly have no idea."

"Can we take two seconds to talk about last night?"

"And how amazing it was?"

She looked at me with a playful smirk. "Yes. Exactly that."

"It was amazing."

"So, the answer to your Nashville question is: yes. I would like to use you for that."

"I think I finally got that when my mouth was on you." This made her smirk grow even more coquettish. "And do we keep doing it until we verbally agree to end it?"

"Correct."

"Man, I'm really liking this tour thing."

She set her plate and banana aside and then cuddled up to me. I wrapped my arm around her shoulders as she sank into my body. As I rubbed her arm, goose bumps popped up on her skin, and I grinned knowing that I was able to give them to her.

"But really," she said, "something we haven't done that we definitely should do: play together. That would be fun, right? At Madison Square Garden? Merge our love for covers on the most famous stage in the world?"

"Um, definitely."

"We can quickly whip something up this afternoon at sound check, right?"

"Absolutely!" I said. "We're professionals."

She shifted so she could face me. I loved how raw her face looked in the morning sun. Free from makeup and showing the perfect light blemishes that speckled across her face. A good night's sleep glowing on her skin. She was so beautiful. She could have asked me to sing some 1970s disco song right then and there, and I would have agreed to it in a heartbeat.

And I hated 1970s disco, for the record.

"We'll need something really fun," she said, luckily not noticing me saving every beautiful detail of her face in my mind. "A song everyone knows and can sing along to. A song that will just get you, me, the guys, and the audience all on the same page in one giant bonding moment."

"I already know the song."

"Well, that was fast. What is it?"

"'Piano Man.'"

People loved singing the song. It swept you up into a cloud of happiness. People went to dueling piano bars, holding their breath as they sat on the edge of their seats so they could hear the pianist finally play the song.

She grinned. "Perfect, Ms. Piano Girl."

❖

My stomach really brewed the nerves that night the more I thought about how significant this show was for all of us and how I desperately wished my family was here to see it. No one was even on stage to entertain them yet, and we could already hear the roaring of the crowd through the cinderblock walls.

As Miles ran in and out of the bathroom, I downed my third tequila shot because my nerves were so strong, SoCo wouldn't tame them, and I seriously debated smoking a second joint. The last time I felt like I wanted to vomit before a show was my first piano recital when I was seven, and then about five minutes later, I butchered Pachelbel's "Canon," and refused to play in front of anyone until high school. If tonight was going to be a repeat of that, my music career would be over, and I would be a laughingstock at Madison Square Garden.

From the corner of my eye, Reagan popped in the doorway, in full concert attire and makeup, looking the same kind of beautiful she had always looked on tour but with an extra glow tonight. Maybe because a memory of her naked under me the night before swept through my mind, or because I knew someone like me was able to get a beauty like her, or maybe her face still glowed from sex.

"Hey, where's Miles?" she asked, leaning against the doorway all confidently and sexy; it made me blush.

"Where do you think?"

"He really gets that nervous before shows?"

"Yup. It's even worse today. He's got the gits."

"The gits?"

"The Garden shits. And my stomach is ready to implode."

"You doing okay?"

"No, I'm completely mortified. My hands just started shaking." I held out my right hand to show the proof.

God, here it was again, the same feeling from the morning.

The choking in my lungs. The shortness of my breath. The warmth blanketing my body, and not the good warmth that should have been there with Reagan showing off those legs and cleavage in her black, sparkly bodysuit. This was a suffocating kind of warmth.

She took a seat next to me and clasped my shaking hands. Something settling ran through me just a little bit. The same kind of settling the tequila I downed a few moments before gave me.

"Oh, Blair, you're really that nervous?" she said, her eyes giving me sympathy.

"I had three shots of Patrón."

"Okay, maybe you shouldn't drink before you perform."

I could feel Reagan's eyes quizzing me but in a different way than before. Before, she looked at me as if she was stripping off my clothes in her head. Now, she looked at me as if she knew something was wrong with me, and I tried everything to keep from crying out how badly I wanted my grandparents—or even my mom—at this show. It would have meant so much to me for them to be there. Gramps always told me that one of the biggest moments in a musician's career was playing at the Garden. And here I was without the fans that meant the most to me: my family.

It didn't seem as thrilling as he made it seem. Probably because when I envisioned myself performing here, he, Grandma, and Mom were always somewhere in the audience.

The way Reagan looked at me, so concerned, free from that impish grin that she always wore, officially cracked me. I let out a long, deep grunt and ran my hands down my face, keeping them there so I could hide my stinging eyes.

"Hey, what's wrong?" she said, rubbing my back with her gentle hand. "Blair?"

"I'm fine."

"No, you're not. Talk to me."

"I just really wish my family was here tonight, that's all. My mom couldn't get off work, and my grandparents…"

I couldn't and refused to let myself cry in front of the girl I just slept with for the first time. It was way too soon in our hookup for me to cry on her shoulder, even though that was all I wanted to do.

She put her arm around my shoulders. "Aw, Blair, I'm so sorry."

"It's fine."

"No, it's not. You have a reason to be upset. But you know that your grandparents would be so proud of you."

"I know. That's why I wish they were here to witness it." I lifted my head out of my hands and stared at the cinderblock wall. "My grandpa always talked about Madison Square Garden, and how he would throw parties for his friends when they had their first Garden show. And here I am, about to perform in front of a sold-out Garden, and he's not here."

Her arm rubbing my back pulled me into her body for a half hug, and I accepted, resting against her. She smelled so good. The very faint smell of the familiar hotel shampoo and bodywash I spent hours rolling around in during the very early hours of the night mixed with a splash of whatever designer perfume she spritzed onto her neck.

"I'm so sorry, Blair. I know that must be upsetting for you, but you better believe he'd be so proud of you. I'm proud of you, if that means anything." I could only shrug because of a lump restricting my ability to speak, but yes, it meant something to me. "Hey, I have an idea."

"What's that?" I choked back the cry hanging in my throat.

"How about we FaceTime your mom? I can get Finn to do it from the soundboard, or we can get him to go where the press is. Or I can do it from the side stage. So she can see your performance. So you have family here to enjoy the show with you. How about that?"

My heart felt as if it dropped into my stomach. The cry in my throat flew right out of me as I studied her to see if she was serious. "Seriously? You would do that?"

She gave me a kind smile. "Of course. Why wouldn't I?"

"That...that would be really great."

"Okay, then, it's settled. Finn and I got you, don't worry."

My blink broke the seals, and I quickly wiped my face to preserve the fresh makeup and so Reagan wouldn't notice. "Jesus, I'm so sorry for getting emotional on you."

"Don't apologize, Blair. Seriously. It's okay, and you're going to be okay, and you're going to kick some ass tonight like you've been doing every show on this tour. Just take a few deep breaths, all right?"

I nodded and spent the remaining time with my eyes closed, practicing the deep breaths Reagan taught me before she left me alone to prepare. But as much as it was settling to know how much Reagan cared and went out of her way to do something so important to me, the feelings in me were too virulent to get rid of in a snap of a finger. My body craved something stronger to replenish the energy that had been depleted from me since the morning.

So, I did two bumps of the cocaine I had hidden in my book bag.

Just to get through this performance, I reassured myself, knowing I would feel guilty about it. *You take shots to get you ready for the show. How is it that different?*

Reagan's manager, Finn, stood in the gated-off front row with the press photographers, holding up my phone while my mom watched all the way back in Los Feliz. She was able to witness how the Garden gave us the most hyped up, loudest crowd we'd ever sung to. Depending on how the crowd was, especially at the larger venues, determined if I would jump on the floor and be a part of the first-row audience or stay on the stage. But this New York crowd really showed up, singing along and head banging the whole time. Everyone on the floor pushed each other toward the stage throughout our set list, which I know annoyed some fans, but I loved it because it was a sign that our music got them hyped up. So, on our fourth song that had an upbeat, bluesy sound, I fully melted into the high and jumped to the ledge that ran along the front of the stage so I could only be about six inches taller than the first row.

They held their hands out, singing, chanting, spilling out all the excitement inside them with cheers and smiles. As I walked along the ledge to the other side of the floor, some of the fans tried grabbing my skinny jeans and shirt. Even though it was jarring to be yanked, I secretly loved it because I could feel their enthusiasm in that little tug. But security didn't enjoy it because they sprinted over to shove the extending hands behind the metal railing. Once I made it safely to the stage, I thought the whole thing was fucking awesome.

When I did the usual, "Are you ready for Reagan Moore?" pump-up talk two songs from the end, I heard how loud twenty thousand eager Reagan Moore fans sounded, and it was even louder when Reagan took the stage with her opening song about Jessie Byrd. She always sang the first verse in total darkness underneath the stage, and then when the chorus came, the lights ignited with flamethrowers attached to the front, and she popped up from the elevator underneath the stage, and the crowd erupted in what I liked to call the concert sonic boom.

I always loved watching her opening song because I loved how hysterical the crowd was at the first couple of minutes of the show, still adjusting to the sight of her. The girls in the front row started crying, throwing their arms over the metal gates, their mouths open from screaming, which was drowned out by the sound of Reagan's voice. She strutted around the stage as if she owned it in the same way we all owned the stage back when we were younger, locking ourselves in our bathrooms, lip-syncing our favorite songs into hairbrushes. Except she did exactly that inside Madison Square Garden, in front of twenty thousand screaming and crying fervent fans. Her confidence was so attractive, it had me glued to her during her whole performance of her angsty breakup song.

And Miles noticed.

"You're smitten," he said into my ear, over the music. I told him about what happened the night before while we got ready, when Corbin wasn't in the room. I didn't want to hear his lecture about how I should be careful. That would be another layer of anxiety I already didn't need; plus, I wanted to feel good about it. "One lay and she has you completely smitten."

I didn't respond because there was no use in lying. He read me like a book from the very first day he met me. Plus, I knew I could trust Miles with any secret. He was the only person I allowed to read my songwriting journal. So, I gave him an answer by not really answering, just sucking in my lips to hide my grin.

"Knew it," he said with an arm nudge.

Halfway into the show, Reagan told the Garden we were coming back on; they gave us the same kind of thunderous energy as before when we stepped back onto the stage. Once I took a seat at her black baby grand piano, I positioned the harmonica holder around my neck, placed my hands on the keys, and looked up at Reagan walking over to me as she adjusted her in-ear.

"I'm following your lead," she said with her smile directed at me. "Whenever you're ready, Piano Girl."

She winked, and my body suffered an intense hot flash.

I inhaled a deep breath until I could feel the oxygen reach the bottom of my lungs. When I was ready, I tickled the keys to my own rendition of the intro, and hearing the echoes of the hammers and strings expelling the notes into Madison Square Garden sent goose bumps down my arms and legs. Then I exhaled the deep breath I just held in and breathed out into the harmonica as I banged away on the chords. While playing the harmonica part, I remembered that this very song was the reason I wanted to learn how to play the harmonica. Nothing seemed more badass to me than playing the instrument and a complicated piano part at the same time in a song that made everyone want to get on their feet and sing as loudly as they could. It took me at least a year to nail down the song as perfectly as a non-Billy Joel could get. Hours upon hours of playing this song on the piano to the point where my mom and grandparents begged me to play something different.

"I'd rather you take up the drums than play that song again," Grandma said, a slight teasing in her voice, but she was ninety-nine percent serious.

So, that Christmas, I asked for my seventh instrument, a drum set, so I could learn my favorite song when I was sixteen: "My Generation" by The Who. By New Year's, my grandma begged me to play "Piano Man" again because she was so sick of the drums.

Mom later told me that she and Grandma begged Gramps not to give me that drum set because they knew I'd put it to good use, and everyone would lose sleep over it. Even me because I would constantly be on the cushioned seat, banging away on the snare and the toms. But Gramps—being a stubborn, music-obsessed guy so desperate for me to stop finding trouble—ignored them and fed into my obsession of musical instruments.

It all paid off on that Madison Square Garden stage.

Reagan took control of the first verse, resting her elbow on the piano while looking at me with those wonderful eyes as if she was singing just to me. I sang the second verse, and we alternated back and forth but sang together in harmony during the chorus. I was so amazed by how my own playing sounded in the arena and how it was even more wonderful to hear the audience react the way they did to the beloved song. They sang every word in a unified roar, and the second time we got to the chorus, they were so loud that there was really no point in Reagan and me singing. She turned to them and used her microphone to conduct their singing.

Then when the time came, I broke out into an improvised piano solo that wouldn't come close to what Billy Joel did every time he played the song, but it was the best I could do, given my piano skills. I practiced my own version of the solo for hours on end. I think that was why Mom and Grandma got sick of the song. Trial and error weren't really pleasing to the ear. But all that practicing, again, paid off when the crowd grew louder after I ran my fingers up and down the piano.

Our cover of "Piano Man" generated an all-time peak of energy during the whole show. Usually, there was only one concert sonic boom per show: when Reagan first took the stage. But after our cover, for the first time ever in my life, I witnessed two concert sonic booms, and it was one of the coolest things I'd ever experienced.

I still heard Gramps whenever I played the piano or the Hummingbird. And I hoped that in his world, when I played, he heard me. When I walked off the stage in Madison Square Garden, a heavy weight hung in my chest but in a good way. Like a hug. And maybe that was a sign that both of my grandparents heard me, and I knew for a fact that if they did, they both sang along and were proud that their granddaughter was in the middle of it all.

CHAPTER SEVEN

"What are you doing?"

Reagan stepped out of her hotel bathroom with a short towel wrapped around her naked body. Even though we'd been sleeping together since New York City, still seeing her in nothing but a towel stopped me dead in my tracks. She made wringing out the excess moisture in her hair sexy.

"Writing," I answered, tapping the pen against the journal.

She hopped on her spot in the bed and pulled my face closer to hers so she could kiss down the column of my neck. I tilted my head backward for a second as she sucked on a good spot, sending goose bumps down my whole body. I guess my answer to her question really excited her.

Yup, this had been my life for the past few weeks. Lots of cuddles. Lots of kisses. Lots of sex. It was a beautiful thing.

"A song?" She pulled her face away. "A new song? Can I take a look?"

"No."

"Why?"

I laughed at my reply that contorted her face into a frown. "Because you're successful, and I literally just wrote it. It's probably still garbage right now."

"Doubt it." She held her palm out for the journal, and I slammed it closed so she couldn't see it. Just because we were sleeping together didn't grant her access to my sacred journal, especially since she had all the hit songs in the music industry, fresh from winning three Grammys, and had the biggest tour of the year. "Please let me read it. I promise to be nice."

"No. It may or may not be about you."

Her eyes rounded. "Well, now I *have* to read it."

I groaned because I knew her insight would actually be beneficial, but my gut told me not to show her. This was practically my heart we were talking about.

And then I had an idea. My eyes widened thinking about it before I said it out loud.

"I have a crazy idea," I said.

"Crazier than sneaking into a pool after hours?"

"*Psh.* Please. That's nothing. This is way crazier."

"What is it?"

"What are your thoughts on collaborating? On our album we're recording—"

She grabbed a hold of my hands. "I would love to collaborate."

"Really?"

"Can I tell you a secret?"

"Of course."

"I've been wanting to write with you for the longest time. Ever since I heard the songs you wrote with the Radicals. And then that song you wrote with Isaac Ball really got to me. You know I'm putting my money on it that you'll be nominated for a Grammy?"

"Okay, you win. That's the craziest idea."

"I'm serious, Blair! That song is amazing. You know how often I hear it on the radio?"

It had to have been the greatest compliment of my career. "Well, geez, you should have told me that you wanted to collaborate."

"I was waiting for the right time!"

"Naked under the towel really is the perfect time."

"So, you wanna write a song?"

"A thousand times yes."

"Now, does that mean I can see this journal of yours?"

"You only get to look at the page I show you. But just, like, be nice when you read it, okay? I literally whipped it up so it's not all finished—"

She sat upright in her spot and snatched the leather notebook off my lap. I sank farther into the bed, wanting to bury my face underneath the duvet as she whipped opened the notebook to the last page of song lyrics. Since the spine had worn in its place, it easily fell open to the page I recently worked on.

She read it silently, and all I could do was watch her eyebrows slowly scale her forehead after she read each line.

Then, with a click of her pen, she hovered the tip over a word, and then eyed me. "Can I make a light suggestion?" she asked.

"Um, go for it."

Without scratching out my word, she wrote in tiny handwriting her suggestion and did this a few times throughout the eight verses.

"Okay, so I know there are tons of verses, but it was just brainstorming, and obviously, I'll delete some," I said.

She smirked and then kissed my cheek. "I love how insecure you're being. For literally no reason because this song is sexy as hell."

"Is it?"

She nodded. "I think this should be the song we collab on. If you're down."

I was stunned. Reagan Moore branded herself as this PG—once in a blue moon PG-13 with a mention of "damn" in her songs—pop singer who would occasionally have a hit song here and there about lust but disguised enough to make the teenagers think that she was singing about just wanting to kiss someone. Now, she was verbally signing herself up for a song that was clearly about sex.

I kind of loved it, and man, would her older fans love it too.

"Now, let me read the rest," she said as she turned back a few pages.

I slammed my hand over hers. "Don't. I said you get one page."

She laughed. "Blair, I'm sure they're all great. You write songs for all the big names. You have nothing to hide."

"Those are lyrics about their life. These are lyrics about mine. I don't even share the whole journal with Miles. He gets one page too."

"How about this," she suggested while closing the book over the hotel pen. "I'll forget about the journal for now only if we have sex, you know, for research, and then play around with this tomorrow on our way to Boston?"

"I'm all for being studious."

She simpered and then jumped on top of me. I quickly loosened the towel around her and got rid of it like the nuisance it was.

❖

Boston was the last American stop of the summer. Then Reagan was off to tour Europe for the next month with a British boy band, the Radicals. I cowrote their first album with them three years back. They were huge across the pond, so I had no idea how two big names would combine over there, but those fans were in for a real treat.

Reagan's camp was already thinking ahead for the next world tour, and the goal was a stadium summer tour. So, to test out a stadium show, our tour stopped in Foxborough to perform at Gillette Stadium with a whopping one hundred and ten thousand people packed into the home of the New England Patriots.

We were all nervous. Stomachaches paining us all day. I had to take a Xanax the night before because I was already on edge. And then in our green room at the stadium, Reagan made a surprise appearance, giving us this terrified expression and asking for a shot of tequila.

Yes, Reagan Moore asked us for a shot before a show.

We'd already taken our two shots, but for a show that was ten times the size of what we were used to on this tour, a third shot was justified, especially when Reagan asked for one.

"You do realize you're going to kill it out there, right?" I said when I handed her a shot glass of Patrón.

"I mean, it's probably no different from the other shows," she said and then looked down at her shot. "Okay, let's cheers." The three of us huddled in a circle, holding the shots out together. "To our first sold-out stadium show," Reagan said.

"With a *hundred* and ten thousand people," Miles reminded us.

"At least there will be fireworks," I added.

We clinked, pounded back the shots, and I made sure I enjoyed the sight that was Reagan Moore tossing back that tequila as if it was no big deal, as if this wasn't her first rodeo. I was dying to see her pound back shots of tequila like that more often. It was hot, not going to lie.

All throughout the stadium, over a hundred thousand lights sparkled from the lit-up bracelets each person got upon entering the stadium. It looked as if all the stars in the universe sat in the seats, twinkling in blues, purples, and greens. It was easy to forget how many people were actually in front of us each show. When the lights went out, they became one massive entity. But when you stuck a glowing bracelet on them, you actually saw every individual person in that speck of color. They engulfed us. The whole time we performed, the goose bumps wouldn't go away because the fans were so loud and filled with energy, I couldn't stop smiling.

They were even louder when Reagan called us back on so we could perform our cover together. For Gillette Stadium, we decided to do "Dream On" by Aerosmith. Reagan and I had the harmonies down, my Fender wailing out the electric vibrations, Miles getting lost in the clashing of the cymbals, and for an added effect—because we had to take advantage of being outside—the flamethrowers ejected bursts of giant orange flames when the climax came around, jolting out every time Miles pounded on the bass drum and cymbals. The crowd was ecstatic. They gave us the loudest and strongest concert sonic booms of our lives. Hearing over one hundred thousand people roaring for us, it totally redefined the concert sonic boom. That was a sound I could keep listening to on repeat for hours and never get tired of it.

With the fire illuminating the stadium, I scanned the enormous crowd, seeing specks of people all around me, above me, extending out in front of me. I couldn't believe this was happening. Miles and I went from performing in our high school talent show to smoky bars filled with people not even listening to us to our little shows of two thousand people and now to performing alongside Reagan Moore, flamethrowers projecting balls of fire up in the air to one hundred and ten thousand people in a sold-out American football stadium.

It had to be the coolest night of my life.

❖

To enjoy the end of the summer and to record the new song the two of us wrote, Reagan invited both Miles and me down to her summer home in Gaslight Shores, South Carolina, a resort town right on the Atlantic Ocean. I might not have been an expert when it came to celebrities, but I was aware of Reagan Moore's Labor Day parties, which were thrown at this very summer house. The gossip media loved to cover her four-day-long rager with her closest celebrity friends, and

I was all ready to witness it and pound back more tequila shots like in Foxborough.

Before her ten other A-list friends filled up the mansion for the last weekend of summer, it was just the three of us in her monstrous oceanfront house with its own saltwater pool as long as the outdoor patio; about an acre of freshly cut, bright green grass as her backyard; and to add to the pristine scene, she had a studio in her house. Her very own recording studio. You know, every musician's dream.

And it was unbelievable.

In the control room, she had a vocal booth, two Mac computers, audio interfaces, studio microphones in the vocal booth, MIDI controllers, and synthesizers, and a massive digital workstation that you would find at an actual recording studio took up most of the length of the wall. She had the works. Miles and I had to stop ourselves from crying about how beautiful her studio was at least seven times.

"This is where I wrote and produced my third album," she said as the two of us practically drooled all over the workstation, cupping our hands to view the dark vocal booth through the glass door.

She was twenty-three and wrote and produced her third album all by herself. The third album that had a sold-out world tour that we got to open the American leg for. Now she wanted to produce a song she cowrote with me. The song wasn't even made yet, and I knew with Reagan's talent and name, it'd be a hit.

We recorded the whole song from start to finish in those two days before all her celebrity friends joined us. Our song, "Patience, Love," sounded amazing, and the best part, we each had our moment to shine. Reagan and I cowrote the lyrics, all three of us added some of our own flair to the melody, I played all the instruments on the track—with the exception of the drums because Miles was way better than me—and even though we each had a say in the producing, Reagan and Miles took the lead on polishing the song. Layered vocals that flitted between our alto voices in the verse and our falsettos in the chorus. Pulsating beats from the bass I played and Miles's bass drum brightened by warm synths that added another sound of subtle flirting.

I couldn't wait to play it to the label when we got back to LA.

After those two work days, Miles flew back to LA to send his sister off to her first day of high school at our alma mater. I told him he was going to miss a hell of a weekend of drinking and beach, but I guess he was being a good brother to his one and only sibling. It was up to me to handle a whole weekend with Reagan and all of her gorgeous friends I'd recognized from all over the internet and award shows. They arrived at the mansion with their designer suitcases, glasses perched on the top of their heads, and beauty after beauty filling up the four walls of the house. From models to actresses to heiresses to singers, Reagan's crew touched every industry in Hollywood, and they wasted no time throwing on their bathing suits, grabbing a margarita from the kitchen, and sprinting outside to the backyard where the pool was warmed up and ready for them to jump in with a backdrop of rentable inflatable slides and a bounce house in the grass.

A part of me worried that this Labor Day weekend in Gaslight Shores would mean that Reagan and I had to pretend that nothing happened or was happening between us. That she would spend more time with the friends she didn't see on a regular basis than me, but that wasn't the case at all. I felt as if the only time Reagan left my side was when we went to the bathroom. We always sat by each other in the group—she even sat on my lap a couple of times, not giving a care in the world about the glances and suspicious smirks her friends subtly made. She was extra handsy with me when we did the inflatable slide races, tackling me to the floor of the slide, completely hidden behind inflatable walls. She crawled on top of me, and in our little secluded world, we made out for a few minutes until the slide started moving from her friends staggering up the stairs.

Honestly, it felt like she was my girlfriend, and I was shocked that it didn't scare me as much as I thought it would. It was…exciting. It drew me closer to her every moment we shared.

The second night, by popular demand, I whipped up a homemade dessert for everyone since Reagan kept begging me to do so. Nothing too extravagant, though, since I actually wanted to be a part of the party. A simple strawberry cheesecake to impress the party, and I made another batch of mango margaritas that we'd all been drinking like smoothies throughout the day.

While making the cheesecake, I noticed her friends circled around her in the pool, occasionally tossing glances at the large kitchen windows overlooking the pool and backyard. I only assumed they were grilling her with questions about me. I didn't mind, though.

Imagining and hoping that she told them that she actually had feelings for me added more warmth to my already sunburned skin.

Then Reagan's best friend, Bristol Perri, came strutting in, wearing an extra-large T-shirt that soaked up the remnants of pool from her bathing suit. She was an A-list actress who'd won an Oscar three years before when she was only twenty-four. She was a beautiful—shocker, I know—familiar face on all the fashion magazines, and what the entertainment media called "The Next Meryl Streep Under Thirty."

"Blair," she said and leaned over the granite kitchen island as I poured the tequila into the blender.

"Bristol," I said suspiciously. From her relaxed eyes and flushed cheeks, I sensed she was feeling pretty good on margaritas, much like the rest of the party. We all started drinking at eleven, and it was now three p.m., so all of us were feeling it. Myself included. Besides saying a few words to each other in a larger conversation with the group, we hadn't spoken one-on-one yet, and her devious tone warned me she was about to yank some info out of me.

"A little birdie told me you're sleeping with the host."

My smooth self flinched at the sudden confrontation, and about a shot's worth of perfectly good Patrón spilled on the counter. This was The Next Meryl Streep Under Thirty we were talking about, so she was doing a really good job pretending to be the lead interrogator at the Gaslight Shores Police Station, all hidden within that famous smile that graced the silver screen.

She drunk-cackled. "So, that spill confirms the rumors?"

"Was the little birdie the host?"

"Maybe."

"My lips are sealed."

She pointed a ruby-red painted nail at me. "You passed the test. Just so you know—as Reagan's best friend—I gotta protect her from dirtbags because the last few people she dated were narcissistic dirtbags." Her words slurred a little bit, and I tried hiding my laughter that she was drunk-grilling me about my intentions.

"I've heard," I replied and poured her the freshly made cocktail, hoping that by giving her the first taste of the new batch, maybe I'd win a couple of extra points with her. "But Reagan and I aren't dating."

She accepted and took a sip. "But then why are you here? Staying in her bed? Getting handsy all fucking day long?"

"Hey, I was fully prepared to pretend like nothing's going on, but little did I know, she likes the PDA."

"And she usually doesn't, for the record. But she's been all over you. We've all been talking about it."

I raised an eyebrow. "We?"

"Yeah. All of us. She's out there telling us everything about you guys. It seriously took you that long to kiss her?"

I rolled my eyes, poured myself a shot, and tossed it back. Bristol tilted her head back in laughter and followed my lead in drinking more of her margarita.

"What else did this little birdie tell you?" I asked.

"That she likes you but *you* don't want a relationship."

Why did I wipe up that tequila when I could have easily taken the shot from the counter? Because with that new information Bristol Perri spoon-fed me, I needed another shot of Patrón right about now. This was uncharted territory we just discovered. She actually liked me? She wanted a relationship? God, I thought we were only sleeping together. Where did all of this come from?

"I just got out of—but she doesn't—she doesn't want one either," I said defensively because I had no idea where else to start with this load of knowledge. "There was a whole *Vogue* feature about it."

"She likes you, Blair. I asked her the lowdown last night while you and Annie were on the unicorn pool inflatable. I asked her what was up with you guys, and she told me that you two were sleeping together but she thinks she actually likes you more than that. But you just got out of a relationship and made it clear this was only sex."

"She's never told me any of this."

"Yeah, because she's an actual child when it comes to her feelings. Like, she won't do anything about it."

"So I've noticed."

"Just a heads-up, don't expect her to tell you how she feels, especially after her last three relationships. She put herself out there, and they treated her like crap. She legit told me after Jessie dumped her that she wasn't going to seek out anyone again. She was tired of it. I can't really blame her."

"I don't know what I'm supposed to do with all of this info."

"Easy. If you really like her, you need to tell her because she won't tell you; as much as I lecture her about how immature she's being, that's where she is right now. Refusing to put her feelings out there. So, if you're just in it to hook up, please don't fuck with her." She said it as if her best friend's love life drained her energy. "It might seem casual to her, but I got different vibes."

I couldn't tell if Bristol Perri was trying to fish out information to give back to Reagan or if she genuinely wanted to take the initiative to protect her friend's heart. For most of the night Reagan sat next to me. At one point, her legs were on my lap, arm locked around mine, and anytime the two of us snuck away to make out in various spots of her property, whether it was in the kitchen, her bedroom, or the inflatable slide, Bristol Perri's dark eyes focused on me as if telepathically trying to tell me she would cut me if I hurt her friend.

I had no idea what we were doing. Bristol probably needed more clarification from Reagan on exactly what we were doing because Reagan didn't really give me any indication we were anything more than just sex on tour…even though I could feel my chest tighten anytime she walked into a room, or I caught her stare, or someone brought up her name.

All signs I was getting feelings.

I guess our feelings were mutual.

Fuck.

❖

Sunday morning, before the whole house woke up, Reagan shook me awake so I could join her on a bike ride around the empty boardwalk during sunrise. And as much as I wasn't a morning person and loved sleeping in until eleven, I couldn't pass up a bike ride through a sleepy Gaslight Shores with her. I hadn't ridden a bike since my Nashville days when I had the space of empty country roads. It'd been eleven years, and to say I lost my balance on two wheels was an understatement. As I tried to get my bike groove back, Reagan circled me, trying to steady her balance as each laugh jerked her handlebars. She offered to give me a helmet and kneepads, but I refused because a twenty-four-year-old woman shouldn't be acting like she discovered a bike for the first time. When I finally got the hang of the bike, we pedaled into town, zigzagging through the desolate streets lined with small beach town shops, and journeyed over to the quiet beach. We tossed our bikes into the sand, and Reagan wasted no time frolicking down to the tide. I trailed behind her, noticing that it was so hard to force the smile back in.

"I love coming out here during the sunrise," Reagan said as she took a seat in the cold sand, collecting a handful of it and letting it fall through her fingers. "It's like the one time I feel safe to come out in public because the town is still sleeping. Every now and again, I see runners or bikers, but it's just for a split second. I'm practically a stranger in a split second."

Her head rested on my shoulder, and the two of us gazed up as the pinks, oranges, and yellows of the sunrise brightened the sky into a light shade of blue.

"The fans every night are pretty great, but so is this," I said. "Right now. Empty beach. Beautiful sunrise. And you."

She lifted her head from my shoulder and assessed me as if a revelation sprouted in her mind. "Thanks for putting up with all my friends this weekend," she said and kissed my shoulder before looping an arm around mine. "You've been quite the trouper. I know we're a lot."

"It's been a lot of fun. Lots of margaritas. You're kinda adorable when you're drunk."

"It doesn't take much. I only let myself loose every now and again, and this weekend is the weekend. I'd figure you'd enjoy that part."

"Oh, I have. Don't you worry about that."

She let out a long sigh. "I can't believe summer is over. I can't believe I'm going to be in Europe for a whole month. Without you." She faltered for a moment and positioned her chin to rest on my shoulder. "Is it weird to say that I'm gonna kinda miss you?"

My mind transported me back to her kitchen the day before with Bristol Perri. If it weren't for her insider knowledge, if Reagan still told me that she would miss me, my stupid brain wouldn't have picked up on the giant clue right in front of my face that she actually had feelings for me. But because I did have that information, it was a clue to me that we shared the exact same feelings. As the weekend flew by, I could feel a dull tug in my chest getting stronger the closer Monday came.

"Why would that be weird?" I said.

She shrugged. "I don't know."

I held my breath, waiting for her to follow up with a statement as to where we stood. An explanation for what we were. I didn't even know what I wanted us to be. After finishing up a few things back in LA for a week, she was going to spend three weeks in Nashville to be with her family before touring Europe for a month. Was I allowed to see other women? Were we going to keep in contact during those six weeks? Was she going to find someone else to fill my void in her tour bus?

"I'll miss you too, if that makes you feel any better," I said with a nudge. "But only a little."

"Yeah, same. Just a little. Nothing too significant."

And we laughed, and then zigzagged back to her house to say good-bye to all of her friends who would leave that day to fly to different parts of the world. When we finally had the house to ourselves for one more night, we had a cookout on her patio. I grilled up some burgers; she made the side dishes. I made the margaritas. She drank all of them, and seeing her buzzed was hilarious because she became extra quirky and talkative and spoke even faster than she did when she was nervous. We floated in the pool illuminated by lights when dusk fell, looking up at the sky to find stars popping through the darkness—stars that I'd forgotten even existed since my Nashville days when I could actually see a shooting star in the dark, suburban skies. And then, we started kissing in the pool and then peeled each other's bathing suits off so we could fully bask in the wonderful touch of our nakedness one last time before we resumed the rest of our North American shows in February.

I was definitely going to miss her. More than for it to be an insignificant hiccup.

The next morning, we woke up bright and early to take Reagan's private jet back to LA.

Yes, the girl I was sleeping with had a private jet.

A jet with beige leather seats; a long, beige leather couch; and a bathroom that could actually fit two whole people in it, unlike commercial planes. Maybe if we got bored, we would join the mile-high club? That was something that would be fun to cross off my bucket list.

As I rested my head on her lap, she leaned back on the couch to answer work emails, and I checked my phone only to find that Miles blew up my screen with three simultaneous text messages. Each text was a different article from a trustworthy entertainment news source.

Reagan Moore Gets Handsy with a Lady Friend This Labor Day Weekend.

Reagan Moore Spends the Long Weekend with a Mystery Girl. Who is She and What You Need to Know About Her.

Is Reagan Moore Dating Midnight Konfusion's Lead Singer Blair Bennett?

"Um, Reagan?"

"Hmm?" she said, eyes still on her phone as she typed.

I shoved my phone screen in her face. "What the hell should we do?"

She took my phone for a better view of the articles. But instead of the reaction I was thinking would play out in front of me, like chucking her phone into my lap, hyperventilating, and calling the pilot for an emergency landing, instead, she rolled her eyes and handed me my phone.

"For starters, you should stop reading the internet," she said. "It's really bad for your mental health."

I was confused. That was her first thought about drones invading her privacy? Hovering over her fenced-in backyard? Did she remember that we had sex in her pool the night before? Did the drones record that?

"You do realize your stalkers this whole weekend were drones, right?" I said as I sat up since this conversation couldn't have been done with my head in her lap. "That this whole conversation about you liking women has started?"

"They've been questioning my sexuality from the beginning. I've said in interviews before that I'm attracted to the person, not the gender. I'm not really worried about that at all. And you seriously didn't see the drones flying around?"

"You did?"

"Blair, they were flying around the tree line, hiding right in there. It's why Bristol was shooting off fireworks during the day. It wasn't for patriotism."

"But they have photo evidence of this whole weekend."

"Bristol was on my lap, too. They'll probably say I'm dating both of you. Hey, go me." She patted herself on the shoulder.

"What about the things you said about Zeke and Jessie? You worried about it then."

"I was in relationships with them, and the media storm was

a million times worse than a pesky drone and a few articles online. Paparazzi were stalking me around every turn. I had rumors about marriage and cheating and pregnancy one month into dating Zeke, and I was nineteen years old."

"You don't think drones flying around your house isn't stalking?"

"I mean, that's kind of bad, but I'm used to it here. It's why I'm asking for a pellet gun for Christmas." She laughed at her own joke.

"So, you're not taking this invasion of privacy seriously because we're not together?"

"Pretty much. There's less to lose."

A dull heat found its way to my stomach. I don't know why the comment bothered me so much, but it did. There was less to lose because everything Bristol Perri told me was apparently for intimidation purposes and not at all the truth. All the cuddling, sex, lap sits, secret kisses in inflatables, and arms locked while watching the sunrise didn't mean anything. It was just sex. Nothing more than sex in her pool, and I was an idiot for having this hope that it actually did mean something more.

"Yeah, you're right," I said, hearing the own disappointment in my voice. "Two completely different things."

Reagan creased her eyebrows. "Yeah…my point exactly."

"Okay, cool. Glad we're all clear now." I lay on my other side, using my own arm as a pillow instead of her lap.

"Blair, what's wrong?"

"Nothing. Just tired and want to take a nap."

"Do you want a blanket?"

"I don't care."

She fanned out the red, green, and yellow plaid blanket she got from the linen closet next to the bathroom and placed it delicately on me, tucking me into my nap.

"You sure you're okay?"

"Totally fine."

She paused. "Can I nap with you?"

"If you want."

"Okay…" I could tell with the uncertainty in her voice and the drawn-out pauses at the end of her comments that she knew that I was upset. "Can I big spoon you?"

"Sure."

My heart betrayed me and fluttered when I felt the warmth of her whole body pressing up against my back and her arm sliding over my side. I was so terrified that I let her beauty and the thrill of chasing her turn into actual feelings. But then I told myself this cuddle wasn't anything worthy of protection. The drones could film us all they wanted; it was as meaningless as if she spooned Bristol Perri.

If she had nothing to lose with me, why did it feel as if I had a lot to lose with her?

Chapter Eight

Now that I was in one city for the next five months and Reagan just performed a show in London, my lesbian dating app resurrected from the Cloud and blew up with matches and messages from girls in the area. Since Reagan had nothing to lose with me, everything Bristol Perri told me went right out the window.

Hello, dating world; it's me, Blair Bennett.

In the few conversations with girls on the dating app, only one conversation didn't eventually lead to them figuring out my job was touring with Reagan Moore. The girl, Paige, asked me what I did for a living, and I told her I was a musician, and I think she probably figured I was really, like, a waitress who said she was a musician but really just busked on Hollywood Boulevard. It wasn't until three days into our conversation that I invited her out to our gig at House of Blues in Anaheim, and I think she figured out then it was more than a hobby. But still no signs of internet research, which earned bonus points from me.

While Reagan toured Europe, during the day, Miles and I finished recording our album. Finally. Only a year later. The summer of sexual frustration, confusion, and feelings really helped fill my journal with songs, and by the time November came around, the album was completed. Over those two months, Reagan and I only exchanged casual text messages a few times a week as if we were just friends who never saw each other naked, talking about finishing up albums and how a VIP fan passed out in Paris when she first saw Reagan backstage. I told her how excited I was to sign more boobs that belonged to a really hot woman after our Anaheim show. Apparently, that was becoming a thing now when we headlined shows. That was something I would always say yes to. Reagan thought it was impressive as well, but it made me wonder if she felt any sort of jealousy. I told myself not to hold my breath on that because not once since Gaslight Shores did we ever crack open our feelings about missing each other.

I woke up to the smell of coffee from our kitchen. Miles always woke up before me and saved me two cups of coffee. He'd been doing this routine ever since we started living together right after I dropped out of USC my sophomore year. We'd spent the night before at a club with Paige, and then I ended the night with her in my bed. So needless to say, I really needed some caffeine.

Taking the first sip of my black coffee, I checked my phone and saw I had a message waiting for me.

Reagan's text read, *Touring isn't the same without you. I really miss our talks. How are you?*

Who needed coffee in the morning to wake you up when the girl you were a giant question mark with sprang out of nowhere and texted you? A text that had feelings hidden underneath. The kind of text message you've only been waiting two months for.

As her text settled in me, Miles came up behind me and said, "So, another successful night?"

"My head is pounding, but I guess." I looked at him skeptically. "Why?"

"Because I was awake. Thank you for the background noise."

I playfully slugged his arm. "Shut it."

"You know, when we're back on tour, I've already decided to make a move on Ethan."

"Yeah, why haven't you?"

"Because the dude is so hard to read. At first, I thought I was going in blind with a straight dude, but now I'm not so sure? He's been texting me this whole time." He wiggled his phone, and this aching of jealousy zipped through me. "'When are you coming back? Why aren't you here?'" Miles said, reading his messages. "'These British openers are fun and all, but you're way cooler. Come back to me soon.' Like, who says that?"

"A guy who wants it. You really need to make a move. I think you got him all smitten."

He tossed his head back until it hit the top of the couch. "Ugh! It's so far away."

"Or you can ask him out on a date like the grown-up you are when they get back."

He shot me a glare. "You're one to talk. How long did it take you to make a move on Reagan? Didn't she tell you she aged, like, twenty years waiting for you?"

He cackled, and I punched his arm again. "I never made a move before."

"Oh, woe is you. You could get any girl you want, and you do, and you're lucky all of them have just thrown themselves at you. It has to be the sleeve."

"That's why I got it," I joked.

"So, when are you guys going to tell Corbin and Finn?" He smiled behind his mug, knowing I was going to toss him a glare, which I did. "Don't you think the managers need to know about this?"

"When it's worth telling."

"You're still mad about her comment?"

"Yes, and the fact we only talk about nothing now. At least you and Ethan talk about how much you miss each other, so please, go ask him out. It'll lessen the blow when Corbin finds out about us doing Reagan Moore and her crew."

I responded to Reagan. *I'm feeling great now that the album is finished. When do you come back?*

Reagan texted back with, *Next week. Can you believe?! Can I see you next Thursday?*

That's our first late show appearance! Yikes!

Oh my God! That's right! That's so exciting!!! I'll make sure to watch it since I really miss your face.

I looked back at Miles, who watched me the whole time.

"You're grinning," he said with a smirk. "Must mean Reagan's texting you."

A blush warmed my cheeks. "Do I smile when she texts me?"

"All the freakin' time. Is she sexting you?"

"No, but she said she misses my face. You know, this is the first time she's admitted that she's missed me...or, you know, has slept with me, since Labor Day?"

"Swallow the pride, Blair, and enjoy this moment. Now text her back something nice."

"If you text Ethan right now and ask him out. They're coming back next week."

"Two completely different things."

"Wanna make out with him or not?"

He rolled his eyes and picked up his phone, and I responded to Reagan, swallowing my pride like Miles demanded. *I kinda miss your face too.*

Reagan: *What about Saturday?*

Me: *Can't. We have a show in San Bernardino. What about Monday?*

Reagan: *Can't. I got album 4 recordings going on.*

Me: *Ugh. Wed?*

Reagan: *Flying out to Nashville to be with the fam for Thanksgiving. Going to spend time with them until the Asia shows in Jan.*

Me: *Well...this really sucks then.*

Reagan: *I know. Now I'm in a bad mood.*

I was too. Now we had to tack on two more months to water down the raging chemistry we had during the summer. Would anything still be left when we resumed our American shows in February?

I needed a distraction. Craved a distraction. I turned to Paige, and we went out with Miles to the gay clubs of West Hollywood. We drank, we danced, and Paige surprised us with some Molly, so the three of us took it and waited for our bodies to feel blissful. The music, the lights, the hot girl in front of me; my body felt so warm and overjoyed, and then Paige started grinding on me on the dance floor, fully enthralled by the high of the Molly. The carefree and weightless feelings of lust reacquainted with my body. I missed those. I needed more of those. Not the timid, heavy feelings that I felt whenever I saw Reagan's face on the internet or that face cream commercial that always played or whenever the thought of her popped in my head.

The morning before Thanksgiving, a few hours after Paige left my bed, my eyes felt as if they were almost glued shut. The downfall of the Molly, feeling as if I hadn't slept in days and my body was hit by a truck. I met Miles out in the kitchen with that same long sulk, knowing we both had to regain all the serotonin we used up the night before. He recapped his bathroom stall rendezvous with a guy he found on the middle of the dance floor when my phone chirped and stole my attention away from the juicy details. Seeing Reagan's name sent a jolt through me, the shot of espresso that I really needed at the moment came from just seeing her name light up my phone screen.

Well, scratch the whole going home to Nashville for Thanksgiving. My flights were just canceled.

I frowned as I typed back, *What?!*

My flight got canceled because of that stupid blizzard Nashville's getting.

Her next text was a screenshot of the radar in Nashville. The whole area was covered in deep blue to signal the blizzard, expected to drop over a foot of snow. In my thirteen years living in Nashville, I could probably count the number of times we got more than over two inches. We never had a blizzard, and any of my sledding experiences involved blades of grass poking through the thin layers of snow.

She responded again. *I'm so upset. I really was looking forward to meeting my niece. I bought her all these adorable clothes and toys and everything.*

Me: *I'm so sorry. You should come spend it with me and my mom so you're not by yourself.*

Reagan: *I don't want to intrude.*

Me: *Oh, stop it. You're not intruding. I don't want you to spend it by yourself, and I kind of really want you to come.*

Reagan: *Aww, really?*

Me: *Really. My mom is going all out this year. It's the first time she's making a whole Thanksgiving meal in her first home ever. She's really excited. You can be my date.*

Me: *Also, please save me because I'll be third wheeling it with my mom and her boy toy.*

Reagan: *Your date?! I really want to be your date!*

Those butterflies unleashed again.

Reagan: *And I'll gladly save you from being the third wheel.*
Me: *Then be my date. It can be our first date…if you want it to be…*

I decided why the hell not. There was nothing to lose, right? So why not take the risk and ask. Plus, if she said no, I'd go to Paige…even though she wasn't as beautiful or funny or talented or mesmerizing or exciting or as great a kisser as Reagan.

I held my breath as I watched the typing cloud appear and disappear and then appear again.

Reagan: *I want it to be.*

It was a date. A real date. With Reagan. I had to learn to breathe through those thoughts.

Now that I had a date for Thanksgiving dinner, I was actually looking forward to it more than I was before. Even though Mom was excited to host her first Thanksgiving, the emptiness of where Gramps should have been sitting with his Johnnie Walker would haunt the dinner table. Then, on top of worrying about being the third wheel to Mom and Greg, I was planning on drinking lots of wine and eating lots of turkey to put myself into a coma to save myself from their honeymoon phase. But now that I had Reagan coming over? I was shocked that I was really looking forward to the day I'd been dreading. The empty space for Gramps would be less noticeable with her there.

She was right on time. I told her to come over at two, and she knocked on Mom's front door at five after two in dark blue skinny jeans, black boots with heels, and a dark maroon sweater with a maroon, mustard yellow, and orange scarf around her neck. Her hair was down in slight waves, and two tote bags dangled from her arms.

She was just as beautiful as I remembered. Must have been all that face cream.

I couldn't believe this was my Thanksgiving date. It was a real shame that she had to skip out on going home because of that blizzard, but I was the real winner for her flights being canceled. And when she beamed at me as I opened the door, I felt pinned to my spot with a tight chest.

"Wow," I said, still studying her and her beautiful, thick blond hair.

"Hey, stranger," she said with a bright smile that warmed my face. "I almost forgot what you looked like."

"Hopefully still hot and charming?"

A light blush dusted her cheeks, and God, it made me feel so great knowing I could do that to her. "Definitely still hot and charming." And as my face heated, she looked down at her tote bags and said, "Okay, so I didn't know what kind of wine you guys like. Which is completely silly because I should know if you like red or white wine. So, I decided to buy all the wine—cabernet sauvignon, pinot grigio, and rosé. Oh, and I brought pumpkin pie…but I don't know why I did that since you bake. That was stupid. You probably made a killer pumpkin pie."

After speaking a million miles per hour, she finally looked up at me, and I laughed by how adorably nervous she apparently was for this dinner. If she really didn't have that much to lose with me, why did she talk at the speed of light?

The overanalyzing gears in my brain kicked in.

"Okay, one: I made a dessert, yes," I said, "but a pumpkin pie is greatly appreciated. And two: you didn't have to bring over three bottles of wine—"

"You didn't have to invite me over, and your mom didn't have to make extra food for me—"

"Three: she was going to make extra food anyways because she's super excited about her five-burner gas stove and her brand-new Williams-Sonoma pots and pans. Four: we love all wine, so any wine you would have brought over would have been perfect. With the exception of blue wine, so thank you for not bringing that. And five: you look really beautiful. Like, amazingly beautiful."

I watched the worry leave her eyes, and her gaze became so soft. "What? Really?"

"Oh, really. If you catch me staring for too long, you know that it's because I'm caught up in all of this." I motioned to her face. "You're gorgeous."

I thought I lost the ability to properly speak around her because I was so nervous about where we left off. But saying those words felt so comfortable that I didn't even get embarrassed when I realized I put my feelings out there.

It could have been that first glass of wine too. Maybe it was a combination of both.

"Wow, thanks, Blair. God," she said, shaking her head as it fell to the ground. "Now you have me blushing, and I haven't even walked in yet." She wiped her cheeks as if that was going to erase the deep red soaked into her skin. "You look good too. As always."

"Now that we have turned ourselves bright red, come in and let's show it off to my mom."

The smells of roasted turkey, thyme, sage, and rosemary scented the whole condo in wonderfulness. Inside the kitchen, Mom and Greg split up tasks of making sour cream and chive mashed potatoes. Greg chopped up the fresh chives as Mom skinned the potatoes. She stopped when she saw Reagan next to me. She tossed the potato on the chopping board and reached her arms out for a hug, luckily not seeming to notice the blush still heating my neck, face, and ears.

"Oh my gosh, hi, Reagan!" She gave Reagan a tight squeeze as if they were long lost best friends.

Reagan gladly reciprocated the embrace. "It's so nice to finally meet you, Ms. Bennett."

Mom pulled away and waved a casual hand. "Oh, please, call me Karen. I'm so glad you're joining us today. And this is Greg."

I was glad I wasn't the only one blushing in the kitchen. When Reagan noticed Greg, it didn't matter if he was in his forties, he knew who Reagan Moore was. If he had any daughters, there was a ninety-eight percent chance they were Reagan Moore fans, much like the rest of the female population. So, Reagan Moore even had the ability to cause middle-aged men to become starstruck.

"Hi, Greg. It's nice to meet you. I'm Reagan," she said in her seamless charm. "I'd like to take partial credit for the shoes Karen wore on your first date."

"It's nice to meet you too," Greg said with a shy smile. "And she really looked beautiful. I approved of the shoes."

"I had to ask Reagan because I don't trust my own daughter's judgment," Mom added with a playful grin to me.

"Hey, I think I look pretty damn okay for Thanksgiving dinner, thank you very much," I said, gesturing to my dark gray cashmere sweater.

"You do," Reagan said, softly enough to probably get away with Mom and Greg not catching it. But just as I thought that, Mom studied the two of us for a split second before Reagan said, "Please, let me know what I can do to help. It's the least I can do after you took in a Thanksgiving dinner orphan. I really appreciate it."

"Oh, honey, don't worry about it. I'm so sorry you can't fly home to your family, but I promise we'll make tonight a close second. We're happy to have you here."

"I have no doubts about that. I brought a few things. I didn't know what bottle of wine everyone liked so I have three options."

"I like her," Mom told me. "She comes prepared."

"And I brought a pumpkin pie, but I don't know what I was thinking since Blair is the baking queen. But, you know, just in case we want to be traditional. Pumpkin pie from my favorite bakery and Cool Whip right here. But I already know I'm going straight for Blair's pie and not this one, so consider this a treat for after Thanksgiving."

"Oh, great!" Mom said and took the pie and Cool Whip container and placed it by my dessert in the fridge. "Blair made a simple caramel apple pie with apple cider whipped cream. So, we have options now, but I love me some pumpkin pie."

She let out a laugh and faced me. "Oh? A simple caramel apple pie with apple cider whipped cream? Doesn't sound simple."

"Try making macarons, and then you'll think it's simple," I told her.

"Oh, I got you a present," she said to me and dug one last thing out of her tote bag as Mom checked on Greg's chive dicing. She pulled out a small rectangular gift wrapped in shimmering blue paper with a white bow on it.

"You got me something? Why?"

"Because I thought of you," she said and then took a step forward, and it was as if we stepped back into our old world. Smelling the designer perfume flowing off her and the lack of space between us lifted that weight off my chest that I'd been carrying around since Gaslight Shores.

I glanced behind her shoulders, and Mom and Greg were now checking on the turkey roasting in the oven. Mom was really worried about messing up a recipe. All the recipes, actually. But mostly the turkey. No matter how many times Greg and I told her that everything was going to taste fine, she continued to worry and kept checking the oven to make sure the turkey was cooking to a nice brown roast.

"Karen, stop checking on it," Greg said every time, a smile in his tone. "It's fine. Stop letting the heat out."

"I just don't want it to be too dry."

"I thought of you a lot, actually," Reagan continued, and I snapped my attention back to her as she assessed the gift in my hands.

Whatever unfamiliar place we were in prior to this moment, we shifted right back to the days of acknowledging the mysterious force between us. A grin spread across her face, and it was small enough to clue me in that it was just for me. A grin that told me she was so genuinely happy to see me. My eyes widened when her confession settled in me, and I remembered what I was up to two days prior, making out with Paige on the dance floor, high on Molly, and rolling around with her naked in my sheets. Now came the guilt. I knew that was the feeling choking my chest. Reagan thought of me a lot while she was gone, and what did I do? I found myself another sex friend because I didn't think she would miss me, and I was wrong the whole time.

If it meant anything, I thought about her a lot too.

"You thought of me a lot?" I asked just in case I heard it wrong.

"Of course. Glad the feelings were mutual." She nudged me in the arm. "I found this at an adorable used bookstore in London. I couldn't believe they actually had this tucked in the back corner of the store. I also don't know how I found it, but I guess it seriously was meant to be, so I knew I had to get it for you. I hope it's not too much."

"Why would it be too much?"

I couldn't stop my curiosity at that point. I ripped the bow off, placed it on her head, and laughed when she let it sit there, a nervous smile finding her lips. Underneath the blue wrapping paper was a dark green book that had seen better days. The binding was worn, the pages aged in a dark yellow tint, each page emanating the smell of all the years that it collected. On the cover was a gold outline of a little boy with a fishing hook next to a small golden outline of a small bear with his paws up.

My stomach plummeted.

"If it's too much, then I'm sorry," she said in that nervously fast voice, the same voice and speed that she gave me at the front door. "I thought of what your tattoo means and how much you miss him. So, if it upsets you, then I'm really sorry. I didn't mean it that way. I just thought—"

I looked at her, trying to hold back the emotions budding in the back of my throat. My eyes stung as my fingers clenched around the book. "This is a *Winnie-the-Pooh* book," I said, interrupting her apprehensive ramble, staring at A.A. Milne's name under my thumbs.

I was amazed at what was in my hand. I was amazed at what she found shoved in the back of a used bookstore in London. This book clearly came from the first few editions printed back in the 1920s. How the hell did she find it?

"Yeah, it's a first edition," she said insecurely. "The bookseller confirmed it."

My heart swelled up like a balloon in my chest. I had no idea how to feel. It felt as if my heart ripped in two all over again at the same time it was being sewn up by this girl who was starting to feel like anything but a hookup to me. I couldn't believe I spent this whole time with another girl at the same time Reagan was buying me a first edition *Winnie-the-Pooh* in London. I was so embarrassed by how I couldn't keep myself from crying. Over a *Winnie-the-Pooh* book. If she thought Southern Comfort was laughable in the name of rock 'n' roll, surely crying over a first edition *Winnie-the-Pooh* would be number one on the list. But a part of me didn't even care because this was single-handedly the best gift anyone had even given me.

I wish I could have shown my grandpa. He would have loved this and would have treasured it as much as I already did.

"Reagan, this is…"

"You look upset. Shit, maybe it was too much. I'm sorry. I just thought—"

I grabbed her hand to make her shut up, and without even thinking, I let go of her fingers and cupped her warm, soft cheek. I could feel the tension that stiffened her body relax into my palm. "This is the sweetest thing anyone has ever done for me."

"Really?"

"Really. I really love it." I let go of her face and quickly wiped away the tears hanging on the corner of my eyes. Something connected us in that moment as we studied each other. Whatever was happening, it overpowered me with the strong desire to kiss her.

"I'm really glad you like it," she said, her eyes holding mine.

I really messed up. This was not what casual hookups bought each other. Holding that book in my hand, any last resistance of having casual feelings for her quickly dissolved, and I could feel myself opening up in a way I never felt before. I felt so warm, and it was only then when I understood what happened with us. She wasn't a hookup to me anymore. She wasn't the girl I used for sex or the girl I allowed to use me for sex. I really, really liked her, and when I finally admitted that to myself, those encumbering, uneasy feelings seeped right out of me.

"I love it," I said. "Seriously. This is…amazing. This is really amazing. You don't even know how much this means to me."

"I think I have an idea."

"I…I really wish I had something to give you."

She grabbed my hand again and traced invisible circles on my skin with her thumb. "You invited me over for Thanksgiving. It's enough."

"It's not."

She squeezed my hand tighter. "It is to me. Trust me."

Right then in that moment, the strong desire to kiss her softly on the forehead overpowered me. A gift like that told me I could probably get away with a kiss too. By the way her eyes held on to mine, I could almost catch a glimpse of how appreciative she was about me inviting her over to my mom's. I guess we were even.

For now.

Well, with that major shift in mood and more tension forcing us together, Reagan and I joined Mom and Greg in cooking. I tried sneaking in my own moments with Reagan, knowing that her feelings for me were on a significantly larger scale after she bought me that book. Still with that white bow on her head, she worked on the green bean casserole with me. I sautéed the green beans in butter and garlic, and once I placed it in the oven-safe dish, she sprinkled shredded Swiss cheese and smashed cornflakes on top of it. As Mom checked the turkey again, I stole a scoop of mashed potatoes with my finger and plopped a dollop on Reagan's nose. In return, she snatched a cornflake off the casserole and tossed it in my cleavage as if she was going for a free throw. When I mixed the cranberry sauce in Mom's new Williams-Sonoma sauce pot, I made Reagan taste it. She opened her mouth, and I shoved the spoon in, purposely trying to get some cranberry sauce on her face. It worked. Just a drop at the corner of her mouth. She backed away, checking to see if any sauce got on her scarf and sweater.

"I hate you," she said, licking her lips to clean up the mess. "That can stain!"

"Your face is already ruined, so the cranberry sauce isn't going add that much more damage."

She laughed and hit my arm. In return, I tapped her butt.

Mom's fears finally died when Greg took out the turkey, and it was a perfect brown. He sliced the turkey, and we set the table and made sure everyone had their pick of the wine Reagan brought. Mom's first attempt at her own Thanksgiving was a complete success. She thought she undercooked the turkey, but the three of us assured her that the turkey was perfect and moist. The wine quickly drained the more we ate, swapped stories, and laughed. Mom found the *Winnie-the-Pooh* book and became just as speechless as I was when she held it. Reagan's face turned bright red when Mom gushed about how considerate it was and then informed Greg about how important Winnie-the-Pooh was to me and Gramps. She made me flash him my tattoo on my left tricep, and what really got me going was when Reagan slipped her hand into mine under the table while we took ten minutes to talk about Gramps and how much we missed him and Grandma. I think she sensed how I started noticing his absence at the dinner table. I squeezed her hand back, and the feeling of her eased the pain of missing him.

After we grazed, the four of us slouched on the couches in the living room, had our fourth and fifth wines, and swapped worldly adventures. Mom and Greg shared the loveseat, and it was the first time I'd ever seen my mom cuddle with a man. While Reagan and I kept about a foot of space between us, Greg had his arm on the back of the loveseat, and Mom snuggled close enough to him that their legs touched. She rested her hand on his leg, and as he told us stories of his younger years traveling the world, Mom gazed up at him as if he was the most interesting person she'd met in a while. That probably filled me with happiness more than that whole Thanksgiving meal. I was so thankful that my wonderful, selfless, and caring mother found a guy who made her feel all the things she deserved to feel.

I thought Greg was going to be a boring, conservative, elitist business executive from Beverly Hills. But the guy was much more than that. He never talked about his work—or gave any indication that he had money—at all. He talked about his three daughters as if they were his gods and looked at my mom the same way she looked at him. He was funny, dorky, and an all-around good person and a good dad.

"Speaking of my middle daughter," Greg said as he shifted his attention to Reagan after modestly bragging about his middle daughter studying pre-med at Cal Tech. "She's a really big fan of yours. Huge fan. You should have seen her trying to buy tickets for your LA show. She almost didn't get them and started freaking out."

I smiled, knowing this confession was sponsored by all the wine we'd had.

"Oh, no! She got some, right?" Reagan said, and her pink cheeks and wine-soaked eyes were the cutest.

"Yeah, eventually. The system kept saying they were sold out, but she finally found some on the upper level."

"The upper level?" Reagan scoffed at that. "Forget that. How about front row and backstage passes?"

Greg's eyes widened, and Reagan casually sipped her wine as if she'd just offered him a ride home. Backstage passes to a sold-out world tour? No big deal.

"What? Really? You'd do that?" Greg said, probably knowing how many bonus points he was about to get with his daughter.

"I know a few people. A friend of a friend of a friend."

"I mean, that would be great. She would be so excited—"

"Consider it done. She deserves a break from pre-med studying. My treat. I'm very happy to do it."

Greg's smile stretched ear to ear when he faced Mom. "Well, I think I finished my Christmas shopping now. The best Christmas present to get a twenty-year-old."

"You're like Santa Claus," I whispered to her.

"It's what I always wanted to be."

"Want me to get you more wine?"

"I probably shouldn't. I'm already feeling it, and I have a forty-minute drive home."

"Spend the night." She looked at me as if I asked her to run away with me to elope. Even though her surprised stare said *what the fuck, Blair*, the small curve of her smile said, *thank you for finally asking.* "I have some clothes I can lend you, and there's a spare room right next to mine that you don't have to stay in at all."

She leaned closer to me and rested a hand on my upper thigh. "I don't want to stay in the spare room."

I wanted that hand to slide farther up my leg. I pressed my lips together for a brief moment to suck back the desire that hit my center, and then said, "Good, you can stay in my bed instead. Now, since you're staying here, can I get you another glass?"

"Only if you're going to have some too."

"Obviously."

As I got off the couch, I grabbed her hand briefly and slowly let my fingers glide off her. Grinning the whole way to the kitchen, I was so thankful that everything was falling back into place. The mindless touching, flirting, deep eye gazing.

Thank you, Winnie-the-Pooh.

Since we still had yet to touch the pinot grigio, I popped open the bottle and poured it into the freshly rinsed wine glasses. This overwhelming sense of contentment ran through me. I felt...whole. It was a feeling that filled me when I was younger with Mom, Grandma, and Gramps during the holidays. It used to be my favorite time of year when my family was still here. But ever since Grandma left us, the holidays became lonelier, and I thought that the first Thanksgiving and Christmas without Gramps and Grandma would be so miserable. Though I still had the urge to ask Gramps if he wanted another Johnnie Walker Blue neat and realized several times there was no Johnnie Walker or Gramps, I felt as whole as one could be. It helped that Mom seemed happy for the first time this year, and it helped that I had Reagan close to my side throughout the whole day.

That was when I found Mom standing next to me. She rested her cheek on her palm with a curious, mischievous smirk etched on her face.

"I see you're fetching her wine?" she said with a playful twinkle in her dark eyes.

"It's the least I could do. Did you see that book she got me?"

"I did, and I want to know what you two are about."

I glanced into the living room and noticed Reagan had scooted into my spot on the couch to get closer to Greg. The two were talking about something, seemingly okay with being alone with each other while my mother dragged the gossip out of me.

"So, something?" Mom said, eyebrows raised, attention right on my face, like a meddling teenager at a sleepover.

"It's..."

"It's what? Tell me!"

I faltered. "It's complicated."

"Complicated? How is it complicated? I've never seen a girl look at you the way Reagan looks at you."

"And what look is that?"

"Like you're everything. And you do it too. You look at her like she's everything."

Warmth crawled up my whole body and took over my face. It was a feeling that I'd never experienced before. A feeling that I always ran away from but not anymore. I embraced it. What was going on with me? Was it all the sage I inhaled on tour? Was it all the wine I already drank?

"Your voice even changes when you talk to her," Mom said. "It gets all high-pitched and goofy. I never thought I'd live to see the day."

Seriously, did Mom have her heat on? Like, at seventy-five? My neck started to sweat from just pouring wine into glasses.

"My voice doesn't change, and you do the same thing with Greg!"

"I know, and it's great." She bit her lip and glanced over her shoulder to take a peek at Greg and Reagan. Reagan had now moved onto the loveseat with Greg, and he showed her pictures on his phone that I only assumed to be of his three daughters. "I really like him," Mom continued. "Isn't he great?"

"He actually is. Consider yourself lucky to find a good person on the internet."

She faced me again. "And I know you like her, Blair. You can deny it all you want, but she bought you a first edition *Winnie-the-Pooh*. That told me everything before I could hear both of your voices change or both of you giving each other these looks like you're completely smitten. I finally get why you broke up with Alanna now. She never made you do that."

I patted her on the shoulder. "Hey, now you're getting it."

"Maybe Reagan's the one you've been saving yourself for."

"Okay, that sounds really religious and disgusting."

"What? It's true. I like to think of your heart as china—"

I made a face. "Like the country?"

"No, like a nice china set. It's beautiful and valuable, but it's always locked up and never put to use. You have so much to offer someone if you allowed them to open the door. But I have a feeling you're keeping that locked up for someone special."

I raised a skeptical brow. "You're referring to my heart as china? Like Grandma's china?"

She rolled her eyes. "I'm no poet, Blair, and I know you understand what I'm trying to say; you're just terrified that I'm saying it. Falling for someone isn't a scary thing, hon. It's a beautiful thing, and if you relax and stop running from it, you'll see how beautiful it could be. Use that good heart of yours. Don't keep it locked up. That's all I have to say about that."

"She's gonna spend the night."

"Then it's a good thing that my room is at the opposite end of the condo, isn't it?" She squeezed my arm and headed back into the living room, leaving me with heat on my face.

Moms knew everything. I hated it.

Mom, Gramps, Grandma, and I had a family tradition on Thanksgiving evening. We always watched *The Polar Express* to celebrate the start of the Christmas season. Grandma loved Christmas, and she would bake an assortment of all the best Christmas cookies the night before to eat while we watched the movie, and Gramps made hot chocolate. In the later years after Grandma passed, Gramps and I snuck into the kitchen to add some whiskey to our hot chocolates and snickered to each other because Mom never caught on. I always looked forward to that little secret we shared for those last five years of his life. Now, we didn't have the cookies, but we had two pies, still tons of wine, and hot chocolate that I spiked with whiskey, an ode to Gramps because I knew he was having the same wherever he was in the universe.

At first, I was wary of getting really comfortable with Reagan on the couch for fear of Mom's teasing, but I noticed Mom relaxed back into Greg's chest, and she was way too focused on the movie and Greg to be paying attention to Reagan and me. But about a half hour into the movie, our legs were touching. We looked at each other, then at the blanket that cloaked our legs, and I forced myself to put my arm around her shoulder. She cozied into me, wrapped an arm around my stomach, and rested her head on my shoulder. For the rest of the movie, I inhaled her shampoo and perfume and absentmindedly started rubbing up and down her arms, and her hand found the inside of my thigh.

After the movie, Mom showed Greg to her room, and I did the same with Reagan. While I gave her privacy to change after presenting her with clothes to sleep in, I went downstairs to grab some water. I found Mom outside on the patio, looking out at the twinkling lights from the homes stacked on top of each other in typical Southern California fashion.

"Hey," I said, creeping outside.

She smiled and gave me a half hug while clutching on to the remains of her pinot grigio with her other hand. "Oh, hi, dear. Are you and Reagan all set up for your big girl sleepover?"

"Are you and Greg?"

"Soon. Just wanted to finish my wine and enjoy the night. He's catching up with his girls. They're with their mother in San Francisco."

I rested my head on her shoulder and let out the longest sigh of my life about the truth I was about to utter. "Mom?"

"Yes?"

"I have a confession."

"Okay."

"Reagan and I...we've...well...we've been sleeping together."

Mom's facial expression made it seem as if I told her that we were engaged. "What? You have? Pause this! I'll grab the wine—"

"No, you don't. That's really it. I mean, it's kinda been put on hold since she's been in Europe, but that's the extent to whatever this is. Just sex."

"I knew it! I knew it the second she walked in. You were watching her sprinkle cheese with this look of full infatuation in your eyes."

"Okay, Mom."

"You don't sound very happy that it's just sex."

"I don't know if she likes me enough to date me or if she just sees me as a hookup."

"Well, she's quite the romantic with her hookups, then, if she's buying you a first edition *Winnie-the-Pooh*."

I shrugged. "She gives me butterflies. Like all the time."

Confirming it felt so rewarding, like finally breathing after holding my breath for so long.

"Oh, honey," she said in the most sympathetic Mom tone I'd heard come out of her. Her grip around my shoulders tightened and turned into a full, motherly embrace. She knew me better than I knew myself. She knew that, for whatever reason that was never psychoanalyzed by a therapist, I had trouble admitting my feelings. "I've never heard you say that about a girl."

"Because it's true. Because Reagan is...well...different. She's so different."

I pulled away from the hug and rested my arms against the patio railing, glancing out at the flickering homes up and down the rolling hills of Los Feliz.

"Then what's the issue?" Mom asked. "Have you told her how you feel?"

"No."

"And why not?"

"She had this whole interview in *Vogue* a few months back where they were asking her about dating, and she said she didn't want to be in a relationship right now. And when we spent Labor Day at her summer house and the internet was talking about us, she said she wasn't worried about it because we weren't in a relationship, and there was nothing to lose. So I was, like, 'okay, I'm just a hookup. I'll find myself another girl while she's in Europe.'"

"Oh, Blair, don't tell me you found another girl."

"Uh, yeah, I did. Because Reagan flat out told me there was nothing to lose with me. She said she doesn't want a relationship in *Vogue*. I'm not gonna be the person to suddenly change that."

"So, she buys you a book, mushes in her seat anytime you speak or look at her, spends all day with you, and then is going to spend the night in your bed?"

I threw my hands over my face. It was all too confusing. Reagan Moore was so fucking confusing the more I analyzed it. "God, I have no idea what she wants."

"Gee, Blair, I don't know, have you ever tried talking to the girl?"

I dragged my hands down my face and then found my mom smirking behind her wine glass as if she enjoyed watching my struggle. "I don't know what to say to her."

"Says the songwriter."

"You don't get it. Ever since Labor Day, everything has felt different."

"Good different?"

"Fucking scary different. I haven't seen her since then, and when

I saw her for the first time today, everything was different. I felt so insecure and nervous. We kept holding hands under the dinner table and blanket, and we've never done that before—"

Mom lowered her wine glass. "Oh my God, she likes you! Now go be a mature adult and talk to her about it."

"The next time we kiss, it's going to mean something. I don't think I see her as a hookup anymore. I even want to kiss her on her forehead."

"You make it sound like that's an obstacle."

"Forehead kisses are intimate, Mom. You don't forehead kiss someone you're using for sex."

"Dear child of mine, those are called feelings. Get acquainted with them. It means you care about her, and I can tell by the way she looks at you that she cares about you too. You're already treating her so much differently than girls you've called your girlfriend."

"That's because she's different. That's because she—"

"Gives you butterflies?"

Just the thought of her gave me butterflies like it was doing at that exact moment. "Yeah." I relaxed into my mom's grip. "That."

"How about you stop acting like this is a game and talk to her. If you don't act, she'll find someone who will."

Then, the patio door slid open. Mom and I glanced back at Reagan stepping out onto the patio in my buffalo plaid sweatpants and my black Queen T-shirt, and holy hell, was she even more attractive in my clothes. How was I supposed to talk to her when all I could do was stare?

"Hi, guys, mind if I join?" she said.

While still studying every inch of Reagan wearing my clothes, I could feel my mother eyeing me.

"Actually, I'm going to follow your lead, Reagan," Mom said and grabbed her wine. "I should get back to Greg and maybe finish reading my book. Today was a long—but good—day."

"Oh, okay. Thanks so much again, Karen, for everything today. It really means a lot to me."

"Of course, honey. Anytime. I'm so glad you spent it with us. You're always welcome here. You two enjoy your talk." And that was when my mother gave me that motherly direct order with a stare and a lightly creased brow. I got these many times growing up. The seventh time she asked me to clean my room. The third time she asked me to stop playing the drums. Anytime I talked back to her, Gramps, or Grandma. The worst communication a mother could give. That motherly stare.

When Mom went back inside, she took all the oxygen on the patio because as Reagan inched closer, I thought my heart was going to sprint right out of my chest.

In addition to never making the first move, it was no surprise that I never told a girl how I felt about her—probably because I never had feelings worthy enough to go into a full-fledged monologue. Alanna and I had known each other since freshman year of college, didn't start casually hooking up until the year after she graduated, and then one day, she told me she wanted to be exclusive. So, I agreed because my thought literally was "why not?" My girlfriend before Alanna, Carrie, those two years I spent at USC, we never put a label on it, but she was the one who told me she really liked me. I also thought she was really, really hot so I thought that meant I liked her a lot too. My high school girlfriend, Rachel, asked me to be her girlfriend senior year, and I wanted a girlfriend because I felt as if that would prove to my friends that I was gay and not just saying shit. But I did like Rachel. She made me laugh, and kissing her gave me tingles on my lips. I liked her the way people liked their high school girlfriend of four months.

Reagan threaded her fingers around my belt loop and pulled me into her. She glanced up, and I wondered what the hell was going through her head because she did a really good job shielding it.

"Why are you so quiet?" she said. "Everything okay?"

"Um, do you...do you think we could talk?"

"Of course."

I scratched the back of my head. "Like, a serious talk."

That prompted her to take her fingers out of my belt loop, and I could already feel their absence. She took a step back and crossed her arms, as if preparing for the serious talk.

"What's wrong?" she said cautiously.

"What's going on with us?"

The scared frown appeared on her face the same way my face probably looked when my mom told me I had to talk to her. Terrified, as if this was the conversation she dreaded the most, which made me feel as if I chugged sour milk.

"Oh wow," she said at the same time she exhaled. "Um...I...I don't..."

I wanted to jump off the balcony. That was what I really wanted to do. How she could tell me she had no idea what we were doing after everything that happened in one day amazed me. And angered me.

"Stop playing a game with me," I said.

"What? What are you talking about?"

"I feel like everything with you is a game. You're really trying to tell me you have no idea what's going on with us after what happened today? You buy all of your hookups first editions of their favorite book?"

Calm down. Take a deep breath. You're sounding aggressive, I told myself.

"No, I don't." The harshness in her tone matched mine.

"Then what are we doing, Reagan? Don't you think we need to have this conversation?"

"Of course, I think we need to have this conversation."

"Okay, then let's have it."

"After you." She motioned me to go ahead.

"Fine," I said, fingers clenching around the railing. "I want to know why you think you have nothing to lose with me."

Her eyebrow furrowed more. "What?"

"On the plane back from Gaslight Shores, you said you didn't care about the drones getting pictures of us because you had nothing to lose with me. Because we weren't in a relationship. That fucking hurt, you know."

"I'm sorry. That's not what I meant—"

"Yeah? Well, I took that as a sign that we weren't anything. So, while you were in Europe, I found someone else to sleep with."

"You did?" She loosened her crossed arms, and it sounded as if my confession knocked the wind right out of her.

"How was I supposed to know anything? All we did was have sex. The whole time you were over there, you gave me no indication that you cared about me more than just some hookup. Not even once. You had an interview in *Vogue* that said you didn't want to be in a relationship—"

"Blair, you broke up with your last girlfriend because you didn't want a relationship. Why would I talk about relationships with someone I'm sleeping with who's terrified of them?"

"I'm not terrified of them—"

"And that interview was done back in April, for the record. More than six months ago."

"You're not answering my question. What are we doing?"

"We're fighting."

I let out a sigh that came from the pit of my stomach. "What. Are. We. Doing?"

"I don't know, Blair!" She threw her hands in the air. "I have no idea what we're doing or what the hell you want or what the hell I want or what the hell we're supposed to do. I don't know."

"Am I just something casual and meaningless to you, or am I something more?"

"I bought you that book. I think that says what you want to know."

God, this woman was difficult.

"I want you to actually say it."

She let out a frustrated sigh and looked at the maroon sky for a second. "You're more than casual."

Finally, my fingers unraveled their grip. I could finally let out that breath I'd been holding. "I wasn't expecting today to be good at all," I admitted. "Because it's the first holiday without my grandparents and everything, but it was actually really great, and that's because of you. I really like you, Reagan, and it really scares me."

She took a step closer to me. "Why?"

"Because I'm selfish and clueless and bad at relationships."

"I'm selfish, not really clueless, and also bad at relationships."

"I don't know what's right for me right now. I thought it wasn't the right time to be in a relationship, but now with you, it doesn't feel right not to be in a relationship. I just know that the thought of you makes me so happy and less lonely, and the thought of you with someone else nauseates me."

"That's how I feel right now knowing you found someone else. I…I don't know how to process it. It keeps playing in my head, you two doing all the same things we used to—"

"She's not you, if that's any consolation."

I could tell by looking at her face she was just as scared as I was. This wasn't supposed to happen. We weren't supposed to catch feelings, and we weren't supposed to care if the other person slept with someone else. We were supposed to use each other for sex and keep each other company during our lonely nights on tour.

I guess that was exactly why we fell into this trap.

"Tell me more about the girl," Reagan said softly.

"She's gone if you want her to be."

Another step closer, and her hands rested on the waist of my jeans. "I want her to be."

"Consider it done."

I tucked a loose tendril of hair behind her ear, and then ran the back of my hand down her soft cheek before I pulled her in for a kiss. She inhaled deeply when her mouth parted, and her tongue welcomed mine, buzzing my lips and everything below my waist. I was right. This kiss was so different. It was hungry and passionate and deep and slow and tender and furious all at the same time. We breathed into each other, cupped each other's faces securely, and when we took turns kissing and sucking on the other's neck, she tilted her head back as if each suck was getting rid of the emotions from her body like venom.

Somehow, we made it to my room, but I wasn't sure how. By the time I kicked my door shut, I had already peeled off the flannel pants and T-shirt. But just like the kiss, the sex was different. Our kisses were deep and hungry. Our movements were slow and tender. I even opened my eyes at one point to marvel at her face, and when I did, I caught her doing the same thing, and we stared deep into each other while warm electrical currents swarmed through me as our naked bodies grinded against each other. We held each other tightly, exchanging soft moans in each other's ears and mouths. This time, I didn't want to rush it. I wanted to fully enjoy the sensation of her breasts against mine. I wanted to take my time sucking murmurs from her neck, tracing circles around her nipples with my tongue, feeling them harden in my mouth, holding her undulating body in my hands. And when we both came, all the feelings I'd been bottling up the past few months escaped me at the same time they escaped her. That never happened to me before. It made me feel so much closer to her that we shared that blissful moment together.

I got the truest sense of how much had changed in that day because this time, as we collected our breaths and wiped the sweat from our foreheads, her arms brought me into her body, and I rested my cheek on her breasts. She cradled my shoulders like the perfect big spoon that she was. I listened to how fast her pulse sped, and I could feel mine beating at the same pace as hers.

But just when I thought I couldn't feel happier and more complete, she kissed me softly on the forehead, and everything felt so right for the first time in a long time.

CHAPTER NINE

"Oh my God, hi!" Reagan yelled from the other end of the hallway backstage in Greenville, South Carolina.

She leapt into my arms, wrapped her legs around my waist, and I caught her, twirling her around while giving her face a kissing attack.

She'd spent all of December with her family in Nashville and then January traveling Asia and Australia.

And now, here we were on the first day of February, and I was so glad to see her again and so glad to be back on tour.

While she clung to me, I scampered to an empty hallway, pushed her back against the cinderblock walls, and took hold of her lips. As our tongues danced sensuously, she fisted my hair and gently pulled on it, and that pull elicited an involuntary moan out of me. I loved it when she pulled my hair like that.

"I've missed you," I said, allowing her to drop to the floor.

"I missed you too." She giggled as I kissed and sucked the other side of her neck. "Geez, Blair, you're in a good mood."

I stopped kissing and met her eyes, smiling when I saw her satisfied grin. "I'm sorry. I had to steal you for a little bit."

"I'm completely okay with that."

"Really? I thought you'd put up a fight. We're kinda being risky right now."

"Well, I'm a little deprived of female attention, so it's worth the risk."

"Okay, good."

I planted my lips back on hers and took in a deep inhale of her taste as our mouths welcomed each other's tongues for a few moments before she pulled away.

"You wanna know what I think we should do?" she said.

I looked up at the wall and attempted to suck in a grin. "I could think of a few things."

"First, we need to celebrate the fact that you're nominated for a fucking Grammy."

That was the best Christmas present when the Grammy nominations came out, and the song I wrote with Isaac Ball was one of the Best Song nominees…along with Reagan's first single off her latest album. I still couldn't believe it. My very first Grammy nomination. There was a lot of crying and celebrating between Mom and Miles, and Mom reminded me that Gramps wasn't nominated for a Grammy until he was in his forties. In total, Gramps won four Grammys: two for songwriting and two for music producing. I was only alive for his producing Grammys, and I remember staying up late with Grandma when I was nine, watching the awards live and screaming with her when he won, and he gave us both a shout-out in his speech. He won his second one when I was fourteen, and he again mentioned me as his inspiration.

I hope he knew that he was my inspiration. He would always be.

"Yeah, I can think of a few ways to celebrate," I said. "With my competition."

Reagan was nominated for two: one for Best Music Video and another for a song she collaborated on with a DJ, a song that wouldn't stop playing in the clubs, the one that was up against my song.

"At the same time we celebrate our number one hit," she said. "How does it feel that a Midnight Konfusion song is number one right now?"

"Pretty fucking amazing. Thanks for reminding me of all the great things happening."

Our song released a few weeks before Christmas, and just like the usual in the music industry, Reagan Moore being attached to our song sent it soaring up the charts. Right before Christmas, we filmed the music video with the director known for having aesthetically pleasing videos, beautiful cinematography, plot, camera angles, you name it. I guess when you're the best in the music industry, you can hire the best director.

Probably what helped the song was the video. Reagan told the director, Devon Gualtieri, that she wanted to take a risk, which floored me as well as her. Reagan wanted the video to match the lyrics and sound of the song—slow yet sultry—and the video portrayed that. We kissed in pink and blue lights, there was a shot where I laid her down in bed, and we kissed some more; we danced under a streetlamp. But as sultry as the song was, Devon Gualtieri made it tasteful. Her shots highlighted our chemistry. It told a story about two girls liking each other, and there was still a bit of innocence behind it that made it sexy but sweet.

So, the song was number one, and the video was number one online and had been for six weeks. It also sparked a lot of media attention because girl-next-door Reagan Moore was getting in bed with someone—something never portrayed in her other music videos. And not just anyone; she was getting in bed with a woman, finally addressing the "is she or is she not into women" question that had been following her around unanswered.

And boy, was the internet excited about that video.

Reagan Moore's Sexy New Music Video with Blair Bennett.

Midnight Konfusion's Blair Bennett Seduces Reagan Moore in Brand-New Video.

Everyone Is Shipping Reagan Moore and Blair Bennet Right Now, and Here's Why.

Plus, on top of all of that, Miles and I were invited to the Meraki Music and Arts Festival, one of the largest music festivals of the season that brought in around three hundred thousand people over the course of the four-day weekend. The opportunity to perform at one of the largest music festivals was beyond exciting.

Plus, our band was on the same lineup as the three big headliners that were on the top of the music industry: Sudden Enemy, a Seattle rock band that had been around since the late 1990s; Taz Jones, a hip-hop artist from the Bronx who'd only been around for four years but had already won six Grammys since his debut album; and Reagan Moore. Along with a bunch of other musicians I'd written for who were attending, like Isaac Ball, Brandy Strong, Rex Silver, and Nora Laine. And in the mix of all that talent, there was our little band, Midnight Konfusion, which I guess wasn't so little anymore if we were going to Meraki.

We had a very great Christmas, to say the least.

"So, to celebrate all the great things happening to you, I have a surprise," she said with a salacious smirk. "Follow me."

She took my hand and weaved me all around the hallways until we made it into her green room. She closed the door, pressed in the lock, and then pushed me into the wall. When she kissed me, I tugged her waist toward me, and I just sort of sank into the wall, remembering how wonderful it was to kiss her again. One hand slid into my hair and grabbed a fistful. Every time she did it, it was like experiencing it for the first time. I murmured into her mouth, surrendering my body, and that was when her hands crept underneath my shirt, feeling my skin, and my arm hairs rose like they always did when she first touched me. As her tongue skimmed my bottom lip, she unbuttoned my pants and pulled down the zipper, and my heart sort of just leapt out of my chest as everything below my underwear begged for her touch.

She made me feel so amazing, I sometimes couldn't handle it.

"Reagan, what are you doing?" I said when I pulled away, nervously laughing at her assertiveness. What happened to the overly cautious Reagan Moore?

"About to get you off," she said.

I pulled away again, and my heart started thrumming. "You know anyone can walk in at any time?"

She blinked a few times. "That's what the lock is for."

She slid her hand underneath my underwear, eliciting a sharp gasp from me. Who the hell was this Reagan? Was this the same girl who was terrified of going swimming after hours? She looked a lot like her.

Her hands crawled down to my center, pushing away the folds so she could go inside me. At the sudden insertion, I had to trap another moan in my throat because I was so terrified about someone walking in, even though the thrill of getting caught caused my pulse to dance faster in my neck. Maybe I was only scared because I thought Reagan would be scared, but once she put her fingers inside me, and I clawed her back, I took that as a sign that she might have started to love the thrills I introduced to her.

"I can't wait until later," she whispered into my ear, and then her fingers sped up, and she lightly bit my earlobe. "I've waited long enough."

I gave up. I allowed her weight to hold me against the wall because all the rhythms inside me were too much for my knees to withstand. Two months without her pressed up against me, mouth on my neck, fingers moving in insistent strokes. I knew this was going to be a quick adventure because Reagan slamming me against the wall and being adamant about giving me an orgasm despite her whole army being on the other side of the door had me instantly wet and ready for her to do whatever she wanted to me.

I nuzzled into her neck as the sensation started to overpower me. I pulled her back for some kind of stabilization to keep my knees gradually weakening from giving out. Her free hand slipped underneath my shirt and crawled up to my breasts, twisting my nipple for even more pleasure, and my whole body buzzed with warmth. My breathing accelerated in unison with her fingers as I moved my hips against her, and it quickly brought me the sharp release I'd been looking forward to since the last time I saw her. I buried my mouth into the fabric of her shirt to mute the strong cries she pulled out of me. As the aftershocks ran from my center, down my shaking legs and up to my chest, I pulled away to look at her only to find a wide, playful grin.

"There, that was my surprise," she said before she retrieved her hand.

I could feel the the blush hit my cheeks. "That was…wow…that was a good surprise. My legs feel weird."

"Good. I did you right, then."

I'm sure she would have wanted to know that, even during our set, I still felt the aftereffects of that intense orgasm and used the very little strength in my legs to prevent myself from collapsing. So, unfortunately for the Greenville crowd, I couldn't hop on the speakers to wave to the upper level or hop off the stage onto the floor to high-five the front row. Nope, my legs were too wobbly from the headliner of the tour fucking me before the show.

During her set, Reagan invited us on the stage to sing "Patience, Love" for the first time live. I spotted all the girls in the front row eyeing each other like the people on Ellen's Twelve Days of Giveaways when Ellen broke the news. It was one thing to know that the song you wrote was at number one. It was another thing to see in the eyes of fans that your song was at number one. Their glowing beams, rounded eyes, hands tossed up in the air: all of that was better than the "one" placed in front of the song name. As we performed, trying to ooze chemistry out on stage, I couldn't erase the smile from my face, knowing how much the crowd loved the song.

And then in Charlotte, Reagan asked me to ditch my own room and bunk with her. So, obviously I didn't have to think more than half a second before I said yes. What was a close second was that Finn didn't ask any questions when Reagan informed him of the change, didn't raise a skeptical eyebrow, or give me a lecture about how I should be careful with Reagan. Corbin gave me a firm, curious eye, warning me with just his strong furrowed eyebrows that I better not fuck it up. And once I got my key and walked into my hotel room with my new roommate, our bodies got even more reacquainted after being apart for so long.

Everything was back to normal…with the added bonus of my hotel room being Reagan's.

❖

We all flew back to LA for the Grammys two weeks later. Walking down the red carpet, Mom—my date—looked absolutely gorgeous in her knee-length, over the shoulder red dress. Miles rocked a velvet tux jacket. Yes, velvet. He thought it was a genius idea as we got ready, throwing it over his suspenders, white shirt, and black bowtie. Oh, and his black-rimmed glasses he brought out on special occasions to trick people into thinking he was much classier than he was. But once we hit the red carpet and a bunch of reporters, paparazzi, and fans crammed underneath the white tent that ran over the carpet, I could tell by the glistening sweat on his face that he severely regretted that velvet. As for me, I decided to go bold and wore an all black pantsuit, the jacket dipping halfway to my belly button and held together by fashion tape on my boobs, and black skinny slacks that stopped at my ankles. Unlike my friend Miles, I opted out of wearing any sort of shirt or cami underneath, and it paid off because the stale air somewhat wafted underneath my jacket and prevented me from overheating on a surprisingly hot February day in LA.

"I'm melting," Miles said through his teeth. The gel that pushed back his hair started melting from the heat.

A million flashes went off in front of us as we posed for the cameras while the paparazzi yelled to get our attention.

Much to my surprise, many of the interviewers and paparazzi yelled at me.

"Blair! Blair! Where's Reagan?"

"Blair! Can you confirm or deny that you're dating Reagan Moore?"

But to fuck with them because it was fun to watch them squirm, I just smiled and waved as I continued down the red carpet.

"Blair, you're not going to go talk to them?" Mom asked.

"Mom, they only want to find out all the juicy info about Reagan. Plus, we need to get Miles into some air-conditioning, or he's going to turn into a puddle."

He fanned his white shirt. "Yes, please. I'm halfway there."

As the three of us were a few steps from making it inside, we heard the fans on the bleachers bellowing out frantic cheers. Like a concert sonic boom made for the red carpet. I turned around to see which celebrity was causing the commotion. Beyoncé? Lady Gaga? Justin Timberlake? But no. It was my girlfriend, wrapped up in a shimmering gold sleeveless dress that hung to the floor. She waved to the fans on the bleachers, who turned into paparazzi by snapping pictures of her on their phones in the same cadence as the actual paparazzi, a storm of flashes and constant clicking taking over the red carpet. She stepped toward the bleachers to let a few fans take selfies with her, and then she hiked up her dress to climb the stairs to talk to the red carpet interviewers. No matter how cold the drinks would be at the bar inside, I couldn't peel my eyes off her.

"Blair. Air-conditioning. So close," Miles said.

"Wow, your girlfriend looks stunning, Blair," Mom said with a hint of teasing in her tone.

She was the most beautiful person on that carpet, so beautiful that I knew if I continued to gawk at her, at least one paparazzo would snap the picture of my drooling, sell it to *TMZ* for the price of one month's LA rent, and then it would make its rounds all over the internet. So, I dragged Mom and Miles inside where the air-conditioning and alcohol would cool us down.

An hour and a half later, I finally got the chance to talk to Reagan backstage since the three of us were pushed back in the sixth row with Isaac Ball. It was an hour into the ceremony, and the three of us prepared for our performance. She opted out of the gold dress and wore her familiar black sparkly bodysuit. That outfit would never get old.

"Hey!" she said, adjusting her in-ear as she flashed her wide smile, and then grabbed my hand for a quick thumb caress.

"Finally, I get to see you."

"I know, I know. How are you feeling? You ready for this?"

I was. Miles had snuck in a flask of Jack in his jacket pocket, which we shared with Isaac, even though Mom kept telling us to put it away so we wouldn't be kicked out. Isaac Ball suggested we switch seats so he could charm Mom into letting us drink. She enjoyed the flirting from a successful, attractive, early thirties musician. So, she hushed and enjoyed the show. At least the whiskey had shoved my nerves deep inside my stomach.

"Born ready."

She squeezed my hand and then took a deep breath. "All right. I'll see you out there. Ready, Miles?"

Instead of her drummer, she invited Miles to play for both songs. He took a deep breath, and then one of the backstage workers in all black, wearing an earpiece walkie-talkie, escorted them out on the stage while the show went to commercial. When the commercial ended, the presenter took the stage, introduced Reagan Moore, and then the music started. The audience stood and danced along to the latest single off her current album. Miles played the drums like the pro that he was, and no one could tell he was extremely nervous getting in front of all those people. She sang half of her single, and then she transitioned into the song we wrote, singing the first verse. When she reached the bridge, that was my cue, and out I walked from backstage. She faced me at the same time the lights shone down on me. The audience cheered at the surprise duet, probably all gleeful that the internet rumors popped up on stage.

As well as all the people in the arena, there were millions of viewers all over the world. I decided that instead of focusing on the cameras that reminded me how many people were actually watching, I focused on Reagan, pretending I was singing to her and only her. By the time the chorus came around again, the stage fright subsided. I was comfortable walking up and down, not holding back on letting my chemistry with Reagan pour out. We walked close to each other, eyes locked, flirtatious smiles naturally seeping out of us, the crowd growing louder. When the song ended and I finally looked at the audience, they gave us a standing ovation, and the group of fans in the general admission section right up on the stage had the same faces as when we first performed the song live in Greenville: mouths dropped, wide smirks, phones out to capture the moment.

The only somber moment of the night came when the In Memoriam played, and Gramp's face and name flashed on the screen above the stage. Mom and I grabbed each other's hand, Miles grabbed my other hand, but the sad moment of missing him didn't last too long because a few minutes later, our night ended with Isaac Ball and me winning the Grammy for Best Song. It completely surprised me because I could have sworn Reagan was going to win it. One moment I was in my seat, the next I was on the stage looking at all the people and the tiers of floors that comprised the Staples Center. All the cameras pointed to me. All the lights heated my body and produced sweat that cascaded down the valley of my chest. Everything in front of me warped in a daze once I clasped that six-pound Grammy. I searched for Mom and Miles in the sixth row. Mom dabbed her eyes. Miles gave me a thumbs-up. And then across the aisle from them was Reagan in the first row. Her eyes fixated on me, and a tooth-revealing beam reached both of her ears as Isaac started off by thanking his manager, his record label, and then he went on about how working with me was an honor, and I was some musical genius. Then he faced me, and words just slipped out of me, and I thanked my family, Isaac, and my grandpa. I tried to make it as brief as possible because I was so warm from shock, the beaming lights, all the people watching me, and the realization that my lifelong dream just unveiled in front of me.

To celebrate, Miles and I begged Reagan to take us to In-N-Out Burger because we were starving and drunk—drunk because we had nothing in our systems.

"Anything for this Grammy winner," she said and kissed me without caring that Miles and Mom shared the limo, and then they teamed up to tease me for the rest of the night.

"Reagan and Blair sitting in a tree," Miles sang, and Mom stooped down to his level to join him, knowing that it would easily get to me.

But Reagan's eyes and smile made it easy for me to block out the heckling.

"I'm so proud of you, Blair," she said and looped an arm through mine. "Even if you were my competition. You deserve it. And you know what, your grandparents are throwing a party up there."

I had no idea what to say. Ever since the presenters said my name and Isaac's for the winners of Best Song, this ball of emotion hung in my throat. I had never been prouder of myself; I had never been happier knowing that I got to share the night with the three most important people in my life. But as much as I was happy, I was so sad I couldn't share it with the man who made me fall in love with music. I couldn't even imagine the night if Gramps was still alive. He would be hollering, probably crying, and then he would have bought the most expensive whiskey out there for us to enjoy together. That ball of emotion prevented me from saying anything because I knew once I tried speaking, my voice would start shaking. I couldn't cry. Tonight was not a night for crying. So, I just kissed her forehead instead.

Miles and I each scarfed two burgers and French fries while Reagan and Mom each ate one. And then, since Reagan and I weren't in the mood to drive all the way out to Calabasas where she lived, the limo dropped us off at our place before taking Mom back to Los Feliz. Once we got to my room, we stripped out of red carpet attire, switched into our pj's, and plopped on my bed, both of us chugging water before curling up with each other. At least with the burgers and fries in my stomach, the world wasn't spinning anymore.

"Did I tell you how amazing you looked in that jacket?" Reagan said with her head resting on my shoulder. "Because damn, I couldn't stop staring at your boobs."

"Did I tell you how amazing you looked? You were, by far, the most beautiful woman on that red carpet."

"That's not even accurate. Did you not see Beyoncé?"

"I did, and she was a very close second to you."

She placed her hand in the valley between my breasts and rubbed the palm of her hand where my skin had been showing all night. "You know, I never went to an award show with the person I was dating."

"Really?"

"No. Knowing I got to dress up and see you all dressed up, it kinda felt like prom. Or what I thought prom would be like, right?"

"Miles snuck a flask of whiskey in his jacket. He did that at our actual prom too."

"Seriously? Blair!" But she laughed.

"What? It makes it all better. Oh, and you came home with me. That's an important detail." I kissed her cheek. "Very prom-esque."

"Yup. That's how I imagined prom would be."

"Wait," I said as I positioned myself so my hand propped up my head. "You never went to prom?"

"I never went to prom. My school only had senior prom, so you could only go if you were a senior or if a senior asked you. The only person I dated in high school was the same age as me."

"The one who used you for your Nashville connections?"

"Yes. Brett."

I shuddered at the name. Anyone named Brett sounded as if they dressed in a camo hat with an over-cupped brim and had a gross toothpick hanging in between his lips…because, you know, that was really sexy.

"By the time I was a senior, I was touring with the Bartlett Belles, and I was homeschooled. So, there wasn't really a chance for me."

"That sounds really depressing."

She shrugged as if it was no big deal. "I mean, I was bummed about it for a little bit, especially when all my friends were talking about what they were going to wear, and what restaurant they were going to eat at, and then I had to hear all their stories, but I felt as if I couldn't complain because I had a record deal and was touring. I went to homecoming all three years, so there's the alternative."

"But prom is like the Super Bowl of school dances."

She laughed. "I kind of find it funny that you're so concerned about my lack of prom experience. You went to prom?"

"Of course I did. I went with my girlfriend, Rachel."

"And did you take forever to ask her?"

"No. She asked me. She wrote me a poem and put it in my locker."

"That's cute, though I'm not surprised you didn't ask her."

I tickled her side. "Hey, I initiated the serious conversation at Thanksgiving that got us into this relationship, so, where's my credit?"

"Okay, you're right. You get credit for that. I don't know what I would do if I saw you in that jacket and boob tape, and I wasn't allowed to kiss you." She kissed my neck.

"Don't worry about high school prom. Touring and a record deal and going to the Grammys is significantly cooler."

"I think the reason why I was bummed about not going to prom was because it's this whole dramatic thing. You dress up, your date gets you flowers, you go to a nice restaurant and feel really fancy. It's just the romance of it that I wish I experienced. Come to think of it, I've never been romanced like that, which is kinda sad. I feel like everyone should be romanced at least one time in their life, and my shitty exes never did that."

Come to think of it, I'd never felt romanced, either; not like I ever craved it. The girl who was the most romantic was Alanna. She wanted all the romance in our relationship, and it was only looking back, when I was in bed with Reagan, that I realized Alanna basically romanced herself, and I was along for the ride. Our only Valentine's Day together, she made us reservations at this restaurant in Santa Monica, making sure we got a table that overlooked the ocean right as the sun set, and we shared a bottle of red wine that I didn't feel fancy enough to drink, and we ate the best lobster both of us had ever had.

But then I imagined going to that same beautiful restaurant with Reagan, and it didn't seem as schmaltzy as the memory was with Alanna. I saw us at the exact same table, drinking wine, watching the sunset, and chatting long into the night like we usually did, until the servers had to kick as out, and then I would tell her I wanted to dig my feet into the sand, listen to the white capped waves crash onto the shore, and kiss her while blanketed by night. Now if any girl of my past told me, in those exact words, that that was their perfect date, my eyes would ache from rolling them so hard. But if Reagan told me, I'm pretty sure my heart would flutter right out of my chest.

I had to give her that romantic date, even if I had no idea how to plan one. Maybe Mom could help me. She sure loved romance.

❖

Two days later, Miles and I flew out to Oklahoma City, meeting Reagan after she did a late show appearance. When we landed at the airport, I flipped my phone off airplane mode, hoping I had romantic text messages from Reagan.

But what I got instead was text after text after text from Reagan, Corbin, and even my mom. Eighteen unread text messages that seemed too much for being out of pocket for a three-hour flight.

When I opened the text from Corbin, my heart plummeted so hard and quickly, I almost threw up.

"Blair, come on," Miles said in the middle of the aisle.

I couldn't really focus on anything. The air on the plane disappeared and my knees forgot how to support my legs. Not as if air would have done me any good, because what I saw on my phone caused me to forget how to breathe. All the energy from the great weekend was left in the Hollywood Hills because what greeted us in Oklahoma City was something that came straight out of my nightmares.

"Blair, what's wrong?" Miles said. "Your face is all white."

I had clicked on the link Corbin sent me. In big, bold, black font on the website for the entire world to see.

Reagan Moore's Racy Text Messages with Blair Bennett Revealed in Mass Celebrity Phone Hacking.

CHAPTER TEN

*A*ll the Celebrity Victims of Recent Phone Hacking Rocking Hollywood.

Bristol Perri Disables Social Media After Nude Photos Leak in Phone Hacking.

Reagan Moore's Text Messages Confirm Relationships with Jessie Byrd, Blair Bennett.

There was a whole list. At least thirty celebrities involved in the hacking. The worst part about it was that my texts with Reagan were nowhere near as damaging as Bristol Perri's nudes. But in the mix of leaked photos was a video of Reagan and me making out in Greenville, in what I thought was an abandoned hallway, which meant whoever took that video of us decided that right after the hacking would be a great time to leak it.

Because Reagan never took sexy selfies of herself, her worst photo was of her in a red-and-white striped bikini on a beach with Jessie Byrd, who was in an all-black bikini, both of them sitting on beach towels with Reagan's head on Jessie's shoulder. I was too traumatized to look at what else was leaked. Plus, since I was sucked into the club of victims, there was no way I was going to intrude on their private stuff. Miles avoided all the articles, but without opening one, he came across that Reagan picture. He claimed that the photo of Reagan and Jessie would have seemed platonic if it weren't for screenshots of her text messages complaining to Bristol Perri about their breakup. The conversation when she came back to LA after touring Europe and said she wanted to see my face? That was out there. The conversation we had in New York City when she told me to come to her room, and she said she wished I was coming? That was out there. Asking her to be my date for Thanksgiving? That was out there too. The texts she sent me while she was in Asia about how she missed my face and body and my tattoos and my mouth? Yup, the most incriminating text conversation out there for everyone to read. I pulled it up on my phone to make sure it wasn't as bad as I thought it was.

Reagan: *Ugh, God, I really miss your face.*

Reagan: *Like, what was I thinking bringing on another band for the Europe/Asia leg? If I knew how magical your mouth was back when we planned this, I'd totally just bring you.*

Me: *Oh, wow, this was an amazing text to wake up to.*

Me: *Ditch your tour and get in my bed. ASAP.*

Reagan: *I really need you right now. I'm deprived. I miss your face and your body and your tattoos. God, the things I'd do to see your tattoos.*

Me: *What sort of things would you do?!*

Reagan: *Riskier things than sneaking into a pool after hours.*

Me: *Why are we not together right now? Damn it!*

Reagan: *Can we make a deal that, once we see each other again in Greenville, we lock ourselves in my green room or bus and just devour each other?*

Me: *I'm not sure how I'm supposed to make it for another few weeks now.*

Reagan: *Just think of me when you do yourself, okay?*

Me: *You don't need to ask me twice.*

So, it was even worse than I originally remembered. I couldn't believe that conversation was out there. A conversation about us fucking each other and masturbating. I could have just run myself through a wall.

The only way I could handle everything on the internet was the vodka I bought from the liquor store closest to our Oklahoma City hotel. As Miles filled me in on everything, I drank to the point that I almost forgot about it, and when I got to that point, Reagan finally made it to our room. The second she came in, I threw my arms out, and she sobbed into my chest. I'd never seen her cry before, and I didn't realize how lucky I was that I hadn't until her sobs sliced through me. I could feel her pain when she cried. I tried so hard not to let my own emotions burst out, but she needed a rock.

I brushed strands of hair out of her face, tucking them behind her ears as she sobbed into my shoulder. She was so upset that she didn't seem to notice that I reeked of alcohol and was really drunk. And if she did, then it didn't matter to her as much as her whole private life up on the internet. There were moments when she stopped and we lay there in silence, and then she started crying again. The fabric of my sweatshirt collected her tears, and I hugged her tighter, occasionally kissing her damp cheek and rubbing her back even after my arm needed a rest, but it didn't deserve a rest until she stopped crying.

"We'll get through this," I said and kissed her forehead as another round of tears ensued. "You won't be alone."

"This is…this is…" She stuttered through gasps of air in between cries. "This is why—"

I grabbed her hand. "I know. I know." And then I pulled her back into me, and her quivering resumed.

"I'm so p…private," she finished. "This is exactly why. It's all out there. It's all…that's…that's my whole life out there. Those texts I sent in Asia!" Her cries became harder. And when the conversation played in my head, the tears started in my eyes too.

I continued to rub her hands and kiss her tearstained cheeks. I felt so hopeless trying to console her because there was nothing to say or do that would take it all back. Whoever hacked into her phone did it effortlessly. Seeing Reagan come apart, crying hysterically, made me so angry. She didn't deserve it at all.

No one did.

I ordered room service, drew her a bubble bath, let her eat during her bath, then cuddled her to sleep. We didn't talk much. I don't even know what we could have said except crying and complaining how this really sucked. She spoke to Bristol Perri on the phone for a little bit after her bath, and I think she got some comfort talking to a good friend, someone who was going through the same stuff as she was. I hated how she went out of her way to protect her private life, made sure she didn't do anything stupid that the media would blow up the internet with, and no matter how hard she tried, it still bit her in the ass.

It was as if Reagan had nowhere to hide. And I felt it too.

❖

I only had about thirty seconds left until I had to meet the rest of the tour to head over to the venue. So, I snorted the very last line I could squeeze out of the eight ball I got before the start of the tour, and then I was pissed when there was nothing left in the bag at the time I really needed it the most. I felt so hopeless that the only thing that I knew would guarantee me just a little break was this powdery concoction.

The line would just be a little encouragement for the evening and would be over by the time we arrived and sound checked. But when I met Miles in the elevator and stepped inside the lobby, I realized that leaving the hotel to get to the bus was a chore in itself. Despite the fact that Reagan used a pseudonym to book hotels, her most fanatical fans still found out the hotel we were staying at and waited for us in the lobby. There was a group of probably twenty, and once they saw Miles and me, their eyes went wide, and their phones snapped out of their pockets and purses, and what started as a brisk walk turned into a sprint as we beelined for the buses. One girl got a nice tug on the back of my shirt, all in the midst of yelling and begging. I almost tripped, but security finally reached us by the time we got to the garage.

And they acted like that just for the openers.

Or Reagan Moore's girlfriend. It was probably that.

As my heart rate calmed down, we got to the venue, and things weren't much different. A group of a hundred something fans and press waited for us to arrive, and I felt like a fish in an aquarium as the fans darted for the bus and pounded on the windows.

"This is fucking crazy," Corbin said as he pulled out his phone. I assumed he was going to notify Finn. He and Reagan were still a few minutes behind us.

"I guess this is what happens when you date the biggest celebrity in the world, right?" Miles said and nudged my arm.

I sank in my seat. Well, there went the rest of that super-short buzz with nothing else to replenish it with. So, I took two extra pregame shots because it was better than nothing.

I decided to use this lively and aggressive Oklahoma City crowd to my advantage. I moved around the stage a little more than other shows, added some extra improved guitar licks to the songs, and jumped on the ledge to entice the audience to push closer to the stage so we could be in one massive heap of crazy. They reached out their hands, I shook some of them and collected some scratches as if a cat clawed me.

They were definitely ready for Reagan Moore that night.

Reagan said that we weren't going to perform our single until the talk about us on the internet died down a little, and I was okay with that. Whatever she needed to gain her security back after that awful breach.

Miles and I drank our way to Wichita while she stayed behind to do her meet and greets—more like I drank my way to Wichita, and Miles tapped out after two beers. Gulp after gulp, I felt the whiskey as it slowly burned its way down my throat, and the discomfort of its potency brought me instant satisfaction. It made my pulse twitch faster, feigning complacency for what was actual discontentment.

A breath from it all.

"Remember in high school when I found that mockup of a yearbook page Brad Politch made with my text messages to him all over?" Miles said as we chilled in his hotel room. I was waiting for Reagan to arrive. Despite what was going on and how rowdy everyone seemed to be, Reagan still insisted to continue the meet and greets after the show. Meanwhile, I lay in Miles's hotel bed, becoming one with the duvet and feeling my head become weightless. "I'm having major flashbacks of that."

I opened my sixth beer, finishing the whole pack I bought before we left for Wichita. "Haven't thought about that scumbag in a while," I said and pulled a large gulp from the bottle.

"I have. He made my life hell. You know how many panic attacks I had when I saw that mockup?"

It was a lot. Brad Politch was the son of Rodger Politch, a big director in the film industry who made many summer blockbusters. That meant he came from tons of money. There was a rumor our freshman year that his bed was stuffed with hundred-dollar bills. Of course, no one believed it, but it became a thing we said whenever we spoke about Brad. He was the first guy Miles ever hooked up with. They made out all the time in the film editing room after school, along with a few hookups here and there. This lasted a whole year, but no one knew about it because those two weren't out. Brad kept insisting he wasn't gay after Miles said that he came out to his family and wanted to date him. Brad got offended by this, got bored in his yearbook class, made a mockup of a yearbook page that had screenshots of all of Miles's texts saying how he came out as bi to his family, telling him he wanted to date Brad, saying he couldn't stop thinking about him, and a few other detailed descriptions of what he wanted to do to him. Brad slipped that mockup in Miles's locker and threatened that if he told anyone about them, he'd print it in the yearbook. For two weeks, Miles kept having panic attacks at school, and I had to pretend to go to the bathroom during my classes to comfort him.

So, one day, I dragged that little asshole out back, slammed him against the brick building, and threatened to break his precious fancy camera his daddy gave him for Christmas if he ever outed Miles. I think that scared him because the page wasn't printed, and anytime Brad saw me in the hallway, his stare flitted in the other direction.

"Too many to count," I answered. "I still get mad when I think about that asshole."

"I get that Reagan's situation is on a way different scale than mine, but the feelings are probably similar, you know? It sucks. More than sucks. I totally feel for her right now. Just wish I could help, that's all."

"Who has nothing better to do than hack people's phones? What do they even get out of it?"

Miles shrugged. "I don't have an answer for you. Brad Politch might know that."

I surveyed my beer that was already halfway done. "I need more. Wanna run out with me?"

Miles laughed. "Blair, you just had a whole six-pack."

"And I have screenshots of a detailed sext conversation all over the internet right now. What's your point?"

"You had six beers in two and a half hours. Plus some whiskey."

"Yeah? And now I need more. There has to be a place somewhere I can grab some." I pulled out my phone to check. "Ah, there's a store two blocks away. Okay, so you want anything?"

"No. I still have the rest of my beers in the fridge."

"Well, drink them. Catch up."

"But you're already wasted. You have your drunk eyes."

"Yeah? I wanna keep it going."

He rolled his eyes and grunted as he got out of bed, grabbing a beer for himself and handing me another one. "Cheers."

By the time Reagan sent me a text that she'd arrived at the hotel, I was eight beers and five shots in and wobbled my way over to her suite. In my defense, I was just following the movements of the earth. That's when I really regretted everything I drank. The sick taste of alcohol hung in my throat, and I could feel all the liquid slushing around in my stomach. A rush of heat consumed my body and gave me this urge to strip off all my clothes to sweat it out. By the time I pounded on the door, I was gagging, and surveying the hallway to find a spot to puke my guts out if Reagan didn't open this door faster. Once it opened, I bolted straight to the bathroom and threw up in the toilet.

"God, Blair!" she said as she walked into the bathroom. I clung to the toilet as if it were a life preserver. I started salivating, and another rush of sweat stuck to my skin. "How much have you had?"

I threw up again and then about three more times. Reagan stayed with me and held my hair back the whole time.

The rest of the night was fuzzy.

❖

No Duet with Midnight Konfusion after Video of Hookup Leaked to Internet.

Reagan Moore Keeps Quiet on the Racy Blair Bennett Texts.

Fans Think Jessie Byrd's New Song "She Knows You're on My Mind" is About Benmoore Romance.

Miles, Corbin, and I listened to that new Jessie Byrd song on our way to St. Louis multiple times to make sure that it was really about me. I only needed to listen to the first verse and bridge of the sensuous, upbeat song to know it was indeed about me.

Did Miles and Corbin need to listen to it five more times? She referenced my sleeve and the lyrics to "Patience, Love," the song I collaborated with Reagan on. I'm pretty sure Jessie Byrd was now out to get me with those threatening lyrics. Knowing what I knew from Reagan, she liked a challenge and a chase, and she seemed so confident that she could win Reagan back. I had no idea why. They'd dated for seven months? Cool. Reagan and I had been flirting nonstop for ten months. Get over yourself, Jessie Byrd.

Even Tony shouted his opinions from the steering wheel and agreed it was about me and referenced all the lines that made him think that. Meanwhile, during the whole hour of debate and analysis over this stupid song, I relieved myself with beer after beer until Corbin cut me off and told me to sleep because I'd had too much. So, I slipped into my bunk, deleted the remaining three Jessie Byrd songs I still had on my Spotify—the ones I really couldn't let go from my purge after the Nashville show—and then passed out.

❖

Since the internet—and now Jessie Byrd—wouldn't shut up, I thought back on that conversation we had after the Grammys, the one where Reagan said her exes never did any romantic gestures. Since I felt bad for throwing up in her toilet and all the crap she had to go through over the last few days, I thought that both of us could use a nice night, so while she met up with Finn to write her public statement, I had our whole hotel room to myself.

And I used it wisely.

If we couldn't go down to the restaurant at the Four Seasons in St. Louis, I'd pull every string to get the restaurant up to us. And all I had to do was say it was for the presidential suite, and bam, they offered everything. A whole three-course dinner of arugula salad, rib eye, and three different sides: French fries, charred broccolini, and polenta, with chocolate cake for dessert. Oh, and we couldn't forget the two bottles of Napa Valley cabernet that the head chef had personally gifted us. The kitchen staff brought up a white tablecloth and some candles, which I didn't even ask for but was beyond grateful for anyway.

And here I just thought my request was going to be a strip steak and French fries.

I tipped them well. I mean, I had to since I hardly worked for this simple request that turned into a five-star restaurant in our own hotel room. As I waited for Reagan to return, I threw on a special outfit that I'd hidden underneath the Egyptian cotton robe—yes, this place had an Egyptian cotton robe. No wonder Grandma insisted on raising me modestly, because touring with Reagan Moore was anything but modest, and these perks were addictive.

Since it took Reagan longer than I expected to write her statement, I broke into one of the bottles because I knew that Reagan would only have a glass or two, and it was practically taunting me. Plus, she wouldn't have known the chef gave us two.

One bottle later, I felt a nice wine drunk. The door creaked open, and the light from the hallway cut through the darkness lit by two flickering flames from the long candles on the table. Reagan's mouth dropped, and for the first time since the Grammys, her eyes softened, and a smile touched her lips. Seeing her smile made my insides flutter.

"Holy crap," Reagan said as she took in the sight of the food in the candlelight. "What…what is this?"

"Dinner for you. Now come sit."

"What? Blair? This is…is that a rib eye?"

I nodded. "Yup. And three sides, a bottle of wine, a salad; oh, and there's chocolate cake in the fridge."

Her eyes lit up. "Chocolate cake? Did you make it?"

"No, but I'm sure this is way better."

"I don't know. That caramel apple pie at Thanksgiving still shows up in my dreams."

"Sit down. Let me pour you some wine. Time to unwind."

I pulled the seat out for her, and she slipped into the chair. I poured us both a nice, liberal glass and then held my glass up for a toast. She followed.

"Remember when you said you were bummed about not going to prom because of the romance?" She blinked a few times before nodding. "Well, I can't give you a prom, and I can't take you out to a nice restaurant because you're a musical genius, and that's your own damn fault, but I can give you the fancy meal way better than you'd ever get at a high school prom and something to hopefully cheer you up. I know how hard this week has been on you, and I know that my walking in drunk last night was the last thing you needed, and I'm really sorry about that. You have every right to be angry, sad, depressed, confused—all the emotions you've been feeling. But you also deserve to be happy and to be treated like a fucking queen because you're an amazing person, and you've made my life so much happier, you've made everyone on this tour happier, and you definitely made all your fans happier for just being you."

Reagan reached across the table to grab my hand and held it tightly. "Blair…that's really sweet. Thank you. I really needed to hear that." Her voice quivered faintly, and she pulled my hand up to kiss it. "This really means a lot to me. This is, like, the nicest thing anyone has ever done for me. You're amazing."

"You deserve it. I know it's a tough time right now, but we'll get through it. You're not going to have to do this alone. I'm here for you, and you have a whole army of people who are here for you. We're not going anywhere. This is all going to pass soon."

"You make this all a little easier," she said, kissing my hand one last time before switching her wine glass for her knife and fork. "I'm so drained from writing that statement with Finn that I don't even want to think about it right now. I just want to enjoy this amazing meal with my super sweet girlfriend. Now, eat your vegetables."

"Can I have a pass?"

"Why?"

"Well, there's another dessert besides chocolate cake, you know. I'm thinking about bringing it out if you allow me to pass on the arugula."

I untied the robe and let it fall to my side. Reagan's eyes widened when she found me in the black lacy teddy I bought back when I dated Alanna but had never used. The lace narrowed down my stomach and to my center, showing off my sides with only a strap wrapped around my waist to hold it all in place. When we were in LA for the Grammys, I figured I might bring it just in case I found the right moment.

Well, the moment was found.

Reagan lowered her utensils without even slicing into her steak. "Holy shit," she muttered.

"So, can I skip that salad?"

Her eyes didn't flinch, but her mouth drooped lower the longer she took in my lingerie. "Um, yeah, wow. You can skip anything you want. Can we pause dinner so I can feel you in that?"

If it weren't for the fact that my stomach had been growling for the past two hours, you better believe Reagan asking to feel me up in my lingerie would prompt me to scoop her up, throw her onto that bed, and have my way with her...or rather, let her have her way with me.

But as much as I really wanted that to happen, I also really wanted those French fries and wine...and maybe to tease her for a bit. Karma for all the teasing she did to me.

"How about we fuel up, and then you can do whatever you want to me?" I said.

"Okay, can you eat your meal like that? Ditch the robe altogether?"

"Sure, if you do the same."

Her grin became crooked as she slipped out of her seat and headed to her suitcase. She peeled off all her clothing, dropped it to the floor, and stood naked as she searched for something. I lowered my utensils.

Seeing her naked was nothing new to me, but she was so beautiful that every time I saw her naked, I lost my train of thought. Nothing else existed except for her and those sexy legs and flat stomach. Oh, and the back muscles. God, how could I forget about those?

She slipped into a red lace bra with matching underwear, both I'd seen at least once before but took on a whole new meaning now that she used it as a ploy to torture and seduce me throughout this whole dinner.

"So, shall we eat?" she asked after she joined me.

I took a large gulp of my wine. "Yes, let's do all the eating."

So, we ate. We downed the whole bottle of wine. She enjoyed me in the teddy while I enjoyed her in her laced bra and underwear. But that only lasted for a few minutes because they did a really good job of disappearing right when we needed them to. Afterward, we blasted eighties music because she said she always did that to make herself feel better. With both of us wine drunk, we listened to all of her favorites. "Nothing's Gonna Stop Us Now" by Starship. I sang the guy's part into the empty bottle of wine. She sang the woman's part into her fist. We jumped on her bed listening to and belting out "The Best" by Tina Turner, and then we slow danced with each other to "Heaven" by Bryan Adams where I got lost in that familiar sparkle of her eyes and her beautiful smile that I missed desperately.

A romantic dinner in, blissful sex, spending an hour listening to her favorite decade of music, and cuddling each other to sleep was the remedy Reagan needed. She smiled the whole night. She laughed. She seemed genuinely happy. It was like I finally got her back, and just for that night, nothing else existed. No hacking. No intruders. No rumors. It was as if we drifted back to all those stolen moments early on in the tour when the world just felt right. When we felt right.

Just us.

❖

Something awful happened right before our Louisville show.

Miles and I discovered that the llama only had enough weed for one more joint.

"Fuck," I said, taking another hit. Great. Awesome. Everything was disappearing. "We're out."

"Seriously?" Miles jolted off the couch and investigated the llama as if to make sure I wasn't telling him an awful joke. "Damn it. You smoke like a chimney, dude."

"It's a stressful time." He gave me a sharp frown, and I raised my hand. "Okay, fine. I'll go find some. I'm sure someone here has stuff."

All I had to do was casually walk around the premises, looking for people smoking out back, and if they vaped, I was one step closer to finding some weed. Miles occasionally smoked a cigarette if he was in the right mindset with a couple of drinks in his system. I wasn't a fan of tobacco. Tried it multiple times, hated the taste and how it lurked on my clothes and made me smell like a stale, filthy, old casino. But these were the sacrifices we had to make. I guess I'd smell like stale, filthy, old casino if that meant I could feel like an inflatable floating on a pool.

I found four guys working the venue, huddled in a circle right outside a backdoor entrance, smoking cigarettes and sharing laughs. I asked them if I could bum one off them, and they happily gave me one and lit it for me, exchanging compliments about our music.

"My girlfriend introduced me to you guys a couple of months ago," the guy who gave me the cigarette said. "I love that song 'Wilted.' So freakin' good. I listened to it nonstop for a week straight."

"The song with Reagan Moore is badass too," the guy who lit my cigarette said. "Not even gonna lie. It's been in my head all night. You guys gonna sing that tonight?"

"Negative," I said and took a disgusting inhale of the tobacco smoke. "Too much attention right now with that phone hacking stuff."

"That's pretty fucked up," the third guy said.

"Tell me about it."

"Man, I was really hoping you guys would sing it," the second guy said.

"I wish we could sing the song for you too. People suck, though."

We chatted for twenty more minutes, when I finally had the courage to ask them if they happened to have any weed. They all turned to the fourth guy, who told me he had some, plus anything else I wanted.

"Well, what do you have?" I asked, feeling like a kid on Christmas Day.

"Almost everything."

It wasn't false advertising. He had everything I needed to replenish my book bag. Weed, Xanax, Ritalin, coke, Molly. My eyes rounded at his supply. All the possibilities to take the edge off and tune out the constant noise and hacking following us around. I bought all five, keeping the fourth guy in business for a few extra weeks. I had to make sure that I had enough stuff to get me to the end of the tour because who knew when I would meet someone as well stocked as this guy?

Since Miles was very against anything that could get him addicted, and I wasn't about to listen to his lecture, I planned to hide the coke from him. Ignorance was bliss, I guessed. But hey, he was much happier when I brought back the weed and even happier to know I also scored some Molly that we'd use at a much later date, preferably if and when we went out to a club.

After smoking the new incredibly strong weed I swear was medicinal grade from Denver, we downed our preshow shots, and then I played around with my newly strung Hummingbird, courtesy of Ethan. I loved the sound of acoustic guitars with fresh strings on them. It was as if they got a haircut and looked so clean and fresh. It was exactly what the guitar sounded like: bold, bright, lively. My nervous plucking was even more enhanced by the killer weed. I felt as if I was sinking into the couch that was really a cloud, and my Hummingbird sounded the best it had ever been, and that thing was forty years old.

We heard a knock on our door. Since both of us seemed glued to the couch, we tossed a pleading stare to the other to open it. I grunted and acquiesced, deciding to be nice for once. When I opened the door, I found a tall security guard looking straight at me, and a rush of paranoia from the strong weed washed through me as I panicked that this was how I was going to be arrested.

"Just the lady I'm looking for," he said and glanced over his shoulder at a man behind him who struggled to make eye contact with me. "I have someone who would like to meet you."

Something about the guy was off. It was as if he was going through an internal battle to look me in the eye. He had to been in his mid to late forties. Dark brown hair with a couple of noticeable gray hairs popping out. Light brown eyes. He wore a VIP lanyard over his black leather coat, which was something I wasn't used to on tour. Most of the

VIPs were kids and teens with their parents or women in their twenties, a very small portion in their thirties. Not grown men who flew solo without a child or a girlfriend.

I offered a friendly smile and a wave, despite still being skeptical. "Hey," I said.

The security guard took a step back and allowed the man to come forward, keeping a cautious eye on him. "Hi. Blair, right?"

Okay, this definitely got weirder the more he lingered. What kind of person dropped a thousand dollars for a Reagan Moore VIP ticket and asked my name for clarification? "Yeah?"

"I, um…" He let out a nervous laugh, and something about his smile seemed familiar. Strangely familiar. The warmth inside me wasn't from the SoCo or the strong weed. It was now laced with actual fear. "I don't know how to introduce myself, so I'm just gonna come out and say it, all right?"

I looked at the security guard, begging him with my eyes that he'd act if this man flinched toward me. We seemed to have an understanding by the way he nodded at me.

"Okay…" I waited.

"My name is Jason Hines. I, um, I'm your dad."

CHAPTER ELEVEN

I wouldn't have believed him if it weren't for that nervous smile he flashed seconds before. I recognized that smile because it was my own. A structured jaw like mine but his was underneath a layer of thin beard. Growing up, everyone said I was a spitting image of my mother. We had the same dark brown hair, the same dark eyes that camouflaged our pupils, and curved, sculpted, thick eyebrows that I once hated but loved now that those were back in style. Mom did say I had some similarities to my dad, but I hated that man so much, I didn't ever care to hear more. He wasn't in the picture, so I never thought he was worth any more of my time other than the phase of wondering why all my friends had a dad in the audience for their recitals, school plays, etc., and I didn't.

"Is this a joke?" I said it more to the security guard then the supposed Jason Hines in front of me. The security guard shrugged as this strange guy fished something out of his wallet.

He then handed me his ID. Sure enough, it said Jason L. Hines on a Kentucky license. Five ten. One hundred and sixty pounds. Oh, he was an organ donor! He was willing to donate his organs to a stranger if he died but never thought about donating his time and father ability to his daughter while he was alive. Cool.

"How did he get back here?" I asked the security guard.

"Because I paid for a VIP ticket," organ donor Jason L. Hines from Kentucky said and showed me the VIP lanyard around his neck as if I couldn't already see it.

I flicked his ID on the ground like a finished cigarette. "Well, if you're really my father, you can fuck off."

"Wait, just…" He snatched his license off the ground and put it back in his wallet. "Just wait."

"Been doing that for twenty-four years. I have nothing to say to you except fuck off." I looked back at the security guard. "Can he please not be back here? He doesn't belong back here."

The security guard grabbed Jason's arm, and he wiggled his way out of his grip. "Wait! Please, wait. I'm sorry. I spent a grand on this ticket just to get back here to talk to you."

"Very charitable. Still not interested."

Right as I closed the door on him, the dude's grimy hands latched on to the door, and he almost risked getting his hand accidentally smashed. Or would it have been an accident? I wouldn't have felt bad at all. I never had full hatred for any person in my life. Not even the girls in my high school's show choir who were mean to me or freaking Brad Politch for all the shit he put my best friend through. I saved all my hatred for my dad. I had so much hate for that man that having to call him my father made me feel as if I chugged a fifth of bottom-shelf vodka, and now I had to violently barf it all up.

"Are you fucking kidding me?" I yelled. "Get out of here!"

"Please, just listen to me—"

"I don't owe you anything. No words. No time. Definitely not money. And not a single more breath of air. You're a piece of shit. I spent twenty-four years thinking you're a piece of shit, and nothing you say or do will ever convince me otherwise."

"Can you give me a second to explain?"

"Explain what? How you left your pregnant girlfriend to raise a child all by herself, and what, now because I have a successful job, you finally decide to be a part of my life? Fuck that."

Jason Hines was a pathetic man for obvious reasons. He was more pathetic because the truth I spoon-fed him made him look like a whimpering puppy. I snapped my attention back at the security guard, whose rounded dark eyes seemed shocked. "Please, get him out of here. Now!"

"Yes, ma'am."

Before the guy could come after me again, I slammed the door shut and pressed in the lock. I turned around and saw Miles with his mouth hanging and his stunned eyes on me. He wasn't sunk into the couch anymore.

"Blair, are you okay?"

I relit that joint, sucked in a deep hit, held it in my lungs only for a short second before I expelled it out in a cough. I hacked for a few moments until I opened my eyes and found Miles still observing me.

I tossed myself on the couch, buried my face in my hands, and sobbed uncontrollably, not caring at all that my eye makeup would streak down my face. Then, I smelled Reagan's perfume and the sage oil clinging to her shirt. I didn't even hear a knock on the door or Miles getting up to answer the door, and just as I processed it, her gentle arms pulled me into her body.

"Hey, Blair, what's going on?" A pause. "You know what happened?"

"Um, yeah, I think her dad suddenly appeared," Miles answered.

I cried so hard that I choked on my own cries. The anger ran through me so potently and quickly that I felt myself losing control of my emotions. I could have punched my fist through the wall, and that was something I never had the urge to do ever in my life.

But then it hit me just as hard as seeing the pathetic excuse for a father standing right in front of me. I could easily let him know what I was thinking—what I'd been thinking my whole twenty-four years. And I had the power to make sure all of Louisville knew how he made me feel. So, I wiped my face, unraveled from Reagan's arms, and stormed out of the green room, hunting down the security guard who was whisking that guy out of my life forever.

No, there was something I needed to tell him.

I found the security guard about to eject him into the main lobby and yelled, "Wait!" Both of them zeroed in on me. "Let him stay."

The security guard frowned. Jason let out a deep sigh. "Thank you—"

"Put him in the press section for our performance."

And then I returned to the green room where Miles and Reagan remained in the same spots. I nestled back into Reagan's arms and buried my face into her chest.

"Blair, what the hell is going on?" Reagan asked, rubbing my hair and holding me close.

I bit my lip for a second to swallow the stutter climbing up my throat. "My dad...he's...um...he bought a VIP ticket."

"God, Blair—"

I pulled away and turned to Miles. "We're doing a cover," I said and dabbed the tears around my eyes. "Or I'm doing a cover."

"We haven't even rehearsed it—" Miles started.

"It's needs to happen." I poured myself a shot of Patrón and savored the burning pain in my throat.

"Blair, maybe you should stop. That's like four shots and three hits of that really strong weed—"

"I'm fine, Miles," I said sharply, even though I knew I wasn't. The weed made me feel as if I was floating like a balloon, but my deadbeat dad showing up was like someone forcing me back on the ground.

"Are you okay?" Reagan said as her fingertips rubbed up and down my arm. "Blair? Please, don't drink or smoke anymore."

I couldn't even look her in the eye. I was so heartbroken and angry and nervous that I didn't feel like a real person. I continued to gaze at the white walls. "I need to be alone right now."

I snatched my Fender off the couch, and then I waited in the darkness of the side stage, resting my head against the wall. I closed my eyes and took deep breaths. I could feel the mixture of the potent weed and the shots mix together into one powerful cocktail in my blood.

When it was time, I floated onto that stage, and thank fucking God I was mellow enough to run through the first four songs of our set. The hardest part about being a singer was performing and pretending that everything was fine, convincing the crowd how awesome they were, and exuding so much lively energy when every part of me felt broken. When I hosted a party, even if I felt as if my insides were crumbling into a massive heap, I couldn't let my guests see that. That was why I canceled all our shows when I knew my grandpa only had a few months left. I had to make them feel as if they were on top of the world when I was stuck at rock bottom, and I knew I wasn't going to be able to do that. And without that strong weed and the shots of alcohol, I didn't know how I was going to show the Louisville crowd a good time when my whole world just shattered.

Then when the time came, Miles ditched the drums and stepped off stage, leaving me out there alone with my piano and the soft white lights above me.

"Hey, Louisville, we're still doing all right?" I said, and I could feel my voice quivering as I placed my mic in the stand. As usual, I got the same eager roars from the arena, mixed in with extra screams that I automatically assumed were from all of the news going on about us. "Awesome. This next song was written by the wonderful Kelly Clarkson. You guys like Kelly Clarkson?" They responded in another thunderous round of applause as I played the first chord on the piano that then trickled into the opening melody. "It's a really good song. Super slow, a little sad, but it's okay if I sing it for you? You guys like sad songs?"

It was a trick question because of course they would cheer for it. I continued to play the opening chords until I choked back the tumor growing in my throat. It was more than a little sad. It was a devastating song, and a song that perfectly fit how I felt about my father in the crowd, standing in a section he wasn't worthy of being in.

Through the tears desperately trying to escape, I performed the song "Piece by Piece," a tearjerker of a song Kelly Clarkson wrote to her deadbeat dad. I related to every single word that comprised it. The audience fell dead silent as I sang Kelly's words about how much of a deadbeat father she had. She wrote about the people who were there for her when her father wasn't. Since I was never going to get a husband, and I didn't have a daughter, I pictured Gramps and Mom and all the wonderful things they did for me. Always encouraging me to dream. Supporting my music. Telling me I was worthy during that phase where I questioned my self-worth because my father didn't want me in his life. Gramps taught me so much. He gave me so much, and it hit me then on that stage that I don't think I ever thanked him for everything he sacrificed for me.

As the song reached the climax, I poured everything I had into the song. I sang the words of how I was going to put my mom first, and I thought of her and how she never got the love she deserved from Jason Hines. I belted the high note an octave higher than the rest of the song, and the silent crowd erupted in loud applause as I sang my heart out, hoping Gramps could hear me, hoping that Jason Hines could see the damage he created. And when I cut the high note off, the stage went silent except for the hammers and strings of the piano, sweeping the arena up in the sound of melancholic melodies, and I ended the song, softly singing the last line.

I sat there for a moment staring at the black and white keys, hearing the crowd roaring. I closed my eyes briefly, swallowed back the tears, and told myself to keep going for the fans, for my grandparents, and most importantly, for myself.

We finished our set list with our two most upbeat and high energy songs to make up for the somberness we'd sent into the crowd. But the second we headed off stage, I collapsed on the couch and sobbed. I didn't even get a minute to myself when Miles crouched down and rubbed my back. He didn't say anything, and I didn't blame him. What was the right thing to say? I didn't even know what I wanted or needed to hear. I think the only thing I knew I needed was someone there for me, and Miles was always there. Had been since we were fourteen. His arm tightened around my shoulders, and his sweaty face and hair rested against my forehead, but it didn't even gross me out like it usually did. His embrace was so comforting, and nothing would make me push that away.

"You're amazing, Blair," he said softly. "And I love you."

He kissed me on the forehead, and that made me cry harder. I buried my face in his shoulder. We sat there in that embrace until I heard the faint patter of Reagan's boots tapping into the room. Miles stopped rubbing my back, and I smelled Reagan and the sage again.

"Babe, come here," she said in such a soft, nurturing way.

As I lifted my head, Miles left the room to give us some privacy, and Reagan slid down to the couch. I wrapped my arms so tightly around her. She squeezed my back, and she let me cry it all out. I only had twenty minutes to do so before she had to go to her hidden stage lift for her first song.

I think the reason I cried so much and hard was because I never really did over the years. Especially over Jason Hines. I remember constantly asking about my dad when I was little, like in kindergarten or elementary school when all my friends talked about their dads, and I started to realize that it wasn't normal to live with your mom and grandparents. What was normal for me was that Father's Day was called Gramps's Day to lessen the blow of my father not being around. But even then, I was more confused than I was heartbroken because I couldn't really be upset over something I never had. But this crying session was holding the suppressed feelings about never having a dad, this awkward strain following Reagan and me around, and missing my mom and my grandparents. All those emotions slipped right out of me, and after our set, I didn't even try to choke them back. I knew I had to let them all out because that weight was getting too heavy for me to carry.

Reagan cupped my cheeks, and her thumbs wiped away the moisture collecting on my face. Her eyes filled up in a thin layer of gloss, looking at me with so much worry.

"For starters, how you got through that set completely amazed me," she said. "You amaze me, and your cover was so powerful and beautiful, and you sang your heart out. You could hear your heart through your voice. Second: if you want him to be removed, let me know so I can do that."

"I don't know what I want anymore." I sniffed and wiped my face.

"Whatever you want, I'll support you. Just let me know what I need to do to make you feel better. Okay?"

During the set, the same question sprouted in my mind every second like a weed: What did he want to say to me? For years, I wanted to know why I didn't have a father. I wondered if he had any regrets, if his heart was seriously as cold as Mom and my grandparents always described it. I wanted to know all the "why" questions, and that piece of shit was the only one who would give me the answers I'd been wondering about my whole life.

"I think I want to know why," I said.

Her eyes widened as if she didn't expect that answer. I guess we were both equally surprised about the truth that came out. "Okay, so does that mean you want me to go get him?"

"I think so."

She hesitated, shifting in her seat as she blinked a few times. "Um, okay, but I'm gonna have to go on stage in, like, ten minutes, so I can't really be here with you."

"I know."

"But I'll be there for you if you want to talk about it after the show. I'm all yours—well, after the VIPs and everything."

I grabbed her hand. She didn't need to explain herself. "I know, babe. Don't worry about me."

"Well, I am worried about you, okay? If you really want to talk to him, I'll go get him. You sure that's what you want?" When I nodded, she kissed my cheek. "Okay, I'll go get him."

The second she left, I went into my bag to grab the extra drugs.

The weed and the alcohol helped, but I wanted something stronger. I wanted something to lift me up, so I took a bump and tossed the small bag way down in a pouch of my book bag, hoping that would get me through this conversation. I closed my eyes when I sat back down and tasted the bitter drip slowly crawling down my throat.

The appearance of two men in the doorway snapped me out of my Zen. The security guard from before escorted Jason Hines into the green room. Jason's eyes were darker than they were before the show, more somber, more reluctant to look me in the eye, and if I did my job correctly, the words I sang to him still haunted him as they continued playing nonstop in his head. Honestly, looking at that man staring at his brown shoes instead of me, I was shocked that he could show any ounce of emotion given the fact he abandoned his pregnant girlfriend and unborn baby, but hey, deadbeat dads had emotions too, I came to find out. I learned something new every day.

"Thank you," I said to the security guard and sat straight up on the couch as the high from the cocaine watered my eyes. "I think we'll be fine for now."

"I'll be right outside if you change your mind," he said.

I gave him a friendly smile, and he shut the door enough to give us privacy but left it cracked open in case he needed to step in. I wiped away the smile and directed my scowl at Jason.

He nervously scratched the back of his head. "So...uh." He whimpered like the coward he was. "You're really talented." His eyes glanced down at me but flinched when our gazes met. I smirked on the inside, knowing that he feared me more than I feared him. I had the power now. "You got a hell of a voice too—"

"I don't fucking care what you think of me, so save the bullshit, okay?" I snapped. He rapidly blinked, took a step back, and his gaze found the floor. "The only reason why you're back here is so you can answer all my 'whys.' Why did you leave my mom? Why didn't you ever try to contact me? Why didn't you try to meet me before? And why the fuck are you here tonight?"

He wiggled into the corner of a chair that I never said he could sit in and scratched the back of his head again, a thing I noticed I did all the time, and I hated that I'd discovered the first habit we shared.

With the cocaine in my system, I had a lot more energy to help spew out all the anger I saved up just in case I ever met him. It made me excited to release some of it. Kind of like going to therapy.

"And how the hell did you even know I was your daughter?" I added.

"Because I knew your grandpa. I saw that he passed a few months back, and the obituary mentioned your name and your mom's, said that you were also a musician. So, I looked you up and saw that you're on tour with Reagan Moore. And a few other gossipy things." I rolled my eyes at that last part. It made me cringe knowing that Jason Hines might or might not have read my text messages with Reagan. "And then I saw you were coming to Louisville, so I told myself that this was maybe a sign or something that I should at least try to meet you."

"Why? Because I'm on tour with Reagan Moore? Because you think I have money now?"

He frowned as if what I said was ludicrous. "No, that's not it at all—"

"Because if you came here asking for money, I wouldn't give a penny to you."

He raised his hand. "I don't want your money," he said sternly. "It's not why I'm here."

"Then why are you? What makes you think I ever wanted to meet you?"

He nervously chuckled. "I, um, I don't know. I guessed I just assumed—"

"Well, you assumed wrong. I never wanted to meet you. I had everything I needed with my amazing mom, who you abandoned, and my amazing grandparents. My life was completely fine without you."

Except that it wasn't anymore. It was in shambles. I had no grip on my life, clearly. But he didn't need to know that.

He finally looked up at me. "I'm sorry. I really am." He caught me rolling my eyes and then continued more firmly, "I know that sounds lame, all right? I know, and it doesn't do any justice by just saying 'I'm sorry,' but I don't know what else to say. I was twenty years old. I never wanted kids. Hell, I was still a kid and didn't even know what the hell I wanted to do for the rest of my life. All I wanted to do was drink, do drugs, sleep with women, and repeat. Your mother and I, we only dated for a few months, and that was even too much for me at the time. When

I found out she was pregnant, I freaked out. I could barely take care of myself. How was I going to take care of two other people?"

It wasn't until then that he had my full attention. My chest constricted when I heard that sentence. It was the exact same thing I told Alanna when I broke up with her. I couldn't take care of myself. How the hell could I be in a relationship? Hell, I was dating Reagan, and every day, I felt as if I was losing more of her, and I had no idea if it was because of me just sucking at being in relationships or if it was because we were trying so hard to protect ourselves from the public after the hacking.

I hated so much that there was something I could relate with him over. The smile and the nervous head scratching were more than enough, but the logic? I had the same logic as child-abandoner Jason Hines?

"You never even tried to reach out," I said. "You weren't at all curious?"

"Of course, I was curious, but if I reached out, I would have had to have been responsible for something I shouldn't have been responsible for. I was a mess. No child should be stuck with a mess. And you know what, a part of me is really glad I wasn't involved. And before you lash out at me for saying that, let me explain why."

It was a smart move to add that disclaimer because I had a whole arsenal of insults that were ready to fire after he said he didn't regret abandoning me.

"I had a father who shouldn't have been a father," he explained softly. "He was awful. Negligent. A drunk. He was also a father who didn't *want* to be a father, and I spent my whole childhood striving for his attention and his approval, and I got nothing in return. Well, the apple really didn't fall far from the tree because when I was twenty, I was a drunk with no ambition or life, only caring about myself. I got this girl pregnant who I hardly knew, and I imagined what my life would be like if I stuck around, if I stayed with your mom to raise you during the worst years of my life. I don't think you would have turned out as successful as you are now, and when I heard how well you were doing—on a world tour with my niece's favorite singer—as much as it sucked and as much as I knew it must have hurt you never knowing your father, I knew it was the right thing. And that's what I wanted to say to you. I saved up a bunch of money to get back here to tell you this: my side of the story and how sorry I am about the pain I caused you. You have every right to hate me. I get it. I hate my father too, and there are things I'll never forgive him for."

That arsenal I had in my brain was depleted. I just sat there, staring at his scruffy beard, caramel eyes, and instead of thinking of something to say to him along the lines of "fuck off," I continued searching for resemblance. I think I had his nose, his flat, narrow nose with narrow nostrils.

My eyes fell back down on the glass of SoCo in front of me. "Do you want a glass?" I offered.

"No, that's fine. I don't drink anymore."

I raised an eyebrow. "You don't drink?"

"No. Went in and out of rehab a few times. Been clean for about seven years."

"Oh, okay," I said and pounded the whole glass back for myself. *More for me then.*

"You know, it's hereditary. My father was an alcoholic; my grandpa was one. I don't know about your mother's family, but—"

"What makes you think I'm anything like you?"

"I see it in your eyes. They're drained and glassy. I don't think that's only from alcohol. Your fingers haven't stopped tapping your leg, either."

I noticed what he was talking about. I was completely unaware that I was doing it, and the fact that he noticed and had the nerve to call me out on it made me want to punch that scruffy beard off him.

"You have a lot of fucking nerve coming back here and calling someone out on the things they may or may not do—"

He raised his hands to surrender. "I, I didn't mean it that way. I just know from experience—"

"If it really bothers you, maybe you shouldn't have abandoned me. Just because my life was fine without you doesn't mean it didn't mentally fuck me up. So, go pride yourself on that and get the hell out of my room."

He sat there for a moment before reaching into his wallet to pull out a business card. "Listen, I know this is a lot, and—"

"Did you seriously not hear me? I said get the fuck out!"

"I just wanted to say—"

I jumped up on my feet, and when I did, the pathetic excuse of a man cowered, holding his hands up again. "Okay, okay."

He placed his white business card on the table.

"Here's my card in case you ever want to reach out again—"

I gripped one of the shot glasses with my fidgety hands, raised it high in the air, and once Jason Hines computed that I was clenching a shot glass and aiming it at him, he beelined it to the door as I chucked the glass at the opposite wall. My heart rate pulsated through my neck. My vision zoomed out of the room like a camera lens. He was gone by the time I focused on the tiny brittle pieces all over the ground. It looked like a little collection of sparkling ice. I guess ruining things was the only control I had left because every other aspect of my life was far out of reach.

I took another bump of coke and pounded back another shot until I finally felt one hundred percent numb to it all.

CHAPTER TWELVE

The four days that followed in between our Louisville show and our Chicago show passed in an unmemorable blur. We'd had shows in Grand Rapids and Indianapolis, but I didn't remember them when I first woke up in my Chicago hotel room.

Last time I went on a bender was when I found out Gramps had stage 4 liver cancer. It happened over the span of four days. I was with three girlfriends I only turned to when I wanted to drink and party…so I guess they weren't necessarily friends, more like three friendly drug connections. We did a lot of coke, Molly at night when we made it to the clubs, and when we went to our favorite lesbian bar, the bartender hooked us up with some free shots. And then we danced for hours, stayed up to at least seven a.m., crashed at one of the girls' apartments, slept in until five, woke up doing more lines, and then repeated. Alanna had a key to my apartment, waited for me to come home the whole weekend, but I was too obliterated and preoccupied to call her back after the numerous missed phone calls. And when I finally returned home four days later, she screamed at me, sobbed, asked me if I did drugs, and I said no, but I knew she was smart enough to know I was lying. And then I collapsed in my bed and sobbed, feeling awful for scaring her the way I did, feeling awful because I got screamed at, feeling awful for what I did to my body, feeling awful about hearing that Gramps got his death sentence, and feeling awful from the withdrawal.

I had no idea why Alanna didn't break up with me then. I never gave her credit for all the shit she dealt with.

Flash-forward a year, I was back at it again. I sort of just woke up in a hotel room, hearing the honking from cars outside. The sun burned my eyes, and I had no idea why the blinds were open when they could have easily been shut. I tossed a pillow over my face, trying to ignore the awful morning sun, while a pulsating pain throbbed in my head. The front, my temples, behind my eyes, the top of my head. Every part of my head hurt.

"Blair?"

I slowly removed the pillow and squinted to find Reagan getting up off the couch on the other side of the suite. She walked over to me in her pj's with her hair in a loose messy bun, the sign she hadn't yet showered.

I wanted to ask her where we were. I had a few memories of the last four days, so slowly but surely, the memories of playing in Grand Rapids and Indianapolis resurfaced. Barely, though.

"Hmm?" I moaned.

"Are you feeling okay?"

As I sat up, the headache grew worse. It felt as if it was ready to implode. "Fuck," I muttered and held my head between my hands, falling back down to the pillows. "Are we in Chicago?"

My question pulled her eyebrows closer together. "Seriously?"

I hesitated. Crap, she was mad now. "No?"

"You had that much to drink last night?"

"No?"

"You puked again. On my bus."

I closed my eyes and felt her glare zeroing in on me. *This is bad. God, this is so bad.*

"I'm sorry, Reagan—"

"Miles, Ethan, and Charles had to drag you up here because you were so incoherent."

"I'm sorry—"

"And were you really that drunk when you were performing? Because you were acting like it."

I opened my eyes again. This knowledge had my heart racing. "How was I acting?"

"You seriously don't remember?"

I pinched the bridge of my nose. "Can you just save the lecture right now and tell me?"

"Slurring your words anytime you spoke to the audience. You

kicked a speaker after you jumped on it. I don't care if everyone was cheering for you. You know the average age of the girls in the audience?"

"We're adults. They know we drink."

"You don't drink on the job, Blair! Oh my God!" She threw her hands in the air and let them land on her head. She got off the bed and paced around a little bit before snapping her scowl back at me. "My reputation is already on the line with this hacking. The last thing I need right now is for my opener to go out there wasted with a bunch of middle and high schoolers." She paused as she gave me a quizzical look. "Have you been sober at all since Louisville?"

The answer was no, but I still looked at the ceiling and thought about it anyway to lessen the blow.

"Wow," she said. "Just wow."

"You never had a problem with my drinking or smoking before."

"That's because it didn't knock you out for four days. You were still able to perform without kicking a goddamn speaker."

"My piece of shit father just showed up in my life. I think I'm allowed to be a little upset."

"Yeah? And my whole phone is out there for everyone to read, but I wasn't incoherent for days. Blair, there was nothing behind your eyes. They were blank. You know how scary that is?"

"I'm sorry."

"Yeah, you really sound like it," she said sarcastically.

I rolled out of bed. I wasn't going to stay in the room to listen to her criticize me. I slipped my shoes on and snatched my phone from the nightstand.

"You know what, I'm gonna leave," I said. "My head hurts way too much to hear you criticize me."

"Yeah, and where are you gonna go?"

"Somewhere that doesn't make me feel like I'm stuck in a prison."

"Um, excuse me?"

I faced her and noticed her eyes blazing with fury. That once beautiful smile that instantly drew me to her was on the other side of the planet because what was in its place was a look I'd never seen on her before. I probably should have apologized or stopped talking right there, but the aching in my head and all throughout my body didn't really help the anger that still remained in me.

"We hide in a hotel room or a bus every night," I said. "Now I can't even drink, apparently—"

"Did you just refer to me as a prison?"

Wait, did I say that, rational me said. But the rational me wasn't in control of my speaking ability at the moment. Hungover me was in charge, and she was irritable and mean.

"I did because we can't do anything—"

"Because that's what happens when you're in this industry, Blair. That's what happens when your phone gets hacked, and text messages and pictures and videos of your personal life are on the front page of gossip magazines for people to talk about at fucking happy hour. Now, if it feels like you're trapped in a prison, by all means, let me snip you free."

"You used to be fun."

"Yeah? You used to be sober."

I rolled my eyes. "Okay, Alanna."

"Alanna?" She belted out a mirthless cackle. "Okay, glad to know you're not just this way with me. If you feel like you're in a prison because I'm upset that you've been intoxicated for four straight days, performed on my tour completely drunk, and made a fool out of yourself, maybe you need to go find someone else."

"Or I need to find someone who can take risks instead of hiding all the fucking time."

"Wow! So, I'm boring because I'm aware that my actions have consequences?"

I shouldn't have said that.

"No—"

She took a step forward and pointed a sturdy finger. "I'm boring because I know that I have little girls looking up to me, and I want to be a good role model for them?"

"Well—"

"I'm boring because I don't want to get shitfaced every night like you've been doing this whole week? Hell, this whole tour? I'm boring because I value my privacy and the close relationships that I have with the very few people I trust? I'm boring because I don't want people intruding on that?"

"No—"

"I took a risk falling for you, my opening act. I took a risk falling for a girl who I knew had the power to completely destroy me because she doesn't like relationships. I took a risk collaborating with someone who I was hooking up with, knowing full well that if it didn't work out, I would forever be tied to that song and that person for the rest of my career. If all of that isn't good enough for you, then leave me, and go find someone else worthier of your time."

"Reagan, I didn't mean it the way it sounded."

"Great. You can sleep with Miles tonight or get your own room."

"Seriously?"

America's Sweetheart really knew how to cut you with her glare. "Does it look like I'm joking?"

I'd never seen her look more serious. Her beautiful warm eyes now darkened with a rage burning inside them.

I raised my hands to surrender. "Fine, I'll leave."

"Good. Bye."

I grabbed my book bag off the ground and stormed out of that room. Having nowhere else to go, I texted Miles to find out what room he was staying in. I waited. Five minutes. Ten minutes. I wandered around the lobby and had to ask the front desk where the buses were, and when they escorted me to the sectioned off underground garage, I also had to text Tony to see if he could give me the keys so I could bunk up. But just like Miles, he didn't respond as fast as I wanted him to.

So, I slid down the concrete wall, hiding behind the buses so I could cry. I wanted to call my mom and tell her what happened in Louisville, but there was only one bar of service in the garage, and I had no energy to aimlessly wander around the hotel again looking for a private spot to cry to her on the phone. I also had no energy to tell my mom that the man who abandoned her twenty-four years ago just popped up from the pits of hell.

A half hour later, Miles finally responded and told me his room. When he let me in, I found him shirtless, in his flannel pj pants, his hair disheveled in every single direction, and Ethan in his bed. My eyes widened at the sight.

"Hey, you're alive," he said, a neutral expression thinning his lips. I recognized the disappointment in his tone.

"Do you think we can talk for a little bit? Privately?"

❖

Admitting to my best friend that I didn't remember the past four days was completely embarrassing. I hated it, and I hated it even more that all this worry detailed his face as I cried. I didn't admit to the coke, and maybe he was a little confused as only a few memories slowly rushed back the more we talked about what happened. I remembered sleeping a lot, and then when I woke up, I started drinking and doing lines of coke. I had a few more shots than I usually did in Grand Rapids, but I remembered that show and the crowd and how a fan in the front row held up a sign, proposing to me, and after our third song, I accepted. Then after the show, I drank, did more lines, and couldn't remember the rest. And Indianapolis got really hazy the second I stepped onto the stage. Miles said he didn't realize how drunk I was until the middle of our set when I hopped off a speaker and kicked it while wailing on my Fender. I was so glad I didn't remember Finn and Corbin lecturing me about my drinking habits once we finished our set. But knowing that it was bad enough for Reagan's manager and our manager to band together to confront me really put things into perspective.

But what really got to me was when Miles said that, despite all of that, Reagan insisted I stay on her bus and her hotel room.

"She took care of you the whole time," Miles said. "You don't remember any of that?"

If I had, would I have still made that awful comment to her? As if guilt didn't already weigh me down. "No, I don't," I muttered.

"You've got quite the girlfriend. Even after you puked on her bus and kicked one of her speakers."

"That's the thing. I don't know if she's my girlfriend anymore."

"What are you talking about?"

I filled him in, wincing when I had to tell him that idiotic prison comment, and he called me a moron, which I rightfully deserved. I told him I'd have to talk to Corbin about getting my own hotel room in Milwaukee, and he said since I was with Reagan, he'd been inviting Ethan to spend time on the bus in between trips. And I was glad he finally found a tour hookup even if mine was falling apart.

Reagan avoided our green room like the plague at the Chicago venue. Our paths crossed once when we finished sound checking, and she was on her way to the stage. Our eyes locked for a brief moment, and then both of us darted away, not saying a word.

"Apologize to her," Miles said once we grabbed a plate of food and hid out in the green room.

"I will. When she hates me less."

"The more you wait—"

"I know, Miles. Just…I need some time."

I only opted for one shot before the show to help loosen the stress coiling inside me. But as I watched Miles take his second before grabbing his drumsticks so we could stand at the side stage, my skin wouldn't stop itching. When was the last time I only had one shot? The more I thought about it, the more I wanted it. The thought of it took over my mind, and it was the only thing I could focus on. The urge to drink another was so powerful, I broke out in beads of sweat, forcing me to clutch my Fender's neck to fight against it. I felt like if I didn't give my mind and body the temporary elixir it begged for, it would be like leaving a snake bite untreated. The craving was such a virulent force that it made me uncomfortable in my own skin.

Here I was, standing in front of twenty-three thousand people in Chicago, and my mind was programmed to think about drinking instead of soaking up the scene of thousands upon thousands of people staring up at me, swaying to the beat of the song. That didn't matter anymore. Having a drink mattered.

The more I told myself to stay away from it, the more my skin crawled with the need to have it. Taming the angel gave fuel to the devil inside me. Drinking was also second nature. Preshow shots were a thing ever since we started performing in high school. Drinking after the show. Drinking at dinner. Drinking on the bus to pass the time traveling. Every night, I'd start drinking around five after we sound checked, then I had shots and continued drinking after our set until I passed out. Then repeated. And since the hacking? Well, I kept the local liquor stores in business, that was for sure.

After the show, I took a minute to collect myself in the green room, alternating between closing my eyes to resist the urge and then opening my eyes to see the bottles of Patrón and SoCo. Miles gave me the hint that he was going to fool around with Ethan for a bit in our bus, so I gave him space by staying in that green room, door closed, looking my demon square in the eye, challenging it.

Then I remembered what I had in my book bag. Weed, cocaine, Ritalin, Xanax, and Molly. For the next five minutes, I told myself to ignore the book bag. Ignore the bottles. I used my pointer finger to dig half moons all up and down my thumb, hoping the pain and studying what resembled a path of footprints on the top of my thumb would distract me from the stifling thoughts.

I couldn't go on the bus because Miles was getting some, and I couldn't go to Reagan because we weren't talking. God, we weren't talking. She hated me. The woman I cared so much for couldn't even look at me.

I broke.

The white powder flew up the rolled-up dollar bill and into my nose. I sank into the couch until my head rested against the back, feeling the cocaine drip down my throat and the warmth flow down my arms and legs. I loved how the drug promised euphoria for the next half hour or so. It was short but blissful, and I loved it when my limbs started tingling. The powder chomped away at the sadness like a game of *Pac-Man* in my bloodstream. Having those toxins in me brought the clarity I was desperate for, shutting out all those cacophonic voices and bringing me peace and silence. It reminded me of my pool hopping days when I loved sitting at the bottom of the pool so I didn't hear anything. It felt like I immersed myself in another world for just a moment. A world of silence. Fucking goddamn silence from my own thoughts.

For the next hour and a half while Reagan performed, and Miles and Ethan used that time wisely until Ethan was scheduled to work right after the show ended, I played with my Hummingbird, did a line, played again, did another line. It killed the time, and hey, I wrote a new song about being sexiled.

And then there was a knock on the door. I shot straight up and glanced down at a rolled-up dollar bill, my ID, and the rest of the eight ball on the coffee table. The doorknob twisted, and as I processed that I needed to discard all the evidence, there was Reagan, her face shimmering from sweat, fresh off the stage and slightly out of breath.

"Hey, Blair? Can we talk for a second—" She observed me and then looked down at the coffee table, staring straight at the evidence, and once that happened, her mouth dropped. "What the hell is—"

"Get out!" I yelled as a reflex.

"What are you…what's that—"

I jumped up and stood in front of the table to hide the evidence. "I said, get out!"

She glanced over my shoulder. "Is that…is that—"

"Reagan, Jesus Christ, get out! You can't just barge in like—"

Ignoring my demands, she lurched closer, but I stopped her with my hands on her shoulders and held her in place. I should have known better than to resist because that just made her body fight me to catch a glimpse of what was behind me. All of that yoga she did every morning paid off. She shifted me to the side to get a better view.

Her eyes flicked back to me, and I could see the anger brewing.

"Are you serious?" she yelled.

Still hyped up on the last bump, it didn't really take much for me to fire back. "I told you to get out—"

"Is that coke?"

"Reagan, seriously le—"

"You're doing fucking cocaine?" She lunged forward to inspect me. "Great. Your pupils are dilated."

"For the millionth time, you need to go—"

"You realize there are fans coming back here, right? Or do you not care about that?"

"Of course, I care—"

"How long have you been doing this?"

"It's not really any of your—"

She pointed a steady finger at me. "Don't you *dare* finish that sentence."

I threw my hands up in the air since that felt like the only defense I had. "You can't just come barging in people's rooms!"

"Seriously, Blair? That's your argument? Are you going to answer anything I asked, or are you gonna continue to yell at me to leave?"

"It's really not that big a deal."

Her eyebrows rose. "Um, what?"

"It's not that big a deal," I repeated slower.

"You know, I wasn't really into you guys pounding back shots and smoking weed before you went on stage, but I bit my tongue. Because you managed to kill it every night. But this? No, not after you can't even remember the last four days and played the Indianapolis show completely plastered. No, this isn't okay at all."

"Reagan, can you please—"

"I'm not gonna have someone high on coke opening for me. That backfires on *me*. That affects *my* reputation just as much as it affects yours. Did you even think of that?" She waited for me to answer, but I had nothing. I was fucking miserable and depressed, and I needed an upper to help me get through the night. That was all I was focused on. "Of course you didn't," she finished.

Miles appeared in the doorway with a smirk, like a nice hour and a half lay session should do to a person. But once he saw me, his grin washed away.

"What?" he said. "What's going on?"

"You know she's doing coke right now?" Reagan said, pointing at me as if he had no idea who I was.

"Say it a little louder please," I said.

Miles checked out the coffee table. Just like Reagan, a frown contorted his face. "Blair, what the hell?"

"Really? So, you didn't know about this? You're not doing this with her?"

"God, no!"

"Cool. So, she's high right now, just so you know. Right before a bunch of fans are about to come back here."

"Oh my God, it wears off in, like, a half hour."

Reagan stepped around me and lunged toward the table. "No. You're not doing this." She snatched the eight ball.

"Don't you dare—"

That was when she looked me straight in the eye and then opened the bag to pour the rest of the cocaine on the ground. Then she snatched the SoCo bottle and poured at least three shots' worth over the powder. All I could do was watch the contents dissolve into the brown liquor on the dirty wooden floor.

"Are you fucking crazy?" I howled and yanked the bottle out of her hands. I was so infuriated, I could feel it piling in my chest.

She dug her boots into the puddle and wiped her feet on the mess as if it was a front doormat. I could feel the weight of pure anger building up in my hands, strong enough for me to want to chuck another shot glass across the room. All the money I spent, all the things I needed to numb the feelings itching at my skin like an army of bedbugs, completely wasted in absolute filth.

"What the fuck, Reagan! What the actual fuck?"

I kicked my boots through the mess, and the concoction splattered up her bare legs. She observed it in utter disgust, as if I spat on her.

"What the hell? Stop it, Blair!" Miles shouted while pulling my arm to prevent another splash.

"She just wasted all of it."

"Good!" she shouted. "Now I don't have to worry about you drinking it like a cat."

"Yeah, because that's something I would have done—"

"Yeah, it probably would have been since you don't seem to give a shit about anything or anyone right now." She tossed a glance at Miles over my shoulder. "She does coke, she's off the tour. Plain and simple." She gave me the nastiest look I'd ever seen on her. Reagan Moore, with her beautiful smile that first reeled me in, the smile all over the magazines and billboards, America's Sweetheart. I guess I'd chased that Reagan Moore away. "You have until Milwaukee to decide what your priority is. In the meantime, I'm fucking done with you, you understand me? One hundred percent done with you."

Just as the burning sensation started in my chest, she swept past me, and I caught the scent of her wonderful perfume that used to comfort me in bed now reminding me of everything I just lost.

And then there was silence. My body felt as if it was filled with cement instead of contaminated blood. The puddle of SoCoke taunted me, splatters scattered across the floor and coffee table. I could feel Miles's burning glare on the side of my face, and when I turned to him, he appeared as disgusted as Reagan. And then I glanced at the white wall behind him, and my limbs felt so clogged with crap that I just wanted to ram my fist through the drywall to get it all out. I had no control over my body. Forget the drugs, the rage that brewed inside me from all these months was more cogent than anything I'd taken in my life. Instead of the wall, I repeatedly punched the couch as dust billowed in the air. A punch for my grandma dying, a punch for Gramps dying, three punches for my fucking deadbeat dad crawling out of the pits of hell, two punches for Reagan's fame sucking up the last bit of passion and romance from our relationship, another punch for the stress relievers Reagan turned into filth and probably a flesh-eating bacteria, and five punches for Reagan being one hundred percent done with me.

As I wound up for another punch, Miles caught my wrist and brought it down to our sides. He spun me around, and that detailed scowl never flinched from his face.

"What has gotten into you, huh?"

I fought to break free. "Nothing."

He let me go, and I tossed myself on the couch, burying my face into my hands. "You better hope to God that Reagan doesn't kick us off this tour, or you're going to lose way more than just your girlfriend."

"Miles, I'm—"

He raised his hand. "Apparently, you have until the morning to decide *both* our fates. So think really hard about that."

And he walked out the door.

CHAPTER THIRTEEN

The drive from Chicago to Milwaukee was so quiet and lonely. Miles's and Corbin's snoring seeped through the white noise machine and past my foam earplugs, but I reached the point of not caring about it anymore. I was more focused on Reagan screaming at me on repeat.

God, did I want to text her how sorry I was, but I was so goddamn pissed at her. For everything. Not just the SoCoke, but for letting the amazing thing we had months ago just fade away. How quickly she discarded me rather than encouraging me to get better because she believed in me and the good person I had living deep down inside.

She didn't even try.

Needless to say, I hardly got any sleep, and that coke Reagan destroyed would have been very beneficial for me in order to stay awake. When the sun invaded the windows, I heard Miles and Corbin on the other side of my curtain, going about their day, chatting in the back room with the door closed. I couldn't make out their muffled words, but I knew they were probably about me and the looming decision I'd have to make once we arrived at the Milwaukee venue.

I forced myself to sleep to waste time until we got there, and I woke up to Corbin yelling at me to get up so we could go to Reagan's bus for an emergency meeting. Aka *the* meeting.

Her bus door was open, and when I stepped in, I found Finn, Reagan, Miles, and Corbin sitting on the couch, waiting for me. I had flashbacks to the very first time I came on her bus with a bottle of rosé and lemon bars in exchange for her noise machine. All the nights we shared on the bus and in her room still lingered in the air, but even those seemed so distant. Reagan had her legs crossed, baggy sweatshirt keeping her warm when it should have been my arms, hair messy in a bun from probably a restless night's sleep when it should have been from my hands, and her eyes drifted to the floor when they should have sparkled at mine.

"Have a seat, Blair," Finn said so professionally that his tone nauseated me.

The great thing about this tour was that we all passed on the professional formalities and acted like a bunch of young people who didn't have to work in an office, dress in business casual, or work nine to five. But now, everyone sat up straight—except for Reagan, the boss of everyone—and formally invited me to sit down. And once I did, Finn clasped his hands together, and I already hated so much where this was going.

I took a cautious seat across from everyone, only resting half my butt against the kitchenette counter. My stare went right to Reagan. A smile didn't brighten her face. It hurt so much seeing the shell of her, knowing it was my fault for making her so upset and angry.

Please, look at me, I tried to tell her telepathically. Please, look at me. I'm so sorry.

"Okay," Finn said and exhaled. "Let's talk about what happened last night. Blair, how about you give your account first?"

A burning sensation swallowed my whole body just knowing how angry I made everyone. Finn, Corbin, and Miles waited for my pathetic excuse with dull looks. I felt awful. Seriously. I felt as if I'd been shredded like a useless document and had taken innocent people with me.

"I don't know what you guys want me to say," I said as I gripped the counter. With two of the most important people in my life refusing to acknowledge my existence, it was hard to find words. Their silence squeezed everything out of me, and I was only left a shell of meaningless words. "I'm sorry I disappointed everyone."

Reagan shook her head, and her soft grunt informed me about the eye roll she just made.

"How many times has this happened?" Corbin said.

"In life or on tour?"

I meant it as an honest question, not trying to be combative. But the three guys' shocked expressions told me they didn't at all take it that way.

"I meant on tour, but we might as well find out now how many times you've done it in general."

"It's not as bad as it looks, all right? I'm going through a rough time."

"Yeah, well, not to diminish what you're going through, but we all go through rough patches, and I don't think anyone has turned to self-destructive behavior like you have." Finn turned to Reagan. "Reagan, how about you talk now?"

"I've already said everything I needed to," she muttered to the floor.

"You have nothing to add?"

She lifted her head and tucked a strand of hair behind her ear, still refusing to make eye contact with me. "Nothing," she said, quickly glancing at Finn and then back to her lap.

"Okay, Miles?"

"I had no idea. About last night or the other times."

"Okay…well…then, Blair." Finn faced me again. "If this is the lifestyle you're going to choose to live, we can't have you join us. Reagan has a clean brand, and your doing drugs is a major liability. Imagine if it gets to the press that a hotel cleaning lady found cocaine in your hotel room or if a venue worker found it, or the VIP fans found out; it would be front-page news, and it would drag Reagan right through the mud. Is that what you want?"

"No."

"And if you guys are sharing a room now, can you see how this is headline news? Cocaine found in Reagan Moore's hotel room?"

"We're *not* sharing a room anymore," Reagan clarified as her head snapped back up. "So, that won't be happening."

Finn paused as if taking in another round of details of his client's personal life. "Okay…we'll go back to getting Blair her own room, then. That is if she decides to stay with us."

This was the lamest intervention. Miles did ecstasy in Honolulu, and it was also his idea to do 'shrooms in Amsterdam. What about all the times the two of us did Molly when we went to clubs? He was pretty excited when I got the new stash from the guy in Louisville. Where was his intervention?

"I'm not gonna do it again," I said, though I really didn't even do a good job convincing myself of that.

"You sound like this is a huge inconvenience for you," Corbin said.

"I think we're being a little dramatic about this, yes."

"Oh my God, I can't do this anymore," Reagan said loudly. I once thought that her eyes were so soft that they didn't have the capability of hurting anyone, but I was wrong. They pierced right through me and caused a burn to rumble through my gut, making me want to scurry out of the stuffy bus to avoid her. "You have no remorse, do you? About anything?"

"Jesus fucking Christ, Blair," Miles said, eyes on me too. "What the hell are you doing?"

"You did ex in Hawaii, 'shrooms in Amsterdam, and you always want Molly when we go to the clubs, yet *I'm* the one getting in trouble?"

"I didn't do them on someone else's tour!" Miles yelled, and he hardly ever yelled. The vein popped out in the middle of his forehead. It took me aback for a second. "I didn't do them before we performed, and I also never performed shitfaced and kicked a speaker in front of twenty thousand people."

"Yeah, because smoking the world's strongest weed is much better. This whole thing is all because Reagan's mad at me from a few days ago. We had an argument, so we might as well blow up the next mistake I do to kick me off the tour. Is that what it is?"

Reagan crossed her arms. "You're really something right now."

"If we were still together, we wouldn't be having this talk. You and I could have easily had a civil conversation without getting Finn and Corbin in on this too. But you didn't want something civilized. You wanted to be angry at me."

"You have a lot of nerve saying all of this right now," Miles muttered through his tight jaw.

"It's the truth! We all know it!" I faced the two managers, who continued giving me this look as if I was crazy and would never climb out of the trench I dug myself. "Finn, I understand your concerns. I really do. And I'm really sorry it happened last night. I never meant to put Reagan's reputation and Miles's reputation in jeopardy. That's the last thing I ever want to do. I'm going through a rough time right now."

"There are twelve shows left," Finn said. "You need to decide what you want to do. Stay off drugs or get off the tour. Only you can make that decision."

"Aka fuck up again, you're off this tour," Reagan said when she got off the couch. "And I think that's a pretty generous offer given the fact that all I want to do is fight."

She stormed into her room and slammed the door.

❖

Fuck up again, you're off this tour.

The anger in her voice kept playing in my head over and over again.

It started out as anger inside me, and then it simmered as I reminisced about the days she explored my eyes in depth. The days when both of us found every excuse in the book to be around each other.

Now, she avoided me. She didn't come out of her green room. I opened for her, got the crowd ready to see her, asked all those fans if they were ready for her show, only for us to stray to parallel paths. All those fans got to see her. I was on her tour and didn't get the chance.

I felt so empty.

It took two shows after our meeting in Milwaukee for me to realize what I had to do. Five days had passed. Reagan went out of her way to make sure our paths didn't cross. Miles only spoke to me when we had to get ready for our performance, but I'm sure he would have joined Reagan if we weren't in the same band. Corbin spoke to me cordially, even though I knew that was the last thing he wanted to do. It was hard to exist in close quarters when everyone around me refused to acknowledge my existence. I couldn't finish the rest of the tour like this. I hated the person I had become just as much as everyone else disliked me at the moment. I hated that I lost my best friend and my girlfriend. Touring with everyone ignoring me and looking at me as if I was a disgusting person ruining the fun vibes was something I needed to remove myself from. Ten shows and three weeks left might not seem like a lot, but to someone who was the elephant in the room, it was a lifetime.

On our way to Minneapolis, the humming of the tires speeding down the highway was the only sound in the bus. Miles and Corbin had their bunks draped shut. I had my curtain shut because I didn't want to look at the wall those two put up. The truth of what was best for me churned nerves and anxiety in my stomach. The hardest part was finalizing what I knew was the right thing. I knew I couldn't do another show on this tour. I needed time to pull away, to view myself and my life from an outside perspective. I needed to properly mourn the loss of my grandfather instead of finding distractions to rid myself of the feelings. The thing with grief is that I had to go through it, and if I tried avoiding it, it would follow me around with a vengeance.

I pushed my bunk curtain aside and stared at Miles's and Corbin's. "Guys?" They didn't respond. I couldn't tell if it was because of the silent treatment, or because they both had headphones in. "Guys, answer me."

Both of them pulled back their curtains and took out their headphones. "What?" Corbin said. Miles just glared at me with one headphone remaining in his ear.

"So, I've been doing some thinking," I said, looking somewhere else than their eyes because the frowns hurt me too much to look at. "We should drop out of the tour."

"What?" Miles's voice rose and finally, the last headphone fell out.

"I'm clearly not doing okay."

"Yeah? No shit."

"I've thought about it a lot...since Milwaukee. I think I really need a break. I need to take time for myself. I need to fix me, and there's a lot of fixing to do. I never meant to hurt you both. I swear. I wanna get better. I really do. But I don't think I'll be able to keep my promise if I finish the rest of the tour. It's just way too easy for me to use in this environment."

Miles played with his headphone cords before he looked back up. "I can't believe we're dropping out," he said and shook his head. His comment hit me square in the chest, hearing how disappointed and heartbroken he sounded. "But I forgive you. It takes a lot to admit your mistakes."

"I second that," Corbin said.

"It does, but I'm in the wrong," I continued. "And I hate feeling this way. I'm tired of it. I want my life back. I want you guys back. I don't want to be a disappointment to everybody."

"We support you in whatever you feel is the right decision," Corbin said and leaned over to catch Miles's reaction. He nodded. "You're not you, and as much as it's disappointing to drop out, you have to think about yourself first and the future of the band. If your gut tells you this is the right decision, maybe it is."

"The thing is: I don't think I can get better by myself," I admitted. "I have all these urges, and I'm so angry and depressed."

"What are you saying?" Miles said.

Here came the thing I needed to admit but didn't want to. It hung heavy in my chest, and it would hang there until I said it out loud. I closed my eyes for a moment as I inhaled a deep breath and then looked back at them. "I want to be on the right track before Meraki. I already messed up this tour. I don't wanna mess up another important milestone in our career. I think…I think I need to get actual help. I can't do this on my own."

Miles's eyes softened on me as his eyebrows puckered. "Like rehab?"

A deep exhale poured out of me. There it was, and honestly, having that word said and floating in between all of us wasn't as scary as I thought it would be. A feeling landed in the pit of my stomach that this was the right move. I had to deal with my issues head-on for the first time in my life. I needed to learn how to avoid the problems that would keep being problems. My depression and anxiety were always going to be a part of me, but the alcohol and drugs didn't have to be. I didn't want them to be.

I also just needed something to believe in again. If I didn't believe in myself at the very least, then what else was there?

"Yeah," I said. "That's where I need to go."

"Whoa, okay, this is really big," Corbin said, probably thinking about all the media work about to come his way.

"I'll be here for you when you get out," Miles said with the thinnest, sympathetic smile. "I promise."

My heart swelled. I never disappointed Miles as much as I did on this tour, but he still stood by my side. This was why I was determined to shake off my demons. If things didn't work out with Reagan, as heartbroken as I would be, at least I had Miles continuing to be my rock.

❖

The thing about being a nuisance as a teenager: I wasn't that remorseful. I couldn't explain why I wasn't. Maybe I thought getting in trouble and disobeying my mom and grandparents was what I needed to do to fulfill my adolescent years. But now, I did feel remorseful. My actions hurt two of the people I cared the most about. Miles had been my best friend since we were fourteen. He was my first friend in California when I moved. I stood by his side during the years he was bullied, and he stood by mine when my grandparents died. We'd been through hell and back with each other, and this was how I repaid him? My stomach had been sinking since he found out about the coke, and I wondered when the hell it was ever going to finally hit the ground.

I knew the morning of our Minneapolis show that this was going to be our last. Corbin, Miles, and I fully discussed it with Finn right as we got to the hotel. He was disappointed just as much as we were, but he agreed with me that it was probably the right thing to do. I apologized for my behavior at our Milwaukee meeting and apologized again for putting Reagan in jeopardy.

Stepping out on the stage that night wasn't thrilling and exciting like it used to be. I was so sad and empty. I looked into the crowd giving me ecstatic grins as far as I could see, and I played upbeat music to get them excited for the star of the show, who currently couldn't look me in the eye or speak to me. Usually, when I performed a song, I felt so powerful with whatever instrument was in hand, melodies I created flowing through the speakers, so loud and heavy, it felt as if they swept me off my feet. I felt so powerful that I had the ability to control the mood of the show. We opened up with one of our head bangers, and then a few songs later, we slowed it down to get everyone in touch with their sensitive sides, and then we ended on another upbeat rock song with guitar riffs and Miles going crazy on the drums.

But when I performed in Minneapolis, it felt as if the crowd wasn't mine anymore. The stage wasn't ours. My life backstage wasn't something I wanted to leave the exciting stage for. Nothing around me was mine anymore because I ruined all of it.

When it came time for the spot in our set list where we'd been performing covers—the ones that I started doing to seduce Reagan—I decided my last cover would be my good-bye song. It was "And So It Goes" by Billy Joel. I knew that the vast majority of fans wouldn't know the song, but being heartbroken and remorseful were two feelings everyone knew. You could hear the pain in every piano chord, every lyric, and I wanted the song to offer a window into what my heart felt like at that moment. My heart was broken in so many different ways.

I wanted Reagan to know that too. And there was only one way for her to find out.

The audience hushed, and I almost forgot there were twenty thousand people in the arena by how quiet they became, as quiet as the song was. I played that song as if I'd carefully crafted each lyric to Reagan about how she was going to break my heart and leave me, which was already done and in the past. Billy Joel wrote the song about his doomed relationship with Elle Macpherson, yet I hated to think my relationship with Reagan was doomed the whole time.

After the set, I debated whether or not to say good-bye to her. After all we went through, leaving her without saying anything didn't feel right in my heart, but it felt right in my gut. Hovering right in front of her closed green room door, I could smell the sage seeping through the crack. I held my knuckles an inch from her door, wondering if I should tell her good-bye, but one last tug in my stomach pulled me away.

So, I left.

❖

It wasn't until the next morning when we finally landed in LA that Miles showed me on his phone the video going around the internet. Reagan responded to my song—like she did in the early days of the tour when we chased each other. She, too, opted for playing on her piano with Charles sitting next to her on his acoustic guitar. She sang "Million Reasons" by Lady Gaga, a song about how there were all these reasons for Lady Gaga to leave her partner if only he'd given a reason for her to stay. I watched Reagan's face closely as she played the piano, and I could see her getting wrapped up into Lady Gaga's words just like how I felt with Billy Joel. And each word was as painful to hear as if she wrote them herself. I could see the heartbreak I felt shimmering in her eyes.

But out of all the songs she could have picked, she chose that one. Did that mean I still had a chance to win her back? My one reason for her to stay would be that I was sober, and that would overpower all the other shit I did. Maybe. But then I kept thinking back to my awful prison comment, and I would understand if she never wanted to speak to me again. But even with that doubt, the slim hope of that Lady Gaga song would be something I clung to during my recovery. I needed something to believe in—something that would give me hope during my withdrawals and my cravings and the hellish days I was about to go through.

I told Mom everything that happened. Details and all. As much as it pained me to see her reaction, I had to. I thought when I was younger that Mom's reaction to a cop bringing me home from pool hopping was a look of extreme disappointment. Or her reaction when Gramps had to explain to her why he was getting a security system and why he wasn't sharing the code with anyone. And her locking herself in her room for two days straight when the school called her to inform her I was suspended for three days for bringing weed onto school property. Those were all teasers to my explanation for dropping out of the tour and checking myself into rehab.

"I just can't...I can't believe this, Blair," Mom kept saying over and over again as she paced around her condo. "How did this even happen?"

She sobbed, blamed herself for it, then blamed Jason Hines and even Gramps, who apparently was a functioning alcoholic, Mom declared, and I had no idea until she said it through thick tears. I guess I was too young and naïve to put all his whiskey drinking and the liver cancer together. And then when I told her that Jason Hines had showed up, she cried even harder and started yelling at him as if he were there to hear it.

"I'm so disappointed in you. So incredibly disappointed in you. And your grandparents would be too. God, I can't believe this."

And then I started sobbing just as hard as she was.

Mom reacted the way I imagined she would react, far worse than when I was suspended. She sternly asked me to leave her house so she could process the info. I kept my drug use pretty hidden from her—from everyone—so I really didn't blame her for needing space. I just really wanted her to hold my broken body in the comforting way like she did the night I broke up with Alanna.

Through thick tears, after I drove back home, I collapsed on my bed, replaying the look of utter disappointment and betrayal from my mom, and that hurt the most. My wonderful mother who'd already gone through so much in her life. And I had the audacity to hand her another huge weight for her to carry.

And then, when I checked my phone to try to get my mind off my mom, I discovered the brand-new celebrity news circling around the internet.

A burning pain erupted in my stomach and crawled up to my chest when I found the answer to my question of who Reagan was going to find to open her last ten shows. If she wanted to have the last jab in our feud, well, up went my white flag. I guess we were both even on the amount of hurt and betrayal we gave one another.

Midnight Konfusion Drops Out of Reagan Moore Tour Due to Personal Issues.

Bristol Perri Was Concerned about Reagan Moore During Benmoore Romance.

Ex-Girlfriend Jessie Byrd to Open for Reagan Moore for Remaining Shows.

Have Benmoore Called It Quits? Blair Bennett Drops Out of Tour, Jessie Byrd Joins.

Move Over Benmoore. Is Jeagan Back On?

Stab to the heart.

All those nights we spent together on her bus? Boom. Replaced with her fucking electric ex-girlfriend for rebound sex. All those songs we sang together? Boom. Replaced with Jessie Byrd, who took a seat on a barstool at the Winnipeg show, fingerpicking her acoustic guitar as Reagan gave her the familiar gaze she gave me when we performed together—steady wide eyes and a flirtatious smirk.

Because who cared about the hacking and the whole world knowing that they dated? Apparently, she didn't care about that anymore.

It was always Jessie. You'll never be anything compared to stupid

Jessie Byrd and her combat boots and her leather jacket and all her rings and her indescribable swag that you'll never have.

Fuck Jessie Byrd. And fuck Bristol Perri for being "concerned" about Reagan. Where the hell did that even come from?

I fought the urge to toss back shots, but it was so hard to do when my mind wouldn't stop spinning with so much ire. I caved. I found a bottle of vodka in my room, about a third of it remaining. I tossed the liquid back straight from the bottle until it was empty, and then I beat myself up for caving when the whole point of dropping out of the tour was to stop drinking and doing drugs. I locked myself in my room and sulked like the drunken mess I was. About drinking. About Jessie Byrd. About Reagan. About Miles. About Gramps. About Grandma. About my fucking father. About my poor mother.

I needed to forget about Reagan until I was emotionally able to handle her moving on. Apparently, she was already on her way there.

So, after that last night of binge drinking, I checked myself into rehab.

CHAPTER FOURTEEN

After spending twenty-eight days in Rancho Mirage for rehab, I came back to LA and craved something totally different. Recording.

I'd had a lot of time with my thoughts and my journal. So much writing that my journal filled up, and I treated myself to a brand-new journal for being one month sober. The second month sober, Miles popped open a bottle of sparkling cider to celebrate being back in the recording studio, and even Corbin was blown away with what we came up with.

"This is a real album," Corbin said three songs into the second full-length album. "I think this is the best way to answer all the questions everyone has."

The first album was a thirteen-song collection we wrote from the ages of eighteen to twenty-three. Songs that dealt with growing up, partying, lust, and one song about death. But we'd grown so much since then, especially within the last year. The second album only had three songs recorded, but we had the list finalized. Songs about falling in love, heartbreak, addiction, and life and death. That gnawing feeling I had when I needed a drink now became a need to record. To get my voice back out there. To tell my side of the all the stories the internet told.

To continue celebrating two months sober, Miles and I went over to Mom's house for dinner with her and Greg. She made my favorite: cheesy chicken casserole with a layer of shredded cheddar cheese underneath a thick layer of cornflakes. It wasn't nutritious in the slightest, but it made my stomach and heart happy. I played her and Greg the three songs we recorded, and the song I wrote during my alcohol withdrawals made Mom cry and even Miles teared up a bit.

"Blair, you know how proud I am of you?" Mom said as she walked up behind me and hung her arms around my neck and shoulders, kissing me on the cheek.

It was a vast difference from when I told her two months prior about the drinking and the drugs. Her reaction was still engrained forever in my memory, and while I shivered, ached, and sobbed during my withdrawals, doubting my ability to make it through, I pictured Mom sobbing while yelling at me when I told her about the coke. Then I wondered what the hell Gramps would have done if he were still alive. That was what kept me going. As hard as it was. All those nights I lost sleep from the desire, from the pain igniting my bones, from the sweat sticking to my sheets. I wanted to get my life back because I really wasn't living if I couldn't even remember what were supposed to be the best days of my life.

Miles and I sat on the balcony, full of cheesy chicken casserole and homemade mashed potatoes—Grandma's delicious recipe with sour cream, chives, and bacon. I had my new journal on my lap, on a page with freshly written lyrics. The words hadn't stopped pouring out of my pen since I entered rehab and began reconstructing my whole life.

And the more I changed myself, the more I thought about her.

"Is it good?" Miles asked, pointing to my journal and opening a can of Coke.

I shrugged. "Just something that popped into my head."

"I wonder who it's about," he said facetiously.

As he sat in the chair next to me, he swept his hair to the side and then looked at a sparkling Los Feliz with a little glimmer of downtown LA in the faint distance. I had to ask him the question that had been stuck in my head.

"Have you seen her?"

He looked at me with a confused stare. "Hmm?"

"Have you seen Reagan?"

"Ah," he said and directed his gaze back at the hills. "I was wondering when you would ask."

"So, that's a yes?"

He took a sip from his Coke. "She invited me over about a month ago."

"A month ago? Well, Jesus, where the hell was I?"

"Here with your mom."

"And I'm just finding this out now?"

"I'm wasn't gonna tell my best friend one month out of rehab that I was going to see her ex-girlfriend. I'm terrified of you relapsing, Blair. I just wanna protect you from shit. I wasn't trying to keep anything from you."

His eyes were soft, and I could see the residual hurt I'd left in him looking straight back at me. I was afraid of relapsing too. They kept drilling in my head that it was so common. And there were so many urges to drink more so than to do drugs. But two months in, I still stood firm, but also felt incredibly vulnerable.

"I'm scared too," I said. "I just...well...did you guys talk?"

"No, we sat around in silence and stared at the walls." He faced me, biting a smile. "Of course we talked."

"You know what I mean."

"We mostly talked about Meraki. Talked set lists, and then we talked about the rest of the tour—"

"And why Jessie Byrd was there?"

"If you want to know the answer to your question, it's yes."

"I haven't even asked a question."

"You don't have to. I already know all of them."

"Oh yeah? And what are they?"

He twisted around, tucking his knees into his chest and then looking skyward. "'Did she ask about me? Does she miss me? Does she still think about me? Does she wonder how I'm doing? Does she still have feelings for me?' The answer is yes."

My heart raced, and all the questions and words that were going to follow vanished in my head because my brain couldn't keep up with all this information. "How do you...how do you know?"

"Because she asked about you. She asked how you were doing, and I told her that you were doing amazing. That your spirits were high, that you're so invested in the second album and staying sober, that you're excited to record, like that's all you want to do is record, and it's sometimes annoying. That you're so ready to get back on the stage for Meraki, and how I'm so fucking happy that I have my best friend back."

"And what about the other questions? Did she mention those?"

"No, that's all we talked about regarding you. But she didn't have to say that she missed you or thought about you or still has feelings for you. I just know by how she asked."

"Well, how did she ask?"

What was up with Miles and all his annoying cliffhangers?

"Like, how you're asking me about her right now. With cautious hesitancy. It was like she was holding in that question all night, the same way I think you were holding it in. Am I right?"

I rolled my eyes because I hated so much when Miles knew me better than I knew myself. But the darkness shielded my eye roll from him, therefore not boosting his pride.

I glanced at the homes below us starting to twinkle in the glow of dusk and thought about her more. Picturing her playing with her fingers as she asked Miles about me with trepidation rattling her voice. I wished she told him more. I wished I knew the depths of how she felt about me because it felt like every day that progressed without her, the deeper my feelings for her became.

When I was sixteen, I asked Gramps how he knew he was in love with Grandma. He said it was when he was twenty-six, and he and Grandma had a falling-out because she wanted to get married and start a family when Gramps was at the peak of his performing career. The two broke up when Gramps continued on with his band, and during those two months, he said he really struggled. He drank a lot, he lost a lot of sleep, and he felt like a shell of himself, despite living out the dream he always imagined. On his drive to Memphis to play a show, he heard a brand-new song on the radio from one of his favorite singers, John Denver. The song was "Annie's Song," and the beautiful melody and lyrics captivated him. He bought the album and listened to it on repeat for the rest of the day. At that Memphis show, Gramps performed a cover of it, and the only person he could think about was Grandma and how John Denver's lyrics described how he felt about Grandma to a T. Every time he heard the song, his stomach sank just remembering the woman he lost. So, a few weeks later, he told Grandma he wanted to start a family too. He took a break from his band, got married, had my mom a year later, and occasionally when he and Grandma had a night to themselves to enjoy a date, he'd put the B-side of *Back Home Again* on his record player so he could share a dance with Grandma to "Annie's Song."

"You'll know you love someone when you listen to 'Annie's Song,' and you feel the love for them in your chest and gut," he said to me after telling me the story. I asked him how he knew he loved Grandma because I wondered if I was in love with Dana Bohlen. So, to put his theory to the test, we listened to the song on his record player in the living room, and I didn't feel a single thing. The lyrics made me roll my eyes, I told him the song was lame, and he told me when I matured and found true love I would appreciate the song. I responded by saying he was full of it.

In rehab, I had a lot of time to listen to music, and the song popped up when my music was set to shuffle. I remembered Gramps's story, and when I fully listened to the song as an adult who missed a woman so terribly, I realized the old man was right this whole time. I could only think about Reagan and all the feelings she injected in me when she kissed me, held me, slept next to me, smiled at me. I didn't have the urge to roll my eyes or deem the song as "lame." The lyrics John Denver wrote for his then-wife perfectly described all the feelings swirling inside me. I was in love with Reagan Moore, and admitting that wasn't terrifying like I always thought it would. It was freeing if anything.

"Can I confess something?" I asked and let out a long, heavy sigh that came from the deepest part of my gut.

"Is it juicy?" Miles asked.

"It's pretty juicy."

He sat straight up in his chair eagerly. "Go for it."

"I think I'm in love with her. Actually, I know I'm in love her."

"Whoa."

"I know."

"Have you ever been in love with anyone before?"

"No."

His eyes rounded. "So, what are you gonna do about it?"

I thought about it for a moment. "I have an idea." I bolted out of my seat as an idea formed in my head.

"Hey! Wait! You have to run your ideas by your best friend!"

I ran inside to my room, shut the door, and grabbed a pen. Flipping to the next blank page in my journal, I stared at the empty lines ready to capture all my words I imagined myself saying the next time I saw her. Without putting too much thought in it, I decided that the most heartfelt apology was one that wasn't heavily edited with too much time, too much doubt, or too much thinking. So, I wrote the first words that came to mind. I wrote as if Reagan stood right in front of me, and I wanted her to hear everything I had to say to her since the last time I saw her.

Reagan,

I have no idea what I'm about to write, but I'm just going to write down everything I feel because it's all coming out at once.

I owe you an apology that's beyond the words I can write right now. I put all the hard work you invested in building your career at risk because of my stupid actions, and it wasn't until I was already off the tour that I was able to fully see the scope of my damage. Hurting you was the last thing I ever wanted to do, and I would take back all the things I said and did in a heartbeat if I could. I want you to know that.

I haven't stopped thinking about you since I left the tour. You won't leave my mind, and the ache I have in my stomach keeps getting stronger the more time that passes without you. I know I said and did enough to make you not want to forgive me, and if you don't forgive me, I understand. But I don't think I could ever forgive myself if I didn't give you the proper apology that you deserve and if I didn't confess all the things I feel about you.

I could go on and on about how I feel about you. Like how you're the most amazing woman I've ever met in my life. How you were the reason I wanted to get out of bed. How every time we kissed, you were able to still give me butterflies. And you still do, Reagan. None of that has changed.

You once asked to look at my journal, and I only showed you one song because it was my most prized possession, and I only gave it to Miles when I wanted him to look over a lyric. But as I finished this book in rehab and I reread all the pages, I realized that ever since last June, you were the theme of all

*my lyrics. I think my journal can better show you the impact
you made on my life better than this letter can.*

*You might think I threw us away, but I hope this journal
proves to you how much you mean to me. No one else has
made me feel this way but you.*

Blair

*P.S. Since this is my most prized possession, I'll need it back
eventually.*

I folded the paper and pulled out the finished journal.
Here went nothing.

A few weeks had passed since I asked Finn to deliver my letter
and my journal to Reagan, and now Miles and I were ready to do our
first show at the Meraki Music and Arts Festival in the open fields of
Tennessee.

I loved taking the stage. It was like walking into a room knowing
you had a surprise party waiting for you, and everyone jumped and
cheered as they emerged from the darkness, all ecstatic to see you.
It never got old. I loved every time Miles kicked the bass drum, and
I felt the rhythm in my throat. I loved hearing the chords I created
with my fingers—whether on guitar, piano, bass, violin, or whatever
instrument—burst through the speakers and elicit another outbreak of
cheers.

The stage was my home. And I was so happy to be back.

Once the stage lights flickered off, the crowd grew together in a
solid "Woo." Miles was already behind his drums and started kicking
quarter notes on his bass drum as the stage lights flashed for every
thump. I stood on the side stage, waiting for my cue, taking one last,
deep breath. As much as I was excited for our performance, I was also
nervous. This was our first performance since the Minneapolis show
back in March. Now here we were in late June, and I wanted our first
ever music festival performance to be epic.

Four measures into Miles's bass drum kicks, I clutched the neck of
my Fender and walked out on stage as the red lights flickered upward to
each bass drum beat. Our very own concert sonic boom evoked screams

that pierced through my in-ears. A clamor of cheers all for Miles and me. We didn't have to share it. We weren't opening for anyone. I couldn't tell how many people showed up to our stage to hear us perform, but I wouldn't be surprised if there were more than twenty thousand. All of them came out for us. The crowd mingled with the sunset quickly encompassing us as the sky turned a light orange and pink. Inflatable killer whales, dolphins, and unicorns bounced up and down, and beach balls frolicked over the canopy of raised hands. Most of the bodies that made up the crowd were cloaked in a sparkling layer of sweat and humidity. Some wore headbands around their foreheads. Many of them wearing colorful mismatched outfits, but matching didn't matter at musical festivals. You could get away with anything.

I waved as I positioned myself behind my looping pedals and the other nine instruments.

"Meraki, how are we doing tonight?" I said into the microphone at center stage, and the audience responded with the same applause that erupted when I walked out. "We're Midnight Konfusion. Let's have some fun together."

After hearing they were ready, I started playing our fun, upbeat, soulful rock song, "1969," and a smile tugged my lips as I sank into the comfort and familiarity of the thing I loved the most: performing.

Being at a music festival was quite the experience. When we graduated high school, Miles and I saved our graduation money to buy Coachella tickets. Everyone was so happy to be there. No one walked around with a frown. Everyone wanted to be friends. Even in the crowd, tall people made sure the shorter people could see the stage. One guy picked up a girl he didn't know—who had to have been only five feet tall—and put her on his shoulders. People shared water, booze, drugs. For a very short time, differences didn't exist. They just came for the music and a good time, and that was all that mattered to anyone. Performing for those people was no different. They projected their energy to the stage, which only inspired us to play with even more heart.

As the night swallowed the sunset and the crowded grass field, glow sticks of every neon color cut through the darkness. All the bodies morphed into a variety of light speckles from their phones, lighters, and glow sticks swaying in the air. I couldn't see them anymore, but

I heard them. Loud and clear. A solid thunderous roar from a drunk crowd pierced through my in-ears. I never heard our lyrics sung that loudly before, it was fucking awesome and addicting.

"Are we still doing okay out there? No one has overheated, right?" I asked, and the roar hit the stage like a wave. "Good." I turned to my maroon digital piano and tickled the keys in broken chords. "So, we took some time off for the last few months. For personal reasons because sometimes you have to pause, take a break, and reflect to make sure you're living your best life. And I wasn't living mine. So, I fixed myself and wrote a lot of songs, and some of those songs are already on the album we're recording right now. But there's one I want to test out with you guys tonight. Are we cool with that?"

The masses wooed, and I pressed the pedal and recorded the first loop on the digital piano, playing those broken chords before switching the piano to sound like a synthesizer for the second loop. Then for the third loop, I strapped my Fender on, and moved my fingers up the neck of my guitar, letting individual strings cry out through the speakers. The song was one of the slowest ones I'd ever written. Most of the time, we kept our soulful rock in every song. But our new song took the form of something completely different, and maybe it was the start of a shift to a different kind of sound for our second album. We ditched the distorted electric guitars wailing out seventies rock and a bit of soul for the touch of synth, acoustic guitar, and the classic sounds of the piano.

The song was different because the girl who it was about was completely different. I had to sing this song for her. I hadn't gotten a response to my journal despite the three weeks that passed by. But I knew Reagan was somewhere on the Meraki premises. I knew she would be watching me. I had to make sure she really knew how sorry I was for everything.

As the loop continued to play, I lowered my Fender so I could play a live layer of piano chords.

"I can feel myself fading from you
Just because I walked away didn't mean I wanted to
The toxic pools I swam in at night
Remind me of all that went wrong
Searching for it all, just trying to belong

All those nights drinking
Now replaced with the thought of us
I'm sober, just not when it comes to my thoughts."

Then the chorus came around, and I switched back to the Fender after a measure, strumming against the loop during the chorus. Miles's drums crescendo was a tease to build up to the climax of the song.

"You're the one thing I've done right in a long time
Now all I have is the memory of your skin on mine
I used to think you were too good to be true
I guess that's just the feeling of falling for you."

And then the drums hushed.

"I can see your smile fading from view
Just because I said those things doesn't mean they're true
All the songs we used to sing
Remind me of how we begged for love
Searching for it all, just trying to belong
All our nights kissing
Replaced with an empty bed
Filled with all the thoughts that were left unsaid."

The second time the chorus came, Miles didn't mute the bass drum, toms, or cymbals. He let them ring out into the audience, who cheered on the progression of the song slowly building. Hearing them send me positive feedback through their cheers and raised hands gave me more courage to sing the rest of the song. If all the people in the crowd seemed hooked by the lyrics and the melody, maybe that meant Reagan would be too. If she was watching.

I hoped she was watching. I performed the song as if I knew for sure she was.

"My love, I regret all the things I did to you
But not for a second do I regret our love
I can still taste our last kiss
Just tell me how to be the girl you miss."

Miles went all out on the drums, and I could picture his hair flipping back and forth as he got lost in the music. I improvised a few licks on the Fender after singing the chorus once more, playing whatever notes felt natural to how I felt in that moment. Hopeful but hurt. Nostalgic but disappointed. The song at its peak. An assortment of stage lights of reds, blues, and whites lambent toward the sky. I strummed the high notes of the guitar's neck, and what started off as a soft song now cried in vibrant sounds with the thousands of people in front of me cheering, with their hands still swaying as if they felt all the feelings that comprised the song too.

And then the drums vanished, my cue to stop playing the guitar. I kicked my foot off the loop so the only thing playing was the piano, the simple chords I played during the first verse. I glanced into the audience that stretched throughout the fields as dusk was almost over, knowing that somewhere Reagan was out there in those Tennessee fields. I sang the last two lines softly, "I used to think you were too good to be true. I guess that's just the feeling of falling for you."

And then the stage lights flickered to black.

❖

The next night was Reagan's night.

Her name lit up the stage in neon pink lights. A sea of people traveled down the hill, a clamor of shrills pierced the night air. I couldn't tell you how many people were in front of her stage, but I wouldn't be shocked if she drew in around seventy-five to one hundred thousand, like Taz Jones did about an hour after our performance. I could hear the audience enjoying themselves all the way from our bus where Miles, Corbin, and I sat on chairs outside, drinking Cokes and listening to the distant, thunderous crowd.

Before we weaved in and out of Reagan's crowd as much as we could to get closer, Miles and I overheard a group of four girls talking about how their friend had been waiting for four hours in her spot up against the metal railings, making sure she was front row for the show. Four hours for us was two shows and a nap ago, and now we stood all the way in the back, far enough that her band was the size of ants.

Since darkness hung in the air, no one recognized us mingled with the rest of the crowd with their hands in the air, ready for Reagan

Moore. As one of the three headliners, she drew in practically the whole festival. Or what seemed to be the whole festival. People pushed to get closer once the lights flickered off, and a wave of roaring quickly crept from the front of the stage to where we stood like a tidal wave, and all the fans circling us nudged us. I loved when fans nudged each other when I was on stage, but when I fucked something up and had to subject myself to the far back of a general admission crowd, no, I hated the nudging. The music poured through the giant speakers, and the stage lights flipped on, and when Reagan walked onto the stage, the jumbo screen behind her projected her beauty and her smile all the way back to us, the crowd of seventy-five thousand created a concert sonic boom just as strong as the one we heard at Gillette Stadium.

Watching her beauty on the screen created this optical illusion that I was much closer to her than I was. For a second, I thought her eyes were on me, that the smile brightening her summer-soaked face was for me. Three months had passed, and her smile still found a way to tangle up my insides. A nice reminder of everything I lost so easily. Her smile was so bright, her eyes sparkling with the same kind of excitement and energy she always had before shows; she almost fooled me into thinking she just didn't go through a breakup a few months back.

A few songs into her hour-and-a-half-long performance, I was already feeling like a pile of crap. Everyone around me bobbed their heads to the beat, singing every lyric. Even Miles. His wide grin matched the ones all around us. Why did I torture myself, insisting on watching her performance, knowing exactly how it would pan out? I waited for her response to my letter because I knew she got it. I didn't even use the postal service, so the letter wasn't lost. Finn handed it to her, knowing that it was my olive branch, and he texted me when he gave it to her. No other details followed. Details like if she was happy or sad, if she ripped open the letter, if she had any lingering hope in her eyes. I didn't hear if she heard my performance. All was quiet on the Benmoore front.

Now, I was unworthy to even catch her eyes from up close. I was pushed so far back that her face blurred into the complexion of her summer tan.

"I'm gonna head back to the bus," I said over the cheering and singing.

"What? Come on. She sounds great!" Miles said, still beaming.

"Yeah, but this is my ex-girlfriend we're talking about."

He turned to me with a frown. "But I thought you wanted to come."

"I did, but I realized it's a bad idea. A very bad idea."

Standing in the crowd really put all my progress to the test, and if I learned anything from my recovery meetings it was that I needed to escape whatever was prompting me to have the urge. And that situation was the anxiety that came with zero closure with Reagan. I practically sent her my heart in the form of my journal and sang her a love song to a whole music festival. Knowing that I hadn't seen her in months filled me with dread, as if all these overwhelming feelings I didn't want to feel would take hold of me. Usually, this kind of anxiety would make me drink, but there was no way I wanted to backtrack. Three months was a long time, a painfully long time, and one sip would erase all of that. No matter how tempting it was. So, I channeled Gramps and bought myself a banjo so that anytime I had the urge to drink, I'd learn more of the banjo. The urge to drink broke out in a burning itch on my skin again. I was no stranger to this after rehab, and the feeling ate at my skin so many times, I played enough banjo to distract my thoughts that I could play the dueling banjos scene from *Deliverance* before it got really fast. Now I was ready to hide from Reagan and cure the immense craving I had for alcohol by perfecting the fast sixteenth note part I'd been avoiding. That was a better way to spend the rest of my night rather than torturing myself by looking at my beautiful, smiley ex-girlfriend.

"Can we go after this song?" Miles asked.

I rolled my eyes and faced the stage. I didn't want to walk back to the bus by myself, so it was worth the wait just in case I got chased. After the song ended, the crowd applauded. I turned to Miles, and he motioned for me to go ahead.

"You guys don't mind if I play a new song, do you?" Reagan asked the crowd. I stopped dead in my tracks and snapped my attention back to her. All the people encouraged her with applause and hands held high to show their enthusiasm, which drew a full smile from Reagan. "I knew you guys wouldn't mind. This is a song I've been wanting to share with you for a while now. You'll let me know after if you like it?"

She strapped on her black acoustic-electric guitar. It was a nice sight to see someone of her fame opt for something as simple as a guitar. Since becoming a superstar, she started incorporating more theatrics like dancing and wardrobe changes, but had originally started out on just piano and guitar. Even on tour when she did play, she still had some theatrics added, whether it was dancers, backup vocalists, or a stunning stage display.

Her band came in, and synthesizers hummed a slow tune, the bassist plucking a deep eighties bass line. A few measures in, Reagan strummed rhythm chords, and my mind traveled back to when I was lucky enough to see her before the shows, close enough to smell her perfume and her hair and the sage scenting her skin.

Now, all I could smell was weed, beer, and stale sweaty outdoors sticking to everyone around me. The stage lights of blue, white, and red highlighted the sweat glistening on her face as her eyes searched the audience. A dull burn brewed inside me, wondering if she was searching for me or someone else.

The melody of the opening measures froze me in my spot.

"In the sun she floats away
As I try to pull her down
She's got a thousand worlds to locate
Spinning me tirelessly around
No two minutes are the same
With a thrill of unknown things
She locks her heart and her mind
Maybe because she's a Gemini."

Miles and I exchanged glances at the same time. Eyes rounded. Eyebrows halfway up our foreheads. My gut hollowed out. I had no idea if Zeke Fowler or Jessie Byrd were Geminis, but I definitely was one. I snatched my phone out of my pocket to do a quick internet search, clenching my teeth, hoping that all the people around me wouldn't hinder my research. But then I got something. Zeke Fowler was born on July twenty-seventh, which meant he was a Leo, and Jessie Byrd was born on November fourth, which meant she was a Scorpio.

I lowered my phone and looked back at Miles, still waiting for an answer.

The brunette in front of me with a tie-dyed bandana tapped her blond friend's arm. "You know this is about Blair Bennett, right?"

The blonde's mouth dropped. "You think?"

"Oh totally. She's probably singing it because Blair Bennett sang that new song last night. The one that was totally about Reagan Moore."

"Oh my God, you're right. But I thought she was back together with Jessie Byrd?"

The brunette shook her head. "I don't know. We haven't seen anything since the tour. Maybe it was just a one-time thing."

I gulped at the same time a warmth spread across my face, and I hoped that those girls didn't turn around and recognize me underneath my black floppy hat.

"Soften soundly in my bed
The only time she's pinned down
All the secrets in her head
She'll keep that part to herself
Your face she'll have memorized
Like the wonders of the world
You'll be the reason she's confined
All because she's your Gemini."

Her band brought on the intensity. Her drummer ditched the muted high hat cymbal and banged on the crash cymbal while his other hand pounded beats into the floor tom and bass drum. The muted guitars that strummed in the background burst open in heavy electric strums on the rhythm guitar and modest riffs on the lead guitar. Reagan stepped away from the mic and got lost in the strumming of her acoustic, which I could barely hear over the drums, electric guitars, and the vibrant synths still adding a mysterious hum to the song. As the climax of the song came alive, the lights on stage swirled upward to the night sky, and the audience roared as they felt the emotion Reagan, the band, and the melody emanated into the crowd. It was powerful enough that my skin broke out in goose bumps, and after a few measures, Reagan stepped back to the mic to sing the climax.

"You see her in the way
She dreams she could see herself
She'll try to save you from her doubts
She doesn't think she's enough
She's a diamond in the rough

But underneath it all she's soft
It's just part of her disguise
All because she's a Gemini.
In the past, you'd run away
As she walks on the razor's edge
But it's something about her air
That coaxes you to come along
She paints your world in colors
When you used to hide in grays
She's made you feel the most alive
And that's why you love that Gemini."

She held out the last note an octave higher, repeating it for several measures with the same climatic intensity. And then the band dropped to the muted hush from the beginning of the song, and she repeated the last line somberly, "And that's why you love that Gemini," four more times until the song faded into nothing.

Was she really in love with me? Because I was really in love with her.

The field cheered, the people all around us raised their hands in the air and clapped, sending their "Woos" to the stage. I stood there with my mouth halfway to the grass, tears stinging my eyes as I watched Reagan take in the loudness of the crowd and the emotion from the power-rock ballad still hanging in the air like the humidity. Her eyes sparkled, and I could see how her body still felt all the words she just sang. I felt it too.

I fucked up so badly, I wasn't sure if I would even take me back if things were reversed. I knew she heard my song because this song had to have been a response to mine—or my letter.

But either way, she was thinking about me.

❖

I hid in our bus as my heart raced, still pumping adrenaline but also mixed with some fear. I had no idea what to do. Did I go find Reagan's bus? Did I call her? Did I text her? Was the ball in my court? Was it in hers? I knew I needed to do something, I just had no idea what.

I turned to the banjo and plucked the strings to the fast part of the

Deliverance scene over and over as Miles sat across from me, texting Ethan so we could all arrange to meet up for the silent disco in the woods after he was done dismantling Reagan's stuff on the main stage.

"You need a new song," Miles said when he looked up from his phone. "I'm getting really sick of this."

"Well, fuck off then."

He gave me a smile. "Wanna sit here and analyze it?"

I stopped playing as I looked at him. "What should I do? If this happened a few months ago, I'd drink to forget about it."

"First, how about you breathe and then recognize that she wrote you a song. That's hopeful, right?"

"I guess." I paused and took a couple deep breaths. "I should go to her bus. Can you get the info from Ethan?"

"Haven't heard from him in ten minutes. I can snoop around for some details about Reagan's whereabouts."

I started playing the banjo again. "Okay. Do that."

About a half hour later, after plotting with Miles on how I could polish up my sweet-talking skills to charm her bodyguards into allowing me to get to her, something from the corner of my eye pulled my gaze.

Reagan stood outside with her eyes on the ground. She flinched toward the door and then backed away. For a second, I thought she would run away, but then she looked up and caught my stare. I'd only been thinking about her nonstop since I left the tour. Getting back together with her was one of the beacons that led me out of the darkness. But then her lips thinned, giving me as much of a cordial smile as an ex-girlfriend without any closure could give, but that was enough for me to open the door. She cautiously took a step inside with my journal in her hands. I backed to my couch, resuming my safe space as the air in the bus wafted out before the door closed behind her.

My heart thudded as hard and loud as a bass drum, and my nerves spiraled inside me. Three months without seeing her or looking at her or talking to her or having anything to do with her. I thought she'd written me out of her life until she sang about me. And here she was standing feet in front of me. Looking at me. Standing so uncomfortably in the entryway as if she was crossing enemy lines.

"Hey," she mumbled as she struggled to make eye contact.

I had no idea what to say, especially since she wore the sexiest black tank top that accentuated the curves of her breasts, almost as if to torture me. I thought of so many things to tell her if this scenario ever played out in real life, but now that she stood in front of me, perfect copper legs, the dip of her shirt, and the curves of her worried eyebrows, I had nothing. It was as if my mind took a leave of absence with no warning sign. Or maybe all the words tried rushing out of me at once so they clogged all up.

"Hi," I said, still holding my breath in my rapidly tightening chest.

"And that's my cue," Miles said as he got off the couch. "I need to go find your guitar tech. You guys say and do the right things," he said with an orderly stare to both of us before he left us alone.

I'm glad I wasn't the only one with warmth spreading across my cheeks after his comment.

"I, um, I read your journal." She spoke softly as she glanced down at it in her hands.

"You did?"

"Yeah."

A silence passed between us. I could hear my heart keeping a beat in my ears while my breaths shortened. I hated the tandem silence. I hated the space. How come she was right in front of me, enclosed in the same four walls, yet she felt as far away as when I was lost in the sea of her fans? I hated how I couldn't just follow my instinct and kiss her. I hated so much how it took all my strength to keep myself on the couch and not focus on her lips.

"I heard your song," she said softly.

"I heard yours."

"Good."

Her response landed in my stomach. The song really was for me. All those lyrics were for me.

She took a step into the bus and held the journal out for me to take. I stood and accepted it, closing in on the large space that held all of our awkwardness.

She looked at me differently than the last time we saw each other. I hoped her observing stare was because she saw a transformed woman in front of her instead of the broken mess who left her. I hoped that I didn't stain all of our memories. They weren't stained for me.

"I read it from the beginning," she muttered.

I swallowed hard. "And?"

"You wrote about me for about thirty-three pages."

"That's it? Seems like it would be more," I said. "Look, I know I fucked up, and I know I hurt you."

"You *did* hurt me. A lot. You broke my trust, and you made me feel like an idiot—"

"That wasn't my intention."

"You were such an asshole to Finn."

"I know."

"And Miles. And me."

"I know. That was probably the worst time of my life because I had so many good things to lose at the same time, I felt like I had no control of my life. And then my dad just shows up and that was it. I was done. I completely lost the very little grip I had. If I could take it back, trust me, I'd do it in a heartbeat."

"I felt like nothing I did or said made you feel happier."

"But that's not even true, Reagan. You were the only thing that made me feel better. At night, I just wanted to fast-forward to the morning so I could wake up next to you and talk to you and experience this rush and thrill of seeing you. That's all you had to do to make me happy. Just being there."

"Then why wasn't it enough? You still got drunk every night. You still walked off this tour without even saying anything."

"I thought leaving the tour was the best thing for both of us. Also, you replaced me with your ex-girlfriend. If you wanted to win the breakup, you did by doing that."

She rolled her eyes. "Jesus, Blair, I didn't want to win the breakup. I asked Jessie to come on because I knew she had the next three months off, and I needed a fast replacement. You might think I did it to get back at you, but I don't do things to purposely fuck with people. I thought about you the whole goddamn time. Every day. Even when she tried coming onto my bus and flirting with me, I pushed her away because I only wanted you."

"She tried getting on your bus?"

She crossed her arms. "That's really the only thing you picked up on? Yes, she tried getting on my bus. She's like a sixteen-year-old boy."

I let out a steady breath, trying to ease the anger and jealousy warming my blood. It didn't matter if Jessie Byrd tried getting with Reagan again. What mattered was Reagan thought about me the whole time. While I thought about her.

"I don't understand how you could perform with her when you knew that everyone knew about you two. But you couldn't perform with me."

"Because I was trying to protect us. Going out on that stage together was inviting the media in, and the worst thing that would have happened would be that I would lose you, and I didn't want to lose you, Blair. I went on stage with Jessie because I don't care if she's pushed out of my life. Probably for the better anyways."

Okay, she kind of made sense there.

"And somehow, I still fucked it up even without the media," I said shamefully.

"You were hurting, Blair. I know now that all the anger was just from you hurting. Maybe that's why I was so hurt because I saw you transform into someone you weren't."

"Look, Reagan, I'm in a better place than I was before," I said and closed the space between us with one more step. Now we stood close enough that it took zero energy to grab her fingers loosely. When I did, her eyes immediately fell as her fingers hooked through mine, and man, that was the best feeling in the world after all the things we put each other through. Even if our raised voices from moments before still echoed in the bus, our fingers still found a way to latch on to each other. "I did it mostly for me because I was so tired of feeling like crap. But I also did it because I wanted to get you back. I want to be with you, and you deserve the best person, and I feel like I'm finally on my way to being the best version of me. I'm nowhere near being perfect, but I like myself a lot more than I use to. I know I was an asshole, and I really wish I could show you how sorry I am. Do you want to know why?"

"Why?" she asked shyly, almost as if afraid of the answer.

"Because I'm in love with you."

Her eyes opened and deepened at the same time my chest swelled as the words echoed. There was nothing truer than what I said. Reagan made me feel things I'd never felt before. I didn't want to sleep because I wanted to be with her. I wanted to kiss her forehead all the time, and she made me realize that "Annie's Song" wasn't lame at all. All the disgusting things couples did, I wanted to do with her.

"You love me?" she asked as if she wasn't sure if she heard me correctly.

"I definitely love you. So much. I think I've known it since Thanksgiving."

"Thanksgiving?"

"The whole night, I wanted to kiss your forehead, then I told myself I couldn't do that because that's an intimate thing to do."

"Kissing a forehead?"

"Yes! You don't do that to someone you're just fucking. It's way too intimate. After we slept together that night, you kissed my forehead and that's when I knew."

She smiled. "I kissed your forehead?"

"You did. Maybe back then I didn't know what my feelings were exactly, but I know what they were now. It was the moment I realized I was falling in love with you. Actually, it was the moment you gave me the *Winnie-the-Pooh* book. That's the first moment I wanted to kiss your forehead."

She looked down at our fingers still intertwined. She gripped them a little tighter before her eyes met mine again. "I think I knew that I loved you when you left the tour without saying good-bye, and it tore me up in a way I never felt before. I was so heartbroken about the things you said, what you were doing to yourself, knowing there was nothing I could do to fix you. Just seeing you crumble in front of me—and us. Blair, those four days you were out of it, you had this look in your eyes I can't forget. After the Indianapolis show, there was nothing there. Your eyes were blank. That was so scary. I thought I was gonna have to take you to the hospital. I was so worried about you. It was like you were all hollowed out, nothing else left in you."

"I'm so sorry, Reagan. I really am."

"I've never seen anyone that obliterated before. Seeing you miserable made me miserable. Seeing you hurt made me feel it too. I officially knew that I loved you when you were gone, and nothing made me feel better except seeing Miles and hearing that you were sober and doing really well. Then it made me feel a little better. It made me feel less broken. And I'm sorry that I wasn't there for you. I should have been there to encourage you to get better and to help you through something I didn't fully understand. But because I didn't understand it, I got angry and ran away from something really scary."

"None of that was your fault, Reagan. It was something that was a problem long before you. You wouldn't have been able to fix me."

"Yeah, well, I should have tried a little harder."

I rested my hand against her cheek as the pain that still lingered inside her resurfaced in her watery eyes. "Reagan, it wasn't your fault."

"It was just awful to see you in so much pain. I was falling in love with you and seeing how amazing a person you were, and you couldn't even see it for yourself."

"No, because I was an idiot. A selfish idiot who hurt you."

"But you're not a selfish idiot. Far from it. You hurt me, yeah, but I still want to be with you because I believe in you—in us. It's because I love you too."

I smiled. "You love me?"

"I sang it in my song, didn't I?"

Hearing someone tell me that they loved me was the best feeling. I'd never heard it before. Well, I guess I did from Alanna, but maybe her words never sat well with me because I didn't feel it back. My chest didn't feel as if it sank into a soft bed after running a grueling marathon. My heart didn't flutter. My mouth didn't involuntarily form a grin. None of that happened with Alanna. If anything, it felt like dry swallowing a pill. I felt guilty that she felt that way about me and I didn't feel that way about her.

But all those things did happen when Reagan admitted it.

"Reagan, this hasn't been easy at all. It's actually the hardest fucking thing I've ever done, but if I want you and Miles back in my life, I know what I need to do. It's the only thing that's really been getting me through it. But I want to get better. I'm still trying to at least. I'm committed to this, and I'm going to try everything in my being to stay sober. I promise. I don't want to hurt you or Miles or my mom or anyone else again."

"Blair, you're not perfect," she said. "And neither am I. Far from it. We've been focusing on all the wrongs we did for the past couple of months; I think we need to focus on all the rights because there are so many more of them. I mean, you wrote me a whole book of love songs without even intentionally doing it."

I smiled. "Yeah, I guess I did. And you bought me a first edition *Winnie-the-Pooh*."

"I did. And you brought me a whole kitchen to our hotel room for a romantic dinner. You gave me my first romantic dinner."

"And you bought me a birthday cake when you hardly even knew me."

"And you took me in for Thanksgiving when the stupid weather ruined my plans."

"And you offered to FaceTime my mom when I was so upset that I didn't have family at Madison Square Garden."

Her smile grew. "And most importantly, you put sunscreen on my back even though it's your biggest phobia. Now that's love."

I laughed, and the space that separated us officially evaporated. "Only for you, though. I don't wanna touch anyone else."

"I'll gladly accept the role. Whenever you have that urge, I volunteer."

"So, does that mean you forgive me? Does that mean we can try this again? The sunscreen applications…and us? Because I really wanna try again. I'm still working on me, but I feel like I'm on an incline for once in my life, and there's no one else I want by my side other than you."

She slowly nodded, as if giving herself the chance to think about it one last time. "I wanna try this again too. More than anything."

I softly grazed her cheek with my thumb as her eyes held mine. "I love you, Reagan."

She grinned. "And I love you, but can you stop talking and kiss me, damn it."

I cupped her face and quickly pulled her in. I couldn't wait anymore. She kissed me back, and no time was wasted letting our lips take hold of one another's, deepening the kiss, our tongues dancing in sync, still having each other's rhythms memorized. Our accelerated breathing in between kisses only encouraged me to push her against the wall. How she softly moaned into my mouth made my brain so dizzy. As she grabbed a fistful of my hair, I snuck my hands under the hem of her tank top so they could be reacquainted with her warm, soft skin. The second my fingers touched her sides, the tiny bumps that broke out on the surface spelled out how much she missed me, and if I had any doubts about that, skimming my hands across her sides and to the small of her back reminded me.

After we kissed long enough to almost make up for three months of lost time, the kiss simmered into an unhurried rhythm, so I could take her in all at once, kissing each atom that made up her lips, fully taking in the taste of her mouth. A taste I never wanted to forget again. The more we kissed, the less I wanted to throw her on the bed and have my way with her, and the more I wanted to take my time, making sure I touched her whole body so that the goose bumps on her skin never got a break, that every part of her was kissed so that our time apart didn't matter anymore.

"Can we go to the back?" I said, the breaths seeping out of me quick and thin. "I want to show you how much I love you and missed you."

"I can't say no to that. Can we utilize a VIP lanyard?"

CHAPTER FIFTEEN

The sun cast its strong morning rays right on me. I stirred in bed and let out a tired moan as I stretched my limbs. Reagan had the most comfortable bed in the world.

When I heard the grand piano downstairs, I smiled. Reagan was in the middle of writing her fourth album, and over the past few weeks practically living with her, I had gotten to wake up to the sounds of the grand piano or Reagan humming melodies beside me as she wrote in her own journal all the lyrics that came to her. Even better, she'd nudge me awake since she was always the first one to wake up to ask me how a certain lyric sounded.

Those became my favorite mornings.

As I walked down the stairs, I found Reagan sitting in an oversize T-shirt and her underwear, her hair in a sloppy, messy bun that tilted to the side and would come undone with a simple shake of her head. She was scribbling lyrics in her journal propped up on the piano's music stand. Next to the music stand was a plate of the baklava Reagan convinced me to make a few days ago. I wasn't stressed at all, so baking something as difficult as baklava really wasn't on my list of things to do. But Reagan begged and pleaded, and I couldn't say no to her. Plus, teaching her how to bake and spending all that time with her gave me a new incentive to bake.

I wrapped my arms around her back so I could kiss the column of her neck which smelled like her and morning. She stopped playing so she could crane her neck and fully enjoy all the kisses I had to give her, all while I marveled at the touch of her toned, smooth legs that had been freed from awful, useless pants.

"Hey, beautiful," I said. "You still eating baklava for breakfast?"

She twisted around on the piano bench and wrapped her smooth legs around mine to hold me in place. "Yes, when it tastes like that, I can't stop thinking about it."

"Does that mean I can ditch the salad today?"

"Mmm, no. But nice try," she said before she kissed me.

"You know how much I'm gonna miss these mornings?"

"I have an idea, but how about you just tell me anyway?"

I kissed her lips. "Okay, for starters, I'm going to miss this whole no pants routine." And then another kiss. "And your piano playing." A third kiss that lasted a little bit longer because her smile kept growing, and that was my weakness. "And the smell of a full pot of coffee and waking up to you writing songs."

"You forgot the kiss," she said and tapped her lips.

I placed my hands on her cheeks and kissed her again, lingering a little bit because I knew once Miles and I hit the American highways yet again for our first ever headlining tour, I was really going to miss all the moments I could have kissed her but didn't.

"You know, you're really sappy, and that's so not rock 'n' roll," she said. "Your sleeve tattoo is misleading."

"Guess what? I don't care anymore."

"Good."

I made myself a cup of coffee and then plopped on the cushioned patio chair that overlooked the skyscrapers poking behind the Hollywood Hills to my right. The view was even better at night when the whole city sparkled.

She followed me outside, clutching what I could only guess was her fourth cup of coffee, given that it was going on eleven o'clock. Her butt pushed my stretched-out legs over so she could join me on my chair.

"So, have you given any more thought about your Louisville show?" she asked and glanced down at the steam billowing from her cup.

After thinking really hard about my life and where I wanted to go from here, asking that question didn't trigger me like it would have in the past. I thought a lot about my dad randomly appearing backstage, everything he said to me, analyzing why he did it. Thinking became a real hobby of mine ever since I dropped out of Reagan's tour. I didn't like all the anger that had accumulated inside me, anger from my grandparents dying to my dad shaking up my broken life even more. That was the one thing I really thought about while I was trying to get sober. My dad and the words he told me as to why he wasn't in the picture. The words that rang so true to me: removing yourself to prevent others from hurting. I didn't think it was okay for him to abandon Mom and me, and I never would think it was okay, but that didn't mean I couldn't be empathetic. I removed myself from Alanna, I removed myself from Reagan's tour, and sure, I wouldn't ever straight up abandon my pregnant girlfriend or child, but hearing his words made him more human than villainous. It made him human because I didn't consider myself a villain for dropping out of the things that I thought I would just make worse. My experiences humanized Jason Hines.

I learned over the past few months that everyone had their demons. Everyone made mistakes, and everyone deserved a second chance if they apologized and truly meant it. I spent my whole life pointing fingers at my father as the biggest villain in my life, then I'd lied to my grandpa and jeopardized Reagan's tour because of my own pain and stupidity.

I guess at the very least, Jason Hines deserved a second chance. He deserved to redeem himself because who I was at twenty definitely wasn't who I was at twenty-four, and I knew that who I would be at forty-five wouldn't be anywhere close to who I was now. At least, I hoped. Maybe Jason Hines was a shitty person when he was twenty, but maybe he was a really great person at forty-five.

Also, it was really tiring to hate someone, and if I wanted to live a happy life, I had to shed as much anger as I could, and that started with giving Jason—I mean, my father—a second chance.

"Yeah, I have," I said.

"And?"

"And…" I let out a sigh as I prepared for the words to make it official. "I think I'm gonna give him a chance."

Reagan lowered her mug. "Seriously?"

I nodded, trying to take in my decision myself, just as shocked as she was. "I wasted too many years hating him, and now that he's fought so hard to make amends, just for me to pile shit on him, I don't think it was fair because that showed a lot of strength and courage. I'm sure it wasn't an easy thing at all, and maybe if he would have found me at a better moment of my life, maybe I would have reacted better than I did. But I'm tired of constantly wondering about him and what my life would be like with my father in it. I think because I lost my grandpa, I have so much room for other people in my life, or maybe now that he's gone, I'm desperate for more. I mean, what do I have to lose? I spent twenty-four years without him; the worst that would happen is that we go our separate ways, but I can survive without him. Look at everything I have right now."

Reagan gave my hand a reassuring squeeze. "You know I support whatever decision you choose."

I kissed the back of her hand. "I know."

"When do you think you'll reach out?"

I shrugged and took another sip of my coffee. "I don't know. Last night I was kinda thinking about today."

"Today?"

She sounded as if I told her something crazy, but the reality of the situation was that Miles and I kicked off our twenty-show tour in a week, starting in Nashville, and our Louisville show was the third show. I couldn't wait until the last minute to call him. Actually, I think I was already hovering in the last-minute territory.

"The show is in a week and a half. I've been putting it off long enough, and today, it doesn't scare me as much as it did a few days ago."

"Do whatever you feel is right, love. I'll be right here if you want me to be?"

I nodded, kissed her hand, gave my body another sip of coffee, and reached for my phone. It was time to pull off the Band-Aid.

With my brain teeming with reflective thoughts, the majority of them concerning my family and my dad, I made myself really familiar with his business card, studying each letter and number as I weighed my options of what to do with it. His phone number was already printed inside my memory, and I already practiced over and over what I was going to say to him, the words I'd say if he was interested in coming to the show, the words I'd say if he wasn't.

As I finished typing his number, my chest dove into my stomach. "Okay, I'm gonna do it now," I said.

Reagan pressed her lips together in a nervous smile as she tightened her grip around my hand.

I let out the last deep breath, clasped her hand to get me through this call, and then I pressed the red phone button.

The ringing sang in my ear, I closed my eyes, listening to each unanswered ring forcing my stomach to sink further.

"Hello?"

My eyes shot open to Reagan still monitoring me, and silence squeezed itself into the phone line as I wondered if that was the same voice as the one I barely listened to in Louisville.

My throat caught my breath. "Hi, um, is this Jason?"

Reagan's eyes widened.

"Yes?" he responded hesitantly in his deep voice with the faintest Southern drawl. "Who's this?"

I exhaled the deep breath. There was no turning back now. "This is Blair. Your, um, your daughter."

The silence grew thicker this time, as if all the stakes sang in a muted chorus. My heart thrummed in my chest, and a ball of nerves evolved in my throat.

"Oh, hi, Blair," he said, and I swear I could hear his smile. "Wow, I wasn't expecting your call."

I nervously scratched the back of my head. "Yeah, um, I guess I gave no good warning."

"No, it's a good surprise, though. I think?"

"Yeah, it's a good surprise, I think too. Um…I know it's been a few months, but…um…" I sighed and ran my fingers through my knotty morning hair. "Look, I was an asshole when we first met. I wasn't really in the best state of mind, so you were kind of doomed from the get-go. But I've gained a lot of perspective since then, probably similar to the perspective you gained since college. The truth is, I always wondered why I wasn't good enough for you. Almost every day, even if I tried so hard to deny those feelings, they were still there. Maybe March wasn't the best time for us to meet because my life was kinda messed up, but now that I think I have a better handle on things, I'd like to at least try. To know you, that is. If you're still interested, and if you're not, I totally understand, and if you want nothing to do with me, I won't hold a grudge—"

He chuckled. "Of course I'd like that. Yes, I'm still interested. I've seen a lot in my life, so an angry musician doesn't really make the list of things to run away from. Sorry to disappoint."

His comment warranted a smile, and Reagan's eyebrows drew together.

"Okay, cool. So, um, my band is going on tour, starting next week actually, so this is really last minute, but I'll be playing in Louisville—"

"That's not a problem at all. I can clear up any day that I have plans."

His comment stopped my words dead in their tracks. I frowned and was just as confused as how Reagan looked. "Really?"

"What's more important than this?"

"I mean, I don't know. I'm sure I could figure out something."

"The answer is nothing. So, go on, what day were you thinking?"

"Right, yeah, um, the show. I have a show in Louisville on the tenth, and I was wondering if you wanted to come. I promise not to sing any Kelly Clarkson songs this time."

He laughed again. "Well, if that's the case, then I'd love to."

I grinned and then gave Reagan's hand another squeeze. "Great! I was thinking maybe you can come to sound check; we can grab dinner, I can pay for your hotel if you didn't want to drive back."

"I'm up for anything, Blair. Really. I'm just glad you reached out."

"Yeah, me too. And I'm sorry for everything I said and did last time."

"It's all right. No hard feelings. It's water under the bridge."

"Cool. Well, I'll let you go. I'll stay in contact with you and reach out again closer to the show. You have my number now, so feel free to reach out whenever."

"Right back at you. I'm really looking forward to it."

"Yeah, me too."

"Have a good one, Blair."

And once the line went dead, I let out the breath that collected in my chest. Reagan squeaked and tossed her arms around me, rewarding me with a kiss attack all over my face.

"Babe! I'm so so happy for you!" she said and cupped my face, planting a long kiss on my lips.

When she pulled away, I couldn't control my grin. I did it. One of the scariest things I'd ever had to do, and I did it. I couldn't believe it. I couldn't believe the man I resented for so long wanted to be in my life. I couldn't believe the man I flipped out on in Louisville still didn't run away from getting to know me. I couldn't believe I had plans with my father in a week and a half.

This was so weird. Did I call him Jason? Did I call him Dad? Was "Dad" even a real word because when I said it over and over again in my head, it didn't sound like a real word.

"Wow, this is really crazy," I said.

"But a good crazy."

I looked down at her to find her hopeful eyes staring up at me. I kissed her nose. "Yeah, good crazy."

My life was nowhere near perfect. I still walked around with a hole vacant from my wonderful grandparents who raised me, who taught me everything about life and love that I needed to learn. Those holes would never be fully filled again, but they could be patched up, and that was what they would have wanted for me. For the first time in my life, my brain was at ease, as if what was once a constant current of swells finally simmered down to a calm ripple, the kind of ripples I peacefully fell asleep to on a noise machine. I'd never seen my mom happier in her own place, spending lots of time finding her own hobbies other than working, schoolwork, and either taking care of me or taking care of one of her sick parents. I'd never seen a person other than Grandma and Gramps who made her smile as much as Greg did. My music career was only starting to launch, and I was so in love with a girl. A wonderful girl. A girl who made me excited for all the unknowns because as long as it was with her, it would all be wonderful.

Reagan nestled her head into my neck and kissed me softly underneath my jaw as she wrapped her arm around my chest. With a long kiss on her forehead, breathing in the smell of her fruity body wash, I exhaled a deep, contented sigh as I continued to gaze at the hills surrounding me and enjoyed all the beautiful things that I had in my life. There were a lot, and in that moment, I didn't want a breath from it all anymore because I was overwhelmed in the best possible way. I wanted to enjoy all of it.

I was eager to keep going. And I would keep going.

About the Author

Morgan Lee Miller started writing at the age of five in the suburbs of Cleveland, Ohio, where she entertained herself by composing her first few novels all by hand. She majored in journalism and creative writing at Grand Valley State University.

When she's not introverting and writing, Morgan works for an animal welfare nonprofit and tries to make the world a slightly better place. She previously worked for an LGBT rights organization.

She currently resides in Washington, DC, with her two feline children, whom she's unapologetically obsessed with.

Books Available From Bold Strokes Books

30 Dates in 30 Days by Elle Spencer. In this sophisticated contemporary romance, Veronica Welch is a busy lawyer who tries to find love the fast way—thirty dates in thirty days. (978-1-63555-498-4)

Finding Sky by Cass Sellars. Skylar Addison's search for a career intersects with her new boss's search for butterflies, but Skylar can't forgive Jess's intrusion into her life. Romance is the last thing they expect. (978-1-63555-521-9)

Hammers, Strings, and Beautiful Things by Morgan Lee Miller. While on tour with the biggest pop star in the world, rising musician Blair Bennett falls in love for the first time while coping with loss and depression. (978-1-63555-538-7)

Heart of a Killer by Yolanda Wallace. Contract killer Santana Masters's only interest is her next assignment—until a chance meeting with a beautiful stranger tempts her to change her ways. (978-1-63555-547-9)

Leading the Witness by Carsen Taite. When defense attorney Catherine Landauer reluctantly becomes the key witness in prosecutor Starr Rio's latest criminal trial, their hearts, careers, and lives may be at risk. (978-1-63555-512-7)

No Experience Required by Kimberly Cooper Griffin. Izzy Treadway has resigned herself to a life without romance because of her bipolar illness but wonders what she's gotten herself into when she agrees to write a book about love. (978-1-63555-561-5)

One Walk in Winter by Georgia Beers. Olivia Santini and Hayley Boyd Markham might be rivals at work, but they discover that lonely hearts often find company in the most unexpected of places. (978-1-63555-541-7)

The Inn at Netherfield Green by Aurora Rey. Advertising executive Lauren Montgomery and gin distiller Camden Crawley don't agree on anything except saving the Rose & Crown, the old English pub that's brought them together. (978-1-63555-445-8)

Top of Her Game by M. Ullrich. When it comes to life on the field and matters of the heart, losing isn't an option for pro athletes Kenzie Shaw and Sutton Flores. (978-1-63555-500-4)

Vanished by Eden Darry. First came the storm, and then the blinding white light that made everyone in town disappear. Another storm is coming, and Ellery and Loveday must find the chosen one or they won't survive. (978-1-63555-437-3)

All She Wants by Larkin Rose. Marci Jones and Tessa Dalton get more than they bargained for when their plans for a one-night stand turn into an opportunity for love. (978-1-63555-476-2)

Beautiful Accidents by Erin Zak. Stevie Adams doesn't believe in fate, not after losing her parents in a car crash. But she's about to discover that sometimes the best things in life happen purely by accident. (978-1-63555-497-7)

Before Now by Joy Argento. The instant Delaney Peyton and Jade Taylor meet, they sense a connection neither can explain. Can they overcome a betrayal that spans the centuries to reignite a love that can't be broken? (978-1-63555-525-7)

Breathe by Cari Hunter. Paramedic Jemima Pardon's chronic bad luck seems to be improving when she meets police officer Rosie Jones. But they face a battle to survive before they can find love. (978-1-63555-523-3)

Double-Crossed by Ali Vali. Hired thief and killer Reed Gable finds something in her scope that will change her life forever when she gets a contract to end casino accountant Brinley Myers's life. (978-1-63555-302-4)

False Horizons by CJ Birch. Jordan and Ash struggle with different views on the alien agenda and must find their way back to each other before they're swallowed up by a centuries-old war. Third in the New Horizons series. (978-1-63555-519-6)

Legacy by Charlotte Greene. In this paranormal mystery, five women hike to a remote cabin deep inside a national park—and unsettling events suggest that they should have stayed home. (978-1-63555-490-8)